Blue by You

1st Sept 2022

Cheryl —

With Best Wishes and Kindest Regards

Vaya con Dios

Jenny

Also By Larry B. Gildersleeve
www.larrygildersleeve.com

The Girl on the Bench
Follow Your Dreams
Dancing Alone Without Music

Blue by You

Larry B. Gildersleeve

to Kathleen

When cancer claimed his young wife, a woman he'd known since they were children, Daniel fled the nation's capital for the remoteness of the Colorado mountains, leaving behind his law practice and everything else that held meaning. He convinced himself there were no do-overs in life, no second chances masquerading as firsts. Nothing left worth living for except his dog Blue.

Then a woman from Nashville swept into his mountain exile for seven extraordinary days and left him a changed man. Decades later and a thousand miles away, a chance encounter reunited them, yet Paula had no memory of him or their previous time together. Daniel fell in love with the same woman twice, a stranger to her both times. A new beginning, but would it end differently?

One

December 4th, 1998
Tuesday, Day One

"I'm lost."

A woman in her late-thirties, tall and slender, flowing auburn hair bouncing off her shoulders, strode confidently up a stone walkway toward a large, two-story log cabin home. It was tucked away at a hillside crevice yet plainly visible from the gravel road where the dust kicked up by her late-model European roadster began settling back down. A man relaxing on the porch touched the head of a pure-bred Australian Shepard at his side as he rose from a sturdy wooden rocking chair.

"Perhaps we can help."

He started down to meet her at the edge of the walkway. She waved him off and he stepped back to watch her effortlessly climb the six wide steps with no hand railing. Had she been shoeless, as he was in heavy wool socks, they'd be about the same height. Her fashionable stilts, better suited for cocktail parties back home in Nashville than outdoors in nowhere Colorado, gave her the advantage. If the difference troubled him, it didn't show. He held her confident handshake a second or two longer than perhaps he should. If it troubled her, it didn't show.

"I'm Daniel. This is Blue."

Blue continued to wag his tail as he had the moment he saw her approaching.

She hesitated a moment, as if trying to remember her name. "Paula," she said, slowly. Then with greater assurance, "Paula Chandler," adding, "what a beautiful dog."

Tiny freckles dotted her flawless complexion, the rest of her hidden beneath a white turtleneck sweater, unbuttoned brown cashmere coat and cream-colored slacks with a crease that mostly held despite hours sitting in the car. In time, he'd know she had freckles elsewhere.

Daniel had the healthy, clean-shaven look of a man who spent a lot of his time outdoors. He motioned toward a matching rocking chair and thought she settled into it as gracefully as an actress performing on a Broadway stage.

"Now that you've found *us*, what were you really looking for?" he asked casually as he sat back down.

His surprise visitor looked straight ahead at the snow-capped mountains off in the distance. Her delicate features, in profile against the canvas of a cloud-streaked early winter sky, began to melt away his nonchalance, yet he struggled to pretend otherwise. He rarely had guests, invited or otherwise, and never one as easy on the eyes as the woman sitting beside him on an unseasonably warm December afternoon. If he'd had a tail, it would be wagging.

"I'm trying to find Three Oaks Manor House. It's supposed to be some sort of meeting place." Her eyes shifted to meet his. "This *is* Three Oaks, isn't it? I mean, if there were signs anywhere, I sure missed all of 'em when I drove in."

Her Southern accent as captivating to him as her countenance.

"Manor House. Nice place. Staying there?"

"I am. Made the reservation months ago. Since you know about it, how do I find it? I mean, I have no idea where I am, so how do I get there from here?"

He did his best to appear thoughtful as he put one foot on the porch railing and crossed his ankles.

"Here would be a good place to start."

He wants to joust, she thought. *I'm tired, but totally up for it.*

"Are you making fun of me, Daniel? It is Daniel, right?" He nodded. "Wait. We've just met." She feigned seriousness with a wrinkled brow and pursed lips. "Let me ask someone who'd know."

He nodded again when she gestured toward the dog lying between them with his head resting on his paws, his tail stilled by sleep. Her eyes, and Daniel's, followed her hand.

"Blue," she asked, as she began to slowly stroke his back with her fingertips, "is your friend here making fun of a damsel in distress? A sojourner at her wits' end in a foreign land. And here I had such a good first impression of him. Have I misjudged him so severely? Please say it isn't so."

The faint sound of Blue's snoring accompanied her smile as she dropped both hands to her lap and turned her silent gaze back to the man in the rocking chair.

She's good, he thought.

"Sojourner, eh?" he asked, holding her gaze.

Her turn to nod.

"Point taken." His tone conciliatory. "I apologize."

"Apology accepted." She guessed him to be about her age. "Now, please begin again. If there's one thing I really love, it's new beginnings."

Still trying for an air of indifference, though he didn't know why, he acted as if he didn't see her wink or hear the flirtation in her voice as he raised his arm and pointed in the opposite direction her car faced.

"Back down the road you came. At the big red barn, take a left. Downtown's a few miles."

"That's it?"

"Yep. One main street. Manor House is white and green. Big sign in the yard. Can't miss it."

"Sounds easy enough. Thank you."

"You're welcome." Wanting to prolong the sojourner's departure, he leaned forward as his feet found their way back to the porch floor. He pointed again. "Don't see many cars like that around here. Mercedes?"

"Beemer." She cleared her throat. "Sorry. BMW."

Her eyes followed his cupped palm as it moved along the sleeping dog's back.

"She's a kindly lady, Blue, she truly is. Making citified jargon easy for simple country folk like us to understand."

She lifted her head when he lifted his, their eyes met, but only one of them smiled.

"Guess I deserved that," she groaned.

His raised eye brows challenged her attempt at pouting.

"Okay. Maybe I *was* being just a tiny bit smug." She paused, then hastily added, "Without meaning to be, of course."

"Of course."

"Still, my turn to apologize." She paused, and he returned her wink from a few moments earlier that wordlessly brought back her smile. "Seems like I've met my match, haven't I?"

He added a slight shrug to his smile.

"Right. Now then, before I go, one last question. Once I'm downtown, on that one main street, which restaurant serves the best lunch?"

"The Diner."

"Does it have a name?"

"It does. The Diner."

"A diner named The Diner." She slowly rocked back and forth, softly tapping the fingers of her left hand on the arm rest. "Who'd have thought?"

"Legend has it a big-time ad agency in Denver."

"You don't say. Well, that answers that. And why do you recommend it?"

"Only one in town."

He was messing with her, was good at it, and she didn't mind. What he had no way of knowing is their spirited exchange might someday inspire a magazine article in a distant city.

"I see. Can you give me directions to The Diner? You know, after I've arrived all the way downtown. From here."

"Sure." He was delighted her questions were delaying her. "Across the street from Manor House."

"I think I can manage that." She hooked an index finger to slide a tan leather driving glove down to look at her watch. "Well, I better get going. Got an early start this morning and skipped breakfast." She looked out at the seemingly endless expanse of peaceful rural surroundings. Nearby trees swayed in a sudden stiff breeze, and she saw a few remaining stubborn leaves twist and swirl as they fell to the ground. "Wouldn't want to get caught up in rush hour traffic and find out they gave my room away."

"Wouldn't want that," he said, hoping she didn't notice he was staring, but not at the leaves.

Realizing her departure had been delayed as long as possible, Daniel rocked forward and stood. Paula planted her feet firmly and held his hand longer than she needed to when he helped her up. Blue scrambled to join them.

"Does Blue shake hands?"

"No. Sorry. Nothing personal. He only got a certificate of attendance at obedience school."

I know I can't stay, but there's something about this man.

"Good one. I can see you're both handsome *and* clever." She bent down to scratch Blue behind his ears. "Did he get his name from his eyes?"

"He did."

"Time for me to go."

When they shook hands, the name of the movie star he favored from years gone by eluded her.

"Thank you, Daniel. Thank you very much."

She had her back to him as she began her descent.

"Elvis."

She stopped on the third step and turned to look up at him. "Elvis?"

"Yeah. He said that a lot."

"Said what?"

"Thank you. Thank you very much."

"He did?"

"He did. Always said them together." He answered her quizzical look. "When the audience applauded. Every Elvis impersonator does it."

"A wild guess. You're a fan."

"Guilty."

Reaching the edge of the walkway at the base of the porch, Paula performed a nimble one-eighty pirouette and took one step back. "Thank you. For the directions, and the dining recommendation." She bowed slightly, kept her eyes fixed on his, and with emphasis added, "Thank you very much."

This time, he made no effort to subdue his staring. In a few seconds, she'd be gone.

"Good-bye, Mr. Elvis Fan."

"Good-bye, damsel in distress."

Paula's fancy shoes slipped twice on the rounded cobblestones, marring the flawless departure she'd hoped for since she knew he'd be watching. Reaching her car, she gave a casual wave to a man she had no expectation of ever seeing again. He waved back.

Daniel wrapped his arm around one of the rough-hewn posts supporting the porch roof and watched her car with Tennessee plates disappear down the unpaved road. He lingered, regretting her intrusion into his solitude had been so fleeting. He wished there'd been more. More what, he didn't know. Just more.

"Handsome woman," he said aloud, as he retraced his steps back to his chair. Blue looked at him. "Tall, too." Blue wagged his tail.

They both remained in place the better part of an hour, Blue sleeping, Daniel consumed with thoughts painting the portrait of a man hopelessly adrift. He'd been pretty much a loner all his life save for his friendship with a girl, and his love for a woman, and they were the same person. When cancer took her from him, he ran away, drawn to the one place he knew would keep her memory alive. Until, he told himself, he could hopefully get on with a life without her.

A year and a half later, he knew he'd crossed over from being alone with memories to being desperately lonely, the loneliness accounting for the ache he felt as he looked down the empty road that had carried his surprise visitor away. He stood, walked to the edge of the porch, leaned against the post and wondered if he'd still be alive come spring when the last snow of the season began to thaw. Doesn't matter, he thought. Nothing will matter once Blue is gone. It'll all be over.

Paula watched the log cabin home grow smaller in her rear-view mirror until it disappeared from sight. Her husband had urged her to fly rather than drive, but she'd told him she needed time away. To think. To reflect. To clear her mind. To pray. But it wasn't time away from her job, which is what she'd told him, rather from her childless, loveless marriage that in her mind had reached a tipping point. She was seeking something to guide her in taking the next right step.

Paula followed Daniel's simple directions and it wasn't long before she steered her car onto the only main street in the small mountain town. She parked around the corner from the front door of Manor House and turned off the ignition. She sat for several minutes, looking around at nothing in particular. What are the odds, she thought, that somehow, in some mysterious way, I've been tipped in that stranger's direction?

Could he be my next right step? Maybe I should turn around and go back.

She stepped out of her car and shook herself, hoping it might dislodge thoughts of a man who'd made her feel as if they'd known each other for years instead of minutes. The only thing dislodged were her keys. She felt them slip from her fingers and heard them fall to the pavement. She bent down, snatched up the key ring, fumbled it and it fell again. "There's my sign," she muttered under her breath as she looked across a white picket fence encircling Manor House. She picked up her keys, dropped them in her purse with a flourish to dramatize an end to her delusion and headed toward the door.

An early evening curtain of darkness, as dark as his mood, descended outside the window as Daniel stood at the sink preparing Blue's dinner in a kitchen any gourmet chef would praise. After arriving from D.C., he'd begun a self-guided culinary journey he hoped would both help pass the time and heal the hurt. Country music, a staple in his life as long as he could remember, filled the house, but not so loud it drowned out the knock. When he opened the front door, a familiar face looked back at him. Her captivating beauty, undiminished by dim porch light and screen-door mesh, left him speechless.

"Hi. Remember me?"

"Of course," he stammered. It took him a moment to recover. "Come in. Please."

Paula pulled open the screen door. Her arrival brightened his mood as quickly as the imposing chandelier illuminated the living room when he flipped the switch on the wall just inside the door. When her eyes adjusted, she realized the home's rustic exterior belied the refined interior.

"This is unexpected." He couldn't think of anything else to say, but he'd soon discover he needn't have worried.

"You're telling me! This has *not* been my day." She caught herself. "Oh, I didn't mean that the way it must've sounded. I'm sorry. I meant it hasn't been my day apart from meeting you. And Blue."

"Paula, we feel the same way."

She liked that he'd remembered her name, at least the name she'd given him, and how it sounded in his resonant voice without a trace of accent. A feminine voice and human scent other than Daniel brought Blue trotting from the kitchen. He made straight for Paula, tail wagging, and she knelt to pet him.

"You can't be lost," Daniel said, closing the door. "We took care of that. Or did we?"

"We did. But you'd know that because I found my way back."

"What then?"

"Well," she answered, standing, "I guess you could say I'm lost in a different way this time."

"Because …?"

"Because my reservation somehow got messed up, and by the time

I got there just a few minutes after I left you, all the rooms were taken. Can you believe that? Every last one of them. A woman named Marlene was nice about it, and I tried to be nice, too. But I'm afraid I became a little unpleasant with her, okay, maybe a lot unpleasant, when I asked for directions to other places where I might stay and she said there weren't any. At least not any within, what did she say, oh, yes, within any reasonable driving distance. I asked her what reasonable is around here and she said about an hour. I don't call that reasonable, do you? I ..."

"On the bright side ..."

"Oh, there's bright side to all of this? That sounds promising. I can't wait to hear what it is because ... why are you looking at me that way?"

"May I finish?"

"Oops."

"You'd be out at the interstate, an hour closer to where you're going tomorrow."

"True," she said, quickly regaining her jousting footing and the breeziness with which her words seemed to effortlessly spill forth. "If I was *going* somewhere else tomorrow. I'm not. You see, believe it or not, I came all the way out here on purpose. To attend a writer's seminar. Three days. To make matters worse, they said on the radio they're expecting snow. Just my luck. And why would anyone schedule an event like this in the mountains in winter unless it's to go skiing? Which we're not. At least I don't think we are. And if we are, I didn't know about it and therefore didn't plan for it. You know. Clothes-wise."

She stopped, anticipating he'd join in. Curious about what she'd say next, and how she'd say it, he didn't. Undaunted, she continued.

"Since you're the only person I've met besides that woman at the Manor House, I thought, hoped really, you'd know a place, any place, a condo, perhaps a house, I can rent for a few nights, you know, until the seminar is over on Friday, I'm guessing probably around mid-day, and I can be on my way home, getting at least as far as one of the hotels she mentioned out there by the interstate an hour away before it gets dark."

Paula paused to take a breath while Daniel marveled at the number of words she'd streamed into a single sentence.

"Then I decided to drive back out here to ask you if you could help me. You know, with any ideas you might have before I started off again on my own searching around in the dark in a place I've never been before and know nothing about. I would've called, but I didn't have your number. So here I am."

He waited until he was certain she'd finished.

"No."

"No? That's it? Just no? Nothing more? That's all you've got to say after all I've said?"

"A longer answer won't change things." Daniel saw frustration clouding the face of an alluring woman standing a little more than an arm's length away. He thought for a moment. "Hungry?"

"Oh, I am! That's another thing. I forgot all about lunch at that place you told me about. Got myself all tangled up and sideways thinking about where I could find a place to stay. Guess I should've thought about that before I came all the way out here again. You know, over the river and through the woods to, well, to wherever this is."

The reclusive Daniel found himself in unfamiliar territory. Awed and intimidated by her appearance, he'd been more at ease sitting with her on the porch in the great outdoors that afternoon than standing so near to her inside. He felt closed in somehow, but the more she talked, and she was clearly the most loquacious person he'd ever met, the more he relaxed. He slowly pulled his hands from his front pockets where he'd nervously shoved them and loosely clasped them behind his back.

"Oh, well, since I know the way, I'll go back to town first before starvation sets in and I fade away to nothing. Then I'll find my way out to the interstate to a hotel. You said it would only take about an hour or so. Now, about food." She narrowed her eyes, pretending to search her memory. "What *was* the name of that place you mentioned? Something memorable, as I recall. Oh, that's it! The Diner."

"No."

"Again, with the no?" Her voice lingered on the last word. "Really?"

"Sorta. You got the name right. The no is to evening meals. Locals do that at home."

"I don't mean to be disrespectful, really I don't," Paula said, hands on her small waist above shapely hips. "But did I also drive past a sign saying I'd left civilization behind when I arrived here?"

The corners of his mouth turned upward.

"What?"

"No offense taken." He paused. "In case you're wondering."

Despite a smile confirming he had a sense of humor, she realized she'd overstepped and offered a chagrined look in reply. Daniel spoke his next words matter-of-factly and with the disarming ease of a skilled trial attorney at summation knowing with absolute certainty he'd won his case.

"Would you like to join us for dinner?"

Caught completely off-guard, she hesitantly asked, "Us? Us? Is there a lady of the house?"

Paula thought she saw a slight change in Daniel's expression before he shook his head.

"Just Blue and me," he said, as her eyes were drawn to his. "You'll be a welcome third."

She made no effort to hide her relief. And that's when the realization came to her. It's not just his words, few as they may be, or the ease with which he spoke. Or his relaxed, non-threatening demeanor. It's his eyes. She'd read somewhere they're the windows to the soul. *He's soulful. Even though I barely know him, that's why I feel so comfortable, so safe, being with him.*

"That's very kind ... and I accept. Gratefully. What a surprise. To tell you the truth, and I'll always tell you the truth, I couldn't help noticing the wonderful smells as soon as you opened the door. Are you sure they'll be enough for both of us? Not that I'll eat that much, mind you."

"Certain of it."

Paula unbuttoned her coat and Daniel draped it over one arm. With his other, he gestured in the direction of the wonderful smells. Aware her host still wasn't wearing shoes, she stepped out of hers and set them by the front door. As her eyes swept the room, she noticed the expensive designer furniture and was fairly certain about three things. It had all been selected by a woman, arranged by a decorator, and appeared to be almost untouched since the day it arrived.

With Blue at her side, Paula headed across the highly polished hardwood floors toward the kitchen, and without turning around, said, "I love country music." She paused for a second, then parroted something he'd said moments earlier. "In case you're wondering."

He carefully hung her coat in the hall closet.

She's quick. Might've been a worthy courtroom adversary.

When she entered the oversized kitchen, Paula looked around and saw four hand-crafted wooden stools, two on each side of a long center island. Her back was to him as she made her selection and sat down, allowing Daniel to continue to admire her shapely figure when he followed behind her.

"Excellent choice," he said, then asked, "chardonnay?"

"Yes, wine would be wonderful. Thank you." When she heard the refrigerator door close, she asked, "And what did you mean excellent choice? All I've done is sit down on this stool. Nothing special about that. Or is there?"

"You chose the one on the end."

"And?"

"Perfect for a left-handed diner."

She looked at her arm as he opened the wine.

"And you know I'm left-handed how? Are you gifted with clairvoyance?"

"Your watch is on your right wrist."

Daniel's courtroom success had been due, in part, to well-honed discipline noticing everything about everything. Jurors, witnesses, opposing counsel. An innate part of him that remained years after leaving his profession. But along the way, he'd shed a trial attorney's stock-in-trade. Being long-winded.

"Well, it's obvious you don't miss a thing, so I better dig deep for my best finishing school table manners." She paused when she heard the sound of the cork leaving the bottle. "Actually, that's not true. And I told you I would always be truthful. I never went to finishing school. I was just turning a phrase. Making conversation." Her host was busy at the impressive gas range, his back to her. Broad shoulders, tapering to a narrow waist. "I feel like I'm being such an imposition. May I at least help in some way?"

"Thank you, no. Everything's ready. We try to eat the same time every evening. Blue can be demanding that way. Your arrival, though unanticipated, timed just right."

An array of copper pans and skillets hung from a rack suspended above them as Daniel set cinnamon-colored stoneware plates on the center island before taking the opposite stool. Poached salmon with dill sauce. A medley of colorful steamed vegetables. Garden salad with homemade blue cheese dressing in a small tureen with matching ladle. Freshly baked rolls wrapped in cloth to keep them warm in a woven-straw basket.

A ringing of expensive crystal as she reached to touch his already raised wine glass, her manicured fingernails in one of a hundred shades of pink.

"To our sojourner guest," he toasted, above the sound of Blue eating in his corner, "and keeping her starvation at bay. At least for now."

He thought her radiant smile lit up the kitchen as much as the chandelier had illuminated the living room.

She sipped the wine. "This is excellent. What is it?"

"Meiomi." He turned the bottle's label toward her. "California."

"May-oh-me." Repeated slowly in an unaffected Southern drawl. "And this is all so amazing! Now *you* tell *me* the truth. You don't eat like this every night, do you? I mean, you weren't expecting me. Were you?"

"I do, and I wasn't."

"Pardon me?"

"I do eat like this every night, or try to. I enjoy cooking, even if it's just for me. Leftovers are lunch the next day. And I wasn't expecting you. Why would I?"

The man who noticed everything about everything saw the slow creeping of scarlet into her fair complexion. He'd embarrassed her and rode to her rescue as he topped off her wine.

"What part of the South do ya'll call back home?"

She recognized the conversational lifeline he'd cast her way and grasped it. "Cute. Real cute." The flush on her neck began to fade away as quickly as it appeared. "Did my accent give me away? Well, of course it did. When did you notice?"

He sipped his wine and pretended to think. "Your first two words."

"Really?" She shifted her weight on the comfortable stool, unable to remember and unwilling to ask. "Just two words, huh? That quickly?"

"Maybe not. Might have been later when I heard river with an *ah* at the end. Or when you stretched wine into two syllables. Or when …"

She exaggerated her interruption. "Are ya makin' fun a me *agin*, Dan-yul?"

"Not for a minute. The only thing more charming than your accent is …"

"Is what?" she impatiently asked, hungrier for a man's compliment than he could've imagined. He had no way of knowing how much she longed to be loved, or for a man to think she was at least loveable in the moment. "What's more charming than my accent?"

Her charisma so natural and unaffected, her every move and mannerism so sophisticated, his answer was both effortless and genuine.

"You are."

The wine, and the closeness of their relaxed dining, kept flirtation on the menu as a second entrée, something neither of them had dined on seriously for a long time. The food was as delicious as Paula anticipated, and she savored each bite. But satisfying her hunger was soon overtaken by a desire to get to know the chef. Her meal mostly eaten, she laid her fork, prongs down, on her plate alongside her knife, laced her fingers together as she laid her arms across the edge of the island, leaned forward slightly and looked across at her host.

"If you'll tell me your story," she said, invitingly, "I'll tell you mine."

A worthy courtroom opponent, perhaps. But it appears I have more experience.

"Ladies first."

Unprepared for his return volley, Paula played for time, gathering her thoughts while pink fingernails tapped out a cadence on the island's granite surface. Her other hand reached for the wine glass.

"It's all so interesting," she said, her response slowly coming together. "My story. So much to share. And, of course, so much to leave out. At least until we're better acquainted. Honestly, Daniel, I wouldn't know where to begin. I …"

"May I help?"

Having no idea what he had in mind, she nodded.

"Begin at the beginning."

Two

Tuesday, Day One ... Continued

O xford, Mississippi was Paula Chandler's beginning, a birthplace where lifelong friendships can be ushered in with deceptively simple yet probing questions asked on park benches beneath spreading magnolia trees on hot summer afternoons. Questions like where are your people from, or where do you go to church? As he listened, Daniel assumed the third glass of wine contributed to her candor.

Tentatively, then hurriedly, Paula unfolded her story, one with all the makings of a Southern coming-of-age novel filled with an abundance of tension and conflict, especially between her and her mother. And in the Cinderella-like relationship with her two jealous sisters, one younger, one older. When her father bothered to notice, and he rarely did, he usually only watched the four-woman family drama from afar, never writing himself into the script if it could be avoided. And it almost always could.

By the time she reached high school, Paula was aware the effect her beauty and maturing had on boys, yet it didn't diminish her popularity with other girls because they'd already learned she didn't pose a threat. Homecoming queen and Miss Anything would have been hers for the taking, but her mother wouldn't allow her middle daughter any recognition based on appearance. Paula told Daniel she knew it also had to do with the certainty neither of her sisters would ever be considered, let alone selected.

"I also wanted to be a cheerleader, but Mother nixed that in a nano-second."

"Why?"

His first question. One she knew he could answer himself.

"The uniform, silly."

His look begged for more.

"Okay, I can tell you wanna hear the naughty details."

A widening of eyes accompanied his nod.

"The skirt would've barely covered my bottom. And I developed earlier than most of the other girls. Mother would have no part of it."

"Why?"

A dinner roll from the basket landed on the floor by Daniel's stool after Paula bounced it off his forehead. He reached down to retrieve it, and when he encouraged her to continue, he could hear resentment in her voice when she talked about life with a domineering mother and distant father.

Her parents owned a small grocery store that consumed most of her father's waking hours. When he was home, he kept to himself, although Paula thought things would've been different if he'd had a son. Limited money was the reason given when their mother denied all three daughters anything, large or small, deemed to be "nice, but not necessary." An oft-repeated phrase Paula came to hate.

"Your sisters. How'd they feel about your mother?"

"Well, let me put it this way. Their life ambition was to get married and have children. Nothing else seemed to matter. At least not the things that mattered to me."

"Sounds like you were complete opposites."

"That's putting it mildly."

"And after high school? No finishing school, right?"

A man who actually listens to me.

"Right. Thought being an Ole Miss Rebel right there in Oxford suited me better. Studied hard and got a full ride. Majored in English and Journalism. It really pissed Mother off … oops, sorry."

"Saying it, or pissing her off?"

"You're not helping."

He steepled his hands together as a silent gesture of apology.

"A sorority had all the things Mother disapproved of. I joined one and *that's* when I pissed her off. My parents weren't paying for college, and I had savings from summer jobs, so she had no say."

"Where'd you see yourself going after graduation?"

In his former life, opposing counsel would have objected to Daniel's leading questions as he lifted the bottle of Meomi.

"Only one place. New York City." She placed a hand over her wine glass. "Had enough, thank you. Probably more than enough, as you can tell. Now, where was I?"

"New York City."

"Right. I papered the walls of my sorority house room with covers of magazines I dreamed would publish my writing."

"How long were you in New York?"

She looked away, then back. "Never got there."

"What happened?"

"I guess you could say Winston Chandler the third happened."

"Your husband."

"How'd you know I'm married? I'm beginning to think you *are* clairvoyant."

"Two things."

"Yes?"

"Well, this afternoon you introduced yourself as Paula Chandler. I used every ounce of my deductive reasoning to ..."

"And the other?"

Paula's hands had been gloved when they first met, and she'd taken her rings off at Manor House before driving back. Daniel rested his elbow on the island, held up his left hand, palm toward her, rubbing his thumb underneath his ring finger. "Ring imprint. Tan line."

She looked at the back of her left hand. "Well, I'll say this. Thin mountain air certainly sharpens one's eyesight."

Paula was aware from the moment they met Daniel's eyes had taken in far more than her finger, and she didn't mind. She'd have minded otherwise. Her husband's lack of interest contributed mightily to reaching her tipping point long before she left Nashville. She'd been the one to initiate flirtation with a stranger and rationalized it as innocent jousting. But now she knew he knew she was married.

"One thing the air here also does, for sure," she continued, "is make my skin dry. Took my rings off in town to put on hand lotion. Didn't want to stain my gloves. That's all. They're in my purse."

He knew he'd embarrassed her and caused an end to her storytelling, not knowing later on he'd read the rest. She looked at her watch while stifling a yawn.

"Tired?"

"More than," she answered, with uncharacteristic brevity. He thought she appeared pensive as her fingers tugged slightly at her lower lip. "Daniel, I have to tell you something so I can ask you something."

"Sounds intriguing."

"Don't know about that. But in our few minutes together on your porch this afternoon, I felt a sort of connection with you. A kindred spirit kind of a thing."

"Sure it wasn't Blue and not me?" he asked, standing. "He's been known to have that effect on women."

"Well, he certainly helped. No denying that. And tonight. I don't know, Daniel. I think that's why I felt safe coming back. Staying for dinner. And that's so strange because I don't even know you. And here we are, out in the middle of nowhere. At least for me it's the middle of nowhere."

Daniel had been in enough courtrooms, listening to enough witness, to often intuitively know what people were thinking before they spoke. An hours' drive at this late hour, hoping to find a room in an inn somewhere, wasn't an option for her now and they both knew it. He leaned against the kitchen doorway and crossed his arms.

"Paula, you wanted to ask me something. Don't get me wrong. I'll happily listen as long as you wanna talk, but a moment ago you said you were tired and ..."

"Yeah, well, about that," she answered, a faint attempt to smile. "I know this is going to sound, well, I don't quite know how it's going to sound, so I'll just ask. Any chance I can sleep on your couch tonight? I won't be any trouble, really I won't. And I'll leave first thing in the morning without disturbing you. Promise."

Daniel uncrossed his arms and shook his head.

"No. But ..."

She made sure he saw her eyes rolling as he passed in front of her. Liquid eyes a portrait artist would paint blue-green.

"I'll say this for you. You sure have a comfortable relationship with that word. I'm sorry I pushed your hospitality too far. You and that Marlene woman said there was no other place around here for me to go. Okay, I'll just get in my car and drive an hour or more back out to the interstate and hope one of those motels has a room left. Otherwise, I'll be sleeping in my car somewhere tonight. And in case that happens, may I borrow a blanket or two? It *is* rather chilly outside, you know. Being winter, and all. I promise to bring them back before I leave." The tinge of sarcasm softened with, "I'll even treat you to breakfast one morning at that place. The Diner. Deal?"

He regretted her anxiety, but she *had* interrupted him.

"If you want." A theatrical pause sharpened to courtroom perfection accompanied Daniel's clearing of their dinner plates. "Or, if you'd let me finish, I was going to say you're welcome to stay in the guest suite upstairs. First door on the right. Has its own bathroom. Tub. Shower. Towels. The works."

"Really?"

"Really."

"Didn't expect this."

"Neither of us did," he said, finishing his chores, wiping his hands on a towel before draping it back over the handle to the stove. "But that shouldn't matter, should it?"

Paula was quiet for a moment. But only a moment.

"Rescued from hunger *and* homelessness, all in one evening. And I do apologize for interrupting you. It's a shortcoming of mine that needs more work. Along with my over-reacting at times. And probably some other things."

She slid gracefully off the stool to follow him from the kitchen.

"No worries. By the way, we bunk down the hall there," he said, his back to her, pointing to his left. "If you're worried we might wander up during the night, there's a lock on the door."

Relief at having a place to stay the night emboldened her to return his flirtation.

"Do you think that might be necessary?"

"Not for me," he said, turning around. "Can't speak for Blue. Always suspected he roams at night when he has a lot on his mind. You'll be his first sleepover."

"And you?"

"Mine, too." She didn't believe him. They reached the bottom of the staircase. "Blue will show you the way while I retrieve your luggage. Keys, please."

"It's unlocked."

Paula admired the rear view his tight black jeans afforded as he walked across the living room. He closed the front door behind him as she got down on both knees and hugged Blue's neck.

"Show me the way?"

The tri-colored dog, mostly black mixed with streaks of rust and white, figured out where they were going. Although the breed is known for its herding instinct, and despite his age, Blue bounded up the stairs ahead of her, slipping twice, recovering quickly. He waited at the landing and followed a half-step behind as she pushed open the first door on the right. Paula barely had time to survey the large room's tastefully appointed western décor before Daniel joined them and set her bags down.

"Will it be a problem if Winston tries and can't find you?"

"Oh my, yes! I totally forgot. Wouldn't want him to think I'd been kidnapped or fallen in with a band of outlaws. Don't quite know how to explain this, though," she said, spreading her arms apart. "I suppose it would be easiest if I fib a little bit and tell him I had to change to a rental house after the reservation mix-up thing."

"I suppose," he repeated. "Phone's there by the bed."

Paula looked at the nightstand. "Do you have an alarm clock I can borrow? I need to wake up by six and don't want to disturb you."

"We're early risers. I'll knock on the door until you tell me you're awake."

"Okay, if you're sure it won't be a bother." He started to leave. "Say, do you have big day planned tomorrow?"

"We'll find out together." He answered her questioning look. "I'm going where you're going."

"Why?"

"That seminar. Same as you."

"I gathered that. But why? It's quite the chivalrous offer, but having made the journey to town once, I can find it again on my own. Really, I can. And I certainly don't need a chaperone. Or are there early-morning dangers out here in the wilds I'm unaware of? You know, me being a city girl and all."

"Paid my fee."

Her head tilted slightly. "You're a writer?"

"Poet's more like it."

"Really? Anything I can read?"

"Maybe. Sometime."

Much as she would've enjoyed talking with her handsome rescuer well into the night, travel fatigue had taken its toll.

"Is this a full-service bed and breakfast?" She laughed when she saw his surprised look as they stood at the edge of the bed. "Breakfast. I *meant,* does your early rising mean breakfast here? Or should we leave in time for me to make good on my offer at The Diner? I'm asking because I'm certain it'll take me a lot longer to get presentable than you, and six o'clock might not give me enough time."

"Here."

"Perfect. Then six works."

He started to leave again.

"Say, I just realized. You know my last name. We've broken bread together, thank you again. We'll be sleeping under the same roof. Different floors, of course. Don't you think I'm entitled to …?"

"Collins," he answered from the doorway.

"Daniel Collins. I like how that sounds." She paused. "You said there was no lady of the house. Since you haven't told me your story, was there ever a Mrs. Collins?"

The pained expression she earlier thought she'd only imagined spread across his face.

"There was."

"Did she leave you?" She scolded herself silently before saying, "Daniel, I'm truly sorry. Sometimes I just can't help myself. I ..."

"Yes," he answered softly. Then he was gone, Blue trailing behind.

When she could no longer hear them, Paula sat at the top of the stairs, hugged her knees, and felt a flood of emotions come over her as a few tears trickled down her cheeks. Happy to have met a handsome stranger, unhappy to have spoken without thinking. Sad for him without knowing why. Wondering what lay ahead in the few days before she left Three Oaks, Colorado at the end of the week.

Downstairs, Daniel's body stretched out fully clothed on top of a bed he made every morning, but Paula's question had sent his mind to another place and time.

Three

1996, Nineteen months earlier
Washington, D.C.

What do you get your wife for her birthday when you both know it will be her last?

The question tumbled into Daniel Collins' thoughts as the room filled with early morning sunlight through a bedroom window framed by heavy white curtains pulled-back and tied in place. More acutely aware of clocks and the calendar than at any time in his life, he knew without looking thirty minutes had passed as he sat in silence before Mallory opened her amber eyes and turned toward where she knew he'd be. He rose unsteadily from his chair on legs stiffened from lack of movement and leaned across the edge of the bed. She often assured him their first kiss would be the highlight of her days, and he lingered to gently lift strands of chemo-ravaged hair away from the eyelashes ensnaring them.

Their morning routine before the arrival of the daytime hospice caregiver drew him to the medicine bottles lined up on the top of the dresser like so many toy soldiers waiting to be called into battle. He counted out the first of the day's assemblage and helped her steady the water glass she raised to her lips. He returned to the well-worn leather easy chair, a legacy from his bachelor days he'd moved from the study to wedge between her bed and the wall. A tight fit, but they both craved the closeness. Daniel would have slept there if Mallory hadn't insisted otherwise. She thought he was sleeping comfortably in their master suite upstairs at night, and none of the overnight hospice attendants ever betrayed his secret. He was on a cot a few steps down the hallway, close enough to hear her labored breathing until one of her toy soldiers relaxed her into a mercifully peaceful sleep. Then, and only then, could he drift off.

Not that long ago, their life together stretched out before them like a Wyoming highway with no curves, no speed limit, no end in sight. An oncologist's words had sent them careening down an unpaved country road, one that would too quickly narrow from months to weeks to one with but a handful of miles remaining. That first night, when they had no more tears to shed and with Mallory finally asleep, Daniel slipped away from their bed to make his way down the winding stairway of their Georgetown townhouse. Outside, cloaked in nighttime darkness away from the glow of streetlights, he paced back and forth on the cobblestone sidewalk. Hidden from prying eyes, he looked up at the sky and cried out, "I can't live without her. She believes in You. If You must take one of us, let it be me. Let it be me."

Disease and drugs caused Mallory to sleep much of the time. During his solitary daylight hours while the caregiver was there, she insisted he write his poetry, though the effort was half-hearted, at best. She also encouraged him to read lawyer novels by Grisham and Turow, a luxury he lacked the time to indulge before. He hated what made it possible now, but welcomed the brief respite of getting lost in the fictional lives of others, while country music played in the background. But his thoughts always returned to Mallory and their life together.

Daniel's parents' tragic deaths in 1973 brought him from a Pacific Northwest farm to live with his grandparents in Arlington, Virginia. His first day at school he met Mallory, hands-down the prettiest and most popular girl in their sixth-grade class at Walter Reed Elementary. Their lockers next to each other and their paths walking to and from school intersected, each school day beginning and ending with them together. His shyness no match for her persistence as she eased his rural-to-urban assimilation among their ten-year-old classmates.

Mallory had her many girlfriends and their shared interests; Daniel a few pals and their activities, especially sports. Given their ages, the unique friendship caused envy among the girls and puzzlement among the boys. She asked him to call her Mel when they were alone together. It was one of the many nicknames for Mallory, and she denied this familiarity to anyone else, creating a special bond between them. Being together almost every day continued through high school until college separated them, Daniel to the University of Virginia in Charlottesville and Mallory to Western Kentucky University, her parents' alma mater, in Bowling Green. If Hollywood ever wanted a script for *Harry and Sally – The Early Years*, screen writers could look to the true story of Danny and Mel.

While apart, they exchanged letters and talked by phone, and spent time together back home in Arlington during school breaks and holidays. They attended each other's graduations but lost contact in a pre-internet world when Mallory left on an extended church mission abroad and Daniel entered law school. Mallory's world was faith-centered; without her, Daniel stopped attending church. He only went because she wanted him to, and he wanted to be with her.

Daniel's grandparents deeded him their North Nineteenth Street home long before their deaths within months of each other in their second year in assisted living. The modest, two-story, mid-century red brick residence was a short walk through the familiar Walter Reed schoolyard to the Westover shopping center where he often caught the downtown bus rather than self-navigate the insanity of weekday D.C. commuter traffic.

One crisp autumn Saturday afternoon as the decade of the eighties came to an end, wearing jeans and a cardigan sweater, Daniel sat outside Common Grounds, his favorite Westover coffee shop. At a nearby table, shaded by an umbrella from the sun's warming rays, a woman looking to be about his age wearing a headset sat down, closed her eyes, and rocked back and forth as she sang a song popular during his senior year in high school. He couldn't believe his eyes, but tempted as he was, didn't interrupt. When the song ended, she blinked and noticed him staring. She removed the earphones, swept back her thick brunette hair and called across an empty table and chairs separating them.

"Love that song. Hope I didn't ruin it for you."

He remained silent for dramatic effect before taking off his UVA college baseball cap with one hand and dark aviator sunglasses with the other.

"Danny? Is that you?" she blurted out.

"It is."

Mallory stumbled as she rushed to his table. After a long embrace, she stepped back. "Did you recognize me?"

"Of course. The moment you sat down."

"How embarrassing! Why didn't you say something?"

"Didn't wanna interrupt. And you were doing such a good job entertaining everyone."

When she looked around, patrons at other tables clapped appreciatively.

"Shame on you." A punch to his arm. "Now I'm *really* embarrassed."

"Shouldn't be. You sing beautifully. Just as you did back in high school."

"You remembered?"

"How could I forget?" He stared at her for a moment. "Join me?"

"Like you could stop me." He pulled back the chair next to his at a table without an umbrella. He helped her peel off a multi-colored wool jacket, and as she draped it across the back of the chair, she asked, "Hey, speaking of music, as I recall, you liked country when absolutely no one else did. Correct?"

"Ahead of the times, it turns out. But I've lived long enough for it to get some of the respect it deserves from my elitist friends. And since we're recalling things correctly, you were in that 'absolutely no one else' group."

"Was I?"

"You were."

"Did you ever try to change my mind?"

"I did. When you said it all sounded like bad garage band music with banjos and fiddles, I gave up."

Her eyebrows arched. "I said *that*?"

"Uh, huh."

"Kinda harsh, I admit. Hearing it now. And you remembered for a long time." She rested her clasped hands on the table. "Too late for an apology?"

"Forget it. I'm sure back then I didn't like everything you did."

"You're just saying that to make me feel better."

"Not true. Let me think." He rubbed his chin theatrically, then moved his hand away and lifted his index finger. "How 'bout this one? You never got me to ballroom dancing class."

"That's right! But I did try, didn't I?"

"You did."

"Okay, fair enough. Now, I don't mean for this to sound like a character flaw. Do you still like country music?"

"I do. Not the new stuff so much."

"What then?"

"The old guys. The country legends. As others have said, I'd pay good money to hear Ray Price sing the Nashville phone book. And then there's Elvis. Not country. But he's my guy."

Only half-listening, Mallory was trying to fully grasp how her life had changed in an instant. She looked at the man sitting across from her as if she'd won the lottery. In a way, they both had.

"Danny, I have to say, you look fantastic!" She waited a few long moments. "Um, that was your invitation to tell me I do, too."

"Not the word I was searching for."

"Well …"

"Hmm. At Walter Reed, I'd have said cute. High school -- attractive. Definitely, attractive."

"Smooth. And college?"

"The word that comes to mind … is beautiful."

"Even smoother. And now?"

"Still searching." In truth, he was. Their surprise meeting, and being with her again, impacted him as nothing else he could recall. "As a placeholder, how about … beyond beautiful?"

"You always did say the nicest things, Daniel Colin Collins."

Mallory was the only person in school who knew his middle name, the fruit of his mother's offbeat sense of humor when her husband insisted their only child become a fourth-generation Daniel.

"Say, are you still writing poetry?"

"Now it's you who remembered."

"How could I forget." She smiled as she repeated his earlier line.

"And the answer is yes. I'm still writing. Some. Not much. My time is all pretty much taken up with work."

"Whatta ya do?"

"I ..."

"Oh, I remember! You went to law school. Is that it? Being Perry Mason and never losing a case?"

"Almost as good. The other side does prevail from time to time. Not often."

"That being the case, I'll wait, not patiently, while my Perry Mason searches for what lies *beyond beautiful*."

****

Despite stellar grades and the law review, Daniel accepted a low-paying public defender job the month after graduation to give him trial experience he didn't think a white shoe law firm would provide a newly minted associate. He wasn't surprised his clients numbered among the worst of the worst on the lower rungs of D.C. society, and after three years of carrying the workload of at least two lesser lawyers, he felt he'd put in his time. Someone else could take a turn behind the battered, government-issued wooden desk in a cramped office with erratic heating and cooling he shared with other overworked and equally disheartened attorneys.

The long hours at low wages ultimately paid dividends as his courtroom prowess gained him notoriety, and when word spread he intended to make a change, several prestigious firms aggressively pursued him. He met with all of them, but at the end of the day, his loner bent prevailed and he went out on his own. A risky decision in a town with more lawyers than trees, but fate smiled favorably. After only a few years, he rang the success bell loudly as the all-important D.C. link to a cadre of Southern trial lawyers who'd launched the class-action takedown of big tobacco companies.

The "link" came about thanks to his grandfather's impeccable reputation and connections, both of which extended after his death well beyond D.C.'s rectangular borders, and Daniel's performance in his lengthy interviews sealed the deal. When tobacco companies settled the lawsuits, his share of the court-awarded legal fees assured his financial independence for several lifetimes. Unless fate intervened.

****

"Mel, where are you living now?" Daniel asked, returning to their table with coffee for both of them.

"In the District. Renting a townhouse at Hillandale across from Georgetown University. If I had the money, I'd buy it. Doubt I ever will, Congressional staff pay being what it is."

"I know the place. It's real nice. Been to parties there a few times."

"Speaking of pay," she said, smiling and pointing to his expensive leather shoes. "Doesn't lawyering earn you enough to afford socks?"

"Don't wear them on weekends. Say, what brings you out this way today?"

"The Westover used book store. Not my first time. Surprised it's taken this long for us to run into each other. And you? Where do you live?"

"Same house you'd remember. Stayed put after my grandparents died. I like having some distance from the downtown lunacy. Helps keep me sane. Or at least I think it does. And it keeps memories alive."

Her eyes pulled his into them. "Am I one of those memories?"

His pulse quickened.

"You are. Happens each time I look out a window and see the swing in the backyard."

"One of *my* favorite memories! We made a lot of plans in that swing, didn't we? Dreamed a lot of dreams."

"We did. And I remember you telling me dreams never come true for those who never dream."

"I said that?" she asked.

"You did."

"Well, I continue to marvel at your memory. Must've been repeating something I read or heard someone else say. I'm not that articulate."

"I beg to differ."

"That's very kind. Anyway, doesn't matter. But now I have to ask. Are your dreams coming true?"

"Still working on 'em, I guess. You?"

A warm feeling came over her. "One came true not too long ago."

"Something you can share?"

"Happily. Being with you again. And Danny, beyond beautiful is just fine. I don't deserve it, but I'm not going to let you take it back, either."

"Not a chance." He let a few moments pass. "Mel, do you have to be anywhere in the next hour or so?"

"I don't. Why? What've you got in mind?"

"Our swing beckons," he said, reaching for her hand.

Instead of an hour or so, from that day on they were inseparable. The rest of the world knew him as Daniel, but to her, he would always be Danny. She'd never made the change everyone else did to calling him Dan when they entered high school.

She was disappointed but unconcerned when she learned he'd stopped going to church, confident it wouldn't be long before he was at her side on Sunday mornings at the Washington National Cathedral a short distance from her Hillandale townhouse. It only took a few weeks, and as the music began, Mallory said a silent prayer of thanks that the man she'd never stopped loving was worshiping beside her. He wore a suit and tie, and she smiled when she first noticed bare ankles between the cuffs of his trousers and his expensive leather shoes. She found his explanation entirely sensible, as would another woman decades later.

Walking out an hour or so later, Daniel squeezed her hand to slow her as they approached a large object inlaid in the marble floor.

"Never seen one like that. What is it?"

"A Jerusalem Cross. It's the cathedral's emblem. Actually, as you can see, five crosses."

"What's the meaning behind it?"

She turned her program to the back page. He read that the five intersecting crosses symbolized each of the wounds Christ suffered at His crucifixion, with the four smaller crosses also symbolizing the spread of Christianity from its Holy Land origins to the four corners of the earth.

He folded his program and put it in his jacket pocket. The next day, Daniel spent his lunch hour with a specialty jeweler down the street from his office.

Mallory's parents had known Daniel since he was ten, yet despite all his success and all his attributes, they couldn't bring themselves to embrace him as a suitable husband for their daughter. Mallory knew the reason without them telling her, though they did anyway -- often, and at length. His ambivalence toward organized religion and how that might impact the lives of their future grandchildren. She asked Daniel not to be drawn into arguments, an agreement that gave rise to an uncomfortable truce between the two generations on the rare occasions they were together.

Despite misgivings about Daniel, Mallory's mother accepted the inevitable and insisted on a big church wedding for her only child. She and Mallory's father chose not to be among a dozen or so close friends who attended the civil ceremony and reception Mallory wanted the summer after the young couple found each other again at a sidewalk coffee shop. It would be a setting that would repeat itself for Daniel in another city decades later.

Daniel often told Mallory he regretted causing estrangement from her parents, especially since he had no family of his own. Each time he did, she assured him everything would heal … in time.

Mallory assumed it was her fiancés' heavy workload keeping him at the office late two nights a week in the months leading up to their wedding, and she never gave a second thought to it always being Tuesday and Thursday nights. Those evenings, before he arrived back at Hillandale where they were living together, Daniel was taking ballroom dancing lessons to surprise her the first night of their honeymoon at a hotel in Hawaii when he reached for her hand and led her to the nightclub's dance floor.

On the island of Kauai, a tropical breeze lifted Mallory's hair from her shoulders as they slow-danced on sunbaked sand at sunset the day before they had to leave paradise and return home.

"Someday," he said, pulling her to him even tighter, "we'll leave that zoo and move to where this all began."

"Back across the river to Arlington? Why?"

"No. Not at all. To Three Oaks."

"Ah, you're thinking of your down-on-one-knee, Rocky Mountain proposal during our hiking trip."

"I am."

"Romantic, yes. But my darling Danny, that's not where this all began."

"It's not?"

"You and I began that morning I showed you how to open your locker at school. Remember?"

"I do. I guess you're right. If you hadn't, there might not be a you and me now."

"There most certainly would," she said, confidently.

"Why are you so certain?"

"I'd have found a way."

"Why?"

"Even sixth-graders can fall in love." Mallory stopped their gentle swaying, reached her hands to each side of his head, drew him to her and kissed him passionately. "I did."

As they had done every evening since their arrival, they held hands and watched the sun slip below the Pacific horizon. In the gathering darkness, Daniel wrapped his arm around Mallory's waist as they slowly walked back toward their oceanfront hotel.

Mallory fingered the handcrafted, eighteen-karat gold Jerusalem Cross dangling on a gold chain around her neck, a Valentine's Day gift, and asked, "Danny, when did you know you were in love with me?"

"It wasn't the sixth grade. But honestly, I can't remember a time when I wasn't. And I don't want to." He wrapped his arms around her. "I let you get away once. Won't ever let it happen again."

"Good to know. And now, Danny Boy, we have all the time in the world."

Four

1998
Three Oaks
Wednesday, Day Two

A s promised, Daniel woke Paula at six o'clock, and an hour later she walked into the kitchen to find a perfectly timed breakfast. She responded in kind to his good morning greeting.

"Daniel, about what I said last night. That last thing. I'm sorry. I ...

"Think nothing of it. I didn't."

"But ..."

"Sleep well?" He approached the center island with a plate for each of them. When he set hers down, he saw both redness and sadness in her eyes and had his answer.

"Like a baby," she lied. "Or at least how I imagine a baby would sleep."

"No children?"

"No children. Doctors say I can't have any."

"But a husband."

Standing at the edge of the center island, she self-consciously twisted her rings. "Yes, you know I have one of those."

"Did you call him last night?"

"I did," she answered, guardedly. "Why do you ask?"

Daniel gestured with the coffee pot lifted from its warming plate.

"Love some. May I have a little bit of cream?"

As Daniel poured, he tilted his head toward the small ceramic pitcher on the island as Paula, dressed similarly as the day before with different selections, perched herself on the left-handed stool.

"Thank you." She stirred the cream. "Why did you ask if I called my husband last night?"

"Wondering if you gave him the number here."

"Read it to him off the phone." She lifted her cup and saw his look. "What's wrong?" Before he could answer, she said, "Oh, I see what you mean. I was so tired I didn't think about him calling and you answering."

"If the phone rings, you answer it."

Rescued again.

She sipped her coffee. "And you. How did you sleep?"

"Soundly." His turn to lie. Memories of life before Three Oaks robbed him of all but a few hours of sleep. "Blue usually sleeps through the night, though he'll occasionally wake me just because he wants middle-of-the-night company."

"Whatta you do then?"

"Read him some of my poetry. Puts him right back to sleep."

Paula's smile found its way to her eyes, wiping away the sadness while leaving some of the redness. Holding a University of Virginia mug in one hand, Daniel sat down on the stool opposite her. She noticed his long-sleeved brown corduroy shirt wasn't yet tucked into his jeans, and liked how his casual, relaxed manner continued to put her at ease.

"Since you mentioned it, I'll ask again. May I read some of your poetry?"

A ringing sound spared him answering.

"It's for you." She handed him the device as she returned to her stool.

"You bet," he told the other person. "We'll be there."

Daniel slipped the cordless phone back into its cradle on the wall and told his breakfast guest the town's only veterinarian had called to confirm Blue's grooming appointment. What he didn't tell her was that the vet was his only friend in Three Oaks, a fellow widower with whom he frequently had breakfast at The Diner. Or that he'd been informally adopted as "Uncle Dan" by the vet's teenage daughter.

"An all-day affair with people fussing over him. Drop off on our way, pick him up coming home."

Though she'd only been there slightly more than half a day, Paula liked the sound of coming home to a residence other than her own, to a man other than her husband, allowing herself to blur fantasy and reality.

"Does that mean I can stay another night?"

"Can't have you homeless, now, can we?"

Heaven help me, am I being tipped his way?

"Thank you. That's very kind." She looked at her watch. "We should be going soon, don't you think? With you leading the way, I presume."

"No."

"You really like that word, don't you?"

"Not much room for interpretation." His best lawyerly voice. "Or misunderstanding."

"I beg to differ. May I?"

A beautiful woman wanting to play verbal volleyball in my kitchen.

"You may."

"Thank you. Now, saying no as you just did could mean many different things." She began counting with her fingers. "That it isn't possible, for what reason I don't know, for me to follow you in my car. Or you don't want me to follow behind you. Or is it because you want me to ride with you? Oh, I guess maybe you want to ride with me. Lots of possibilities, don't you see? I respectfully ask for an interpretation. You know, to avoid any possible misunderstanding."

Standing in the center of his kitchen, he conceded good-naturedly. "Pleased with yourself?"

"I am. A carefully conceived and articulately expressed response. If I do say so myself. And I do. Say so myself, that is." She looked at him over the rim of the coffee cup she held in both hands, elbows resting on the island. "Your turn."

"Okay. Another way to think about it, possibly, is my four-wheel drive with winter tires spent the night in the garage. Your car, probably without winter tires is, like the road to town, covered with snow."

"It snowed last night?"

"Happens here this time of year. Do you remember saying you heard it forecast on the radio?"

"Ah," she said.

"Speechless?" Asked in the friendliest of taunts, softened with a grin.

"Seldom. Just a lot to think about, that's all. Let's see. To summarize. Last night, hunger and homelessness had me in their clutches before I stumbled my way here. And thank goodness I did. Look at what I found. Food. Shelter. And now, transportation. Through snow, no less.

Meeting all my needs." *Well, almost.* "But we haven't discussed price. Or if you take credit cards."

"Your company is more payment than Blue and I have any right to expect."

Daniel was satiating Paula's hunger for male compliments, and the sincerity with which his words came created a warmth inside her she'd feared was gone from her life forever.

"Well, I'll admit I do enjoy my own company, and I'm pretty certain one or two others do, as well. Always been a social kinda gal. Have a flair for it, I guess. Since that's going to be my payment, and if Blue's okay with it, too, I hope I don't disappoint."

"No chance."

He glanced at the simple, battery-powered clock on the wall opposite the six-burner gas range that cost as much as a late-model used car. A study in contrasts, something Paula would come to learn also applied to Daniel. But he'd keep the darkest ones from her. As he had from everyone else.

"Time to go," he said. "Doubt any effort's been made to clear the roads."

"Would those be the roads less traveled?" she asked, nimbly easing herself off the stool and straightening her sweater where it touched the waist of her tailored slacks. He answered wordlessly with a look she could easily read. "Sorry, couldn't resist."

"I see you're getting an early start on your writing seminar," he said, motioning toward the door. "Careful. You may find the road to being teacher's pet a heavily congested one."

"Good one. Actually, really good. Your home field advantage means I'll just have to work harder."

On the slow drive to town, tires crunching snow that glistened in the morning sun on uncleared roads, Paula asked again if he'd tell her his story.

"Some other time. Maybe."

"I'll take that as a yes." She hungered for more physical contact, but only reached to elbow him lightly. "Okay, in the few minutes we have now, will you at least tell me how you became a poet?"

"At best, aspiring."

"That's why you're attending the conference."

"Are you asking, or answering?"

"*Very* good, Daniel. Very good. Keeping me on my toes. Now, here *is* a question. Have you ever been published?"

"A few times. Small journals, here and there. No big deal."

"Oh, getting published, anytime, anywhere, is laudable. Take it from someone who knows."

"And how is it you know?"

He maneuvered his Jeep to the opposite side of the road to avoid a snow drift.

"That'll cost you. Let's say, lunch. Today. What a bargain. Back to you. Do you have an editor? If not, is there anyone you let read your poems before you send them off to a publisher?"

"Does reading to Blue count?"

Daniel pulled into the animal clinic's parking lot as Paula turned to look at the rear-seat passenger who recognized their destination and eagerly anticipated what the day held in store for him. She smiled at the canine's excitement before looking back to the driver.

"To use your favorite word, no."

Daniel's hand-tooled cowboy boots leveled the height disparity with Paula as they signed in for the seminar at the town's largest historic home, a testament to Gold Rush money in the late 1800s. They went their separate ways after agreeing to forego the event-sponsored buffet and meet for lunch across the street. Hours later, she found him already occupying his favorite corner booth at The Diner, home to a limited comfort food menu but bottomless coffee pot. Seeing her approach, he folded the newspaper he'd retrieved from the post office three doors down and put away his reading glasses.

An unfriendly waitress took their sandwich orders. After she left, Paula said, "Wonder what *her* problem is." Daniel shrugged and fiddled with his napkin. "Anyway, your session must have ended early, too. Think we'll get our money's worth?"

"I won't. Not going back."

"Why? What happened?"

Daniel had registered almost a year earlier when his outlook on life had been somewhat brighter. He wouldn't have been there today were it not for a lady from Tennessee.

"More what didn't happen. No other men. I felt like an intruder."

I doubt any of the women were unhappy, though he'd definitely be distracting.

"And the instruction wasn't to my liking. Expected more, I guess. Or different."

She started to ask him to explain, but decided instead to push against the door he'd closed on the drive to town.

"On the way here this morning, when I asked you to tell me your story, you said some other time. By my watch, it's some other time."

The attractive waitress in her early thirties returned, giving Daniel a reprieve. She silently served their lunches as if they, especially Paula, were in some way diseased. They watched her depart, bumping unapologetically into another waitress carrying a heavily laden tray. Despite the pungent aroma of jealousy in the air, Paula acted as if nothing out of the ordinary had happened, unwrapped stainless steel flatware from a paper napkin sheath, and waited.

He knew what she wanted, but he'd come to enjoy their repartee and wanted to see if he could wait her out. She gave in.

"It's *still* some other time."

He set his uneaten grilled cheese sandwich back on the plate next to the bowl of tomato soup.

"Okay." Elbows on the table, he creased his napkin as he spoke. "Only child. Parents died when I was ten. Went to live with my grandparents. I loved them, and they me. University of Virginia, undergrad and law. My grandparents died within a few months of each other while I was practicing in D.C. Hired a money manager so I wouldn't have to be bothered with such things. Then my wife died. Gave up law and moved here. Got a dog."

Daniel thought he was finished. Paula thought otherwise.

"That wasn't your story. That was your way of telling me you don't want to talk now. That's fine. You'll tell me later."

"Perhaps." He took his first bite of sandwich. "You know, cold grilled cheese isn't half-bad. Anyway, your turn. The reason I'm buying your lunch. Tell me how is it you know so much about publishing?"

"Sure, why not? I'll be as brief as you. Or try. I'm a writer. Newspaper and magazines. Started small, worked my way up to the big time. Or at least as big as it gets in Nashville."

"Explains the fancy car."

"May I continue?"

"Sorry," he answered, dipping a spoon into his soup, bringing it to his lips. Cold. He set the spoon down and gave all his attention to the beautiful woman with a Southern accent.

"I like the research part since I mostly write lifestyle pieces. Restaurants and entertainment. Usually a mix of fine dining and comfort food. Country music, of course. Came here for the seminar because a friend from Kentucky is one of the instructors. Met you. And your dog."

"Wow. Less than a minute. Including my rude interruption."

Paula returned his smile as they touched raised glasses of iced tea. Their waitress saw the gesture as she approached and managed to convey unpleasantness with a single word.

"Finished?"

Daniel looked across to Paula, then nodded.

"One check or two?"

Daniel raised his hand.

"Figures." An edge to her voice as the she dropped the bill in front of him before leaving.

Paula leaned in and whispered, "Let me guess. The two of you. History?"

He winced slightly but remained mute.

"Thought so. Now," she whispered playfully, "if this were a history class, would we be in ancient times or current events?"

This lady certainly has a way about her.

Paula heard the unmistakable sound of yet another door closing when her question went unanswered.

As he slid around and out of the booth, Daniel dropped a twenty on the table for a twelve-dollar meal, the generous tip preferable to prolonging their departure.

"Speaking of class, you have one of your own to get back to. What time do you want Blue and me to pick you up?"

That evening, helping prepare a dinner of freshly caught, mountain-stream rainbow trout from a local market, Paula delighted in their closeness and rubbed her elbow lightly against his.

"It's later." She pointed to the clock on the wall. "Again."

"Later?"

"As in you were going to tell me later. You know. Your story. The rest of it."

"I believe my exact word was perhaps."

She turned toward him and slowly raised the paring knife in her hand while unsuccessfully trying for a menacing look.

"Well, since you put it that way," he said, grinning. "Guess I have the same problem you did last night."

"And that would be?"

"Where to begin."

"How 'bout you follow your own advice."

"And that was …"

"Begin at the beginning. And more than half a minute this time, if you please."

Knowing she was a journalist, Daniel sensed Paula wouldn't be satisfied just hearing him tell his story his way. She'd poke and prod to peel back his layers. She didn't disappoint.

"And I'll help get us started." She wanted him to loosen up, to move from inward resistance to outward sharing. "Where were you born?"

"George, Washington."

"No, seriously."

"Seriously, that's where."

"Well, I didn't think it would be a secret. But if you don't want to tell me, then don't tell me."

"Not a secret. Mid-way between Seattle and Spokane."

Paula looked dubious. "Tell me more."

"Sure. It's a small town in the high desert where the hills seem to roll on forever. Skies are seldom cloudy, or at least that's my recollection."

He left her side to adjust one of the burners on the stove, returned, and continued.

"When the wind blows, as I recall it always seemed to, the air fills with the smells of whatever crops are in the ground or being harvested at the time. Could be wheat or corn. Maybe alfalfa. Even has its own zip code. 98824, I believe. In the fall, the leaves turn to orange and gold. Then winter comes and every day the sky threatens snow, and ..."

He sure got loose in a hurry.

"Okay, okay." Her interruption punctuated with laughter. "I get it. I'm sorry. I'm sorry I doubted you. I apologize. It'll never, ever, *ever* happen again."

His expression conveyed how pleased Paula knew he was with himself. To give full measure to his moment of one-upmanship, she allowed an interlude before asking how he got from George in Washington to living clear across the country near George's Mount Vernon home on the Potomac River.

"Guess there is a certain symmetry," Daniel allowed, as they brought their food to the center island. "My parents were farmers, and they worked the fields together at harvest time. One year, they got behind because of unseasonably heavy rain and were out long past dark one evening. They were driving home on a narrow road and were killed when stuck by a large truck headed to a grain elevator. My paternal grandfather was a congressman. He sold the farm and I went to live with them in the other Washington. He used the money from the farm to pay for my education."

Daniel felt his answer sufficient, but as they sat down after he'd served Blue, Paula's demeanor indicated otherwise, a calculated, though wordless, peeling back. He decided to accept it for what it was and continue, knowing she was a married woman living half a country away he'd never see again. And he liked that someone, especially someone as intriguing as Paula, was this interested in him. If only for a few days.

"My grandfather grew weary of the Congressional swamp and chose not to campaign for re-election after several terms. He and my grandmother often talked about returning to Washington State, but never did. They stayed in D.C. and he took a job as a lawyer with a non-profit advocating for human rights and the environment."

"You said at lunch you were an only child."

"Like my mother and father before me." He spread his cloth napkin across his lap. "Let's eat."

She reached across the island. "Daniel, would you mind if I said a quick blessing?"

She took his hands in hers, and when she bowed her head, he followed. He listened as she gave thanks for the food, the hands that prepared it, and for chance encounters that put people in the paths of others. It was the closest he'd been to praying since leaving D.C.

They finished dinner and their second glass of wine. Paula began stacking dishes in the dishwasher, helping without asking, making herself at home as if their evening together was a family affair.

"Where'd you learn to cook?"

"Are you asking as a writer?"

"I doubt you'd be all that interesting to my readers."

"Because I'm not part of the Nashville scene?"

"There's that, and well, because I don't know enough to write about you." Peeling away. "Now, where did you learn to cook?"

"Promise you won't write about me?" he asked, wiping Blue's dish and water bowl with a paper towel before adding them to the dishwasher.

"Promise."

"Prison."

She'd wrongly doubted his birthplace, and earlier told him she'd never, ever, *ever* doubt him again.

"Really?"

"No."

Hearing his favorite one-word answer, she curled her upper lip as Daniel's hero Elvis often did. He got the message.

"Sorry, force of habit. The truth lies in a college apartment with roommates. I had a choice. Cook or clean. All of us were more interested in beer than food, so just simple things. Quantity over quality."

"And you've obviously improved over time." With no effort at segue, she asked, "Where did you meet your wife?"

Daniel hesitated before giving voice to what had kept him awake most of the previous night.

"Mallory and I met in elementary school."

"Really?"

"Yes. And I've been keeping track. You say really more often than I say no."

"Touché. Now, details, please. You know, meeting Mallory.

"None worth sharing. It's just where we met, that's all."

"Such a beautiful name. Don't think I've ever known anyone named Mallory."

"Time for me to take Blue outside for his after-dinner business. Won't be gone long."

This man sure can close doors.

When they returned a few minutes later, Paula followed them into the living room where Daniel pointed to matching soft-leather chairs in front of the fireplace. Blue settled on the floor between them. Conversation over red wine and cheese continued late into the night, long past when Daniel let the fire burn out. Paula had been right. Daniel had never before entertained anyone in this room, and it was the first time a fire had ever burned in the fireplace. But she hadn't noticed, focused instead on her disappointment he hadn't asked for more of her story. She knew most women, and some men, would have asked. Looking at his profile in the dim light and shadows, the name of the movie star he resembled came to her.

Upon reaching adulthood, Daniel often heard he reminded others of the late actor Steve McQueen, perhaps best known for driving a 1968 highland-green Ford Mustang fastback in an iconic car chase scene through the streets of San Francisco. Both men were handsome, fit, five-ten, sandy-colored hair worn short, blue eyes. The actor had been known to delete words script writers allocated to his characters supposedly because of his difficulty memorizing, his acting as dependent upon facial expressions and body language as spoken words. In court, Daniel had been the master of expressions and body language, as well, but could speak at length when it was called for. And it often was. Back then.

Paula didn't count a single attorney among her friends, and only a few as acquaintances, yet Daniel didn't fit her image of a successful trial lawyer. Her instinct was dead-on. He'd changed in many ways following Mallory's death, notably his transition from an intense courtroom combatant to a man of relatively few but carefully chosen words. From the moment they met, Paula was aware the scale balancing the number of words spoken between them tipped heavily toward her. Gazing into the fire, her bare feet resting against Blue's back, she asked if he thought she talked too much.

"Certainly not. Refreshing change from Blue. I can only guess at what he's thinking. Except when it's about food. Or going outside."

Paula turned to look directly at him, and there was sufficient light for him to see her narrow her eyes. Her Elvis lip curl still fresh in his mind, he was catching on she also could say a lot without saying anything.

"Seriously, living as I do out here creates hunger for the sound of another's voice." He took a swallow of wine. "And I especially like the sound of yours."

She leaned toward him. "You mean the southerness?"

"If southerness is a word, it's a new one to me. But yes. What you say, and how you say it."

Before the fire burned out, with Paula gently prodding, Daniel opened up about his years as a public defender. His words were "a gladiator for the downtrodden." He told her he did his time but left disheartened by the hopelessly overburdened court system and lack of client gratitude, especially from those who returned to crime wholly unrepentant after he'd skillfully kept them out of prison.

"Were you good? As a gladiator, I mean."

"Like to think so. Never considered it a calling, though."

"Did you find your calling?"

"Once. Helped lawyers from your part of the country make some big companies do the right thing. Their sins cost them a lot of money."

"Did you get some of it?"

"The money?"

Paula nodded.

"More than I dreamed possible. Left the zoo with all its two-legged animals behind and moved here."

"But why?"

"To write poetry." Not within striking distance of a truthful answer.

"You could do that anywhere. Why here? Why a place so far from all that you'd known?"

Daniel stared into the fire. "Came to spread my wife's ashes. Stayed."

Paula knew for a second time in as many days he'd gone to a far-away place, leaving her behind. She now knew something else. A ghost was haunting a log cabin home in Three Oaks, Colorado, and the ghost had a name.

Five

1996, Eighteen months earlier
Washington, D.C.

When Twilight Comes
When twilight comes across the quiet land,
I crave your presence, you who understand
The comradeship of word and look and smile;
The gentle talk and laughter after a while,
And homeward walk across the wave-worn sand.
How will it be, I wonder, when the grand
Full midday glow of life has vanished, and
The sun's last rays fall coldly on the dial,
When twilight comes?

Oh, that we two together still may stand;
Undone, perchance, the deeds we hoped and planned,
Tired and very old, yet missing naught
Of tenderness or olden word or thought,
God grant that life may leave us hand in hand,
When twilight comes.

The march of time after discovery of Mallory's cancer scorched calendar pages like a wind-blown fire, laying waste to their *forever more* in a matter of months. Lying in bed, her head rested comfortably against a small embroidered pillow. On it, her grandmother had stitched the words *I believe in angels*. When years ago, Daniel asked, "Do you?" Mallory answered, "Of course. Don't you?"

With her thirty-third birthday only a few days away, the gift question flickered back into Daniel's mind like the persistent quivering of a neon storefront light.

"That's so sweet of you to ask." She reached for his hand. "A bracelet from Tiffany, heavily laden with their ridiculously expensive charms, lots of them, would be nice."

Thinking her answer a serious one, and not wanting to deny her anything, he edged forward in his chair.

"Which charms?"

"I was only trying for a bit of fun with you." She slowly turned her head from side to side, smiling. "Jewelry is the last thing I'd want."

"Okay, what then?"

"Honestly, Danny, I haven't given it any thought because the one thing I want, no one can give me."

He knew the answer. Time.

Her face revealed the serenity she felt, at peace with their narrowing road.

"There is something else, though."

"What?"

"Promises."

"Promises?"

"Yeah. Since you asked, that's what I want for my birthday. Got something to write with?"

"I'm sure there's something here somewhere. Why?"

"Please get it." She released his hand. "Dictation time, counselor."

He returned a few minutes later to the ground-floor guest suite in their Chancery Court townhouse in Georgetown. Looking out the window, he could see the roof of the French Embassy a short distance away.

"At the top, write: I promise Mel."

He did, then straightened up in his chair and turned to look at her. He would regret forever neither of them had been much for taking pictures. And now it was too late. As was their decision to delay having children. In truth, it had been Mallory who insisted they wait.

"Here are the promises. And remember, you asked." She spoke slowly as he wrote. "I will blame nothing or no one. I will pray daily. I will go to church often." She paused to let him catch up. "I will treasure my friends and keep them close. I will keep lawyering. I will write my poetry. I will get counseling."

Hearing the last promise, Daniel's expression gave his thoughts away.

"You'll need it but think you don't." Both would turn out to be true. "Write it down. Please."

He did, and sensing she'd finished, laid pen and paper aside.

"One more." She gestured in the air as if she had the pen in her hand. "After Mel is gone … you're not writing. After Mel is gone, I won't just listen to my head. I'll go where my heart leads me." When their eyes met again, she said, "I have something to help you."

She reached for her grandmother's Bible, the leather cover softened and smudged by three generations of faithful hands. She feathered the pages open to the place marked by an attached silk ribbon and withdrew a small, fragile piece of paper yellowed with age. A poem with a title, *When Twilight Comes*, but neither author nor date. She handed it to Daniel and asked him to read it to her. The piece of paper fit in the palm of his hand. He squinted slightly at the small newspaper print as his courtroom baritone filled the small room. When he finished, she reached out her frail hand and he gently grasped it.

"The hand in hand when twilight comes. Danny, it's what I wanted for us. Now promise me it will happen for you. With someone else."

With the same care Mallory had shown, Daniel returned the poem to its place of safe-keeping. He felt the warmth of tears he couldn't subdue. There were times when Mallory couldn't focus much farther than her arm could reach, and he hoped for one of those times as he dried his eyes. She didn't notice.

"Oh, one more thing," she said.

He attempted to lighten the moment as he put his handkerchief away. "That would be your second one more thing."

"Clever. But it does show you're paying attention. That's good. Something I'm counting on."

He waited several seconds. "And?"

"And what?"

"The one more thing."

"Oh, yes. Remember. A promise is a promise. Going where your heart leads you. Finding someone else."

When she grew quiet, he thought of another quick-witted reply, but let it pass unspoken. He wanted to hear her voice, not his.

"Where was I? Oh, I remember. She has to be someone I'd approve of."

"How will I know?"

"You'll know. And hopefully, your new wife will have a more optimistic name."

It wasn't until they were in high school that Daniel learned Mallory in French meant "unlucky."

Daniel left the notebook and pen on the floor by his chair. While Mallory slept during the day, when he wasn't reading novels or attempting to write poetry and failing miserably, he filled the hours scribbling page after page, recording memories both seminal and trivial he could cling to after she was gone. When was the last time they slow danced? Watched a sunset? Made tender, familiar love on a Saturday morning before or after reading *The Washington Post* in bed together? Ate at their favorite restaurant near DuPont Circle? Was their last chardonnay Cloudy Bay from New Zealand or Meiomi from coastal California? Though it made him crazy, knowing he couldn't turn back time, he kept at it, day after day.

During increasingly fewer lucid moments in her final days, Mallory reminded Daniel. "You must keep those promises. For both of us."

Memorizing the short list posed no challenge, but he knew *Twilight* would never happen. What he had with Mallory so rare, so wonderful, stretching back to their childhood, there would be no one else after she went away. No do-overs in life. No room in his heart for another woman. Mallory knew different.

The first week of April, the end of their road coming into view, Mallory laid her head back as Daniel returned the toy soldiers filled with pills to parade rest. She spoke so softly he strained to hear her.

"I want you to do something for me."

"Anything."

"I want you to begin wearing my cross."

"Are you sure?"

Daniel was certain she hadn't taken it off since that Valentine's Day dinner in an elegant D.C. restaurant when he completely surprised her. Those six plus years now seemed like six days.

"I am. But I'll need your help."

Daniel wasted neither words nor time in asking 'why.' He gently pushed down the pillow and slipped his hands beneath her neck. He kissed her forehead and both cheeks before returning to his chair.

"In my prayers, I ask for three things. Will you do the same?"

"Of course, Mel. Just tell me."

He fumbled around fastening the lobster claw clasp to secure the dainty chain with the Jerusalem cross.

"Three things. Not much pain. My dignity. I won't die alone." She closed her eyes, and he feared the passing of her cross was her way of letting him know they'd finally come to the end. He held her hands for what seemed to be an eternity before her eyes opened, and she whispered, "Will you pray those for me?"

"I will." His raspy, trembling, broken voice would have been unrecognizable to those who knew him.

"Danny, the first two are in God's hands, the third in yours."

God came through for her, and so did Daniel. Three days later, the antique grandfather clock in the townhouse foyer chimed eleven times in the darkness when Mallory left one to be with the other.

Daniel waited several hours before making the calls he knew he had to make, then went outside as daylight began breaking over the city. He looked up at the orange-red sky on the eastern horizon, the aftermath of the storm that passed through during the night. He fell to the ground ... and wept.

After Mallory died, Daniel burned the notebook containing both the handful of promises she'd dictated and the countless memories he'd recalled. All the promises but one went unfulfilled. Not because he tried and failed. He never tried. He blamed himself for the time away from Mallory spent lawyering before she was diagnosed.

Overcome with grief, one by one he distanced himself from those he'd promised to treasure and keep close. They feared he might do something to follow her, to be with her again, and their fears weren't unfounded. But the harder they tried, the greater his distancing. Eventually, they all stopped trying and he got what he wanted. To be left alone. How different things might have been if he'd ever darkened the door of a therapist of any kind. It would take years before the only promise he did keep -- writing poetry – would become the pathway to fulfilling a second. One he'd so strongly discounted. The last one. *Twilight*.

The weakness of Daniel's faith disappointed Mallory but didn't diminish her love for him. "Danny," she'd once said, "you're trying to come to Christ with your mind. As if becoming a true believer is somehow like winning a big case. It doesn't work that way. You also need to open your heart. And you must pray. Try this. Think of prayer as a watering can, and water your garden every day. You'll be amazed at what will grow."

Much as he wanted to share his beloved Mallory's belief in watering cans and gardens while she was alive, her death put an end to it all. He had one awkward meeting with her parents after the funeral before he shuttered his legal practice and sold their townhome to newly arrived foreign diplomat. One hot summer day in early June, Daniel Colin Collins went away, leaving behind everyone he and Mallory had known, never once sharing where he was going. As a high-powered Washington, D.C. attorney, Daniel recorded his days in the fifteen-minute increments billed to clients. Soon, thousands of miles away, he'd measure his life by the changing seasons in a place only Mallory would have known where to look. It was there he cast her ashes into the wind at the spot where he'd proposed to her.

The week after Thanksgiving that same year, Daniel sat alone on a hard bench in a remote Colorado mountain town. His *Washington Post* subscription, the only enduring connection other than Mallory to his previous life, arrived by mail at the Three Oaks post office a few days after the front-page date. It lay open on the faded green laminate tabletop in the corner booth of the town's only diner as he sipped a steaming cup of black coffee while reading about Queen Elizabeth II. In the story, the writer referenced a famous quote from a speech the queen had given to an assemblage at Guildhall in London on her fortieth anniversary as monarch. Speaking in late November, the Queen reflected on that year by saying: "1992 is not a year on which I shall look back with undiluted pleasure. It has turned out to be an *annus horribilis*. I suspect that I am not alone in thinking it so."

Annus horribilis, the *Post* article explained, is Latin for "horrible year," the Queen's intentional twist on John Dryden's 1667 poem Annus Mirabilis – year of miracles. In March, Elizabeth's second son, Andrew, separated from his wife, Duchess Sarah Ferguson. In April, Princess Anne, the Queen's only daughter, divorced Captain Mark Phillips. In May, the book *Diana: Her True Story in Her Words* documented for a voyeuristic world her fractured marriage to the Queen's oldest son, Prince Charles. In the succeeding months, the British tabloid press recounted in excruciating detail the alleged infidelities of both Charles and Diana. On November 20th, four days before the Queen's speech, a fire destroyed a portion of Windsor Castle, the historic royal residence in London.

Okay, Daniel thought, she had a rough year back then. And now, this is my *annus horribilis*. He gazed out the window at the gently falling snow being swept along the side of the diner by an occasional gust of wind. Every morning, he carefully refolded the newspaper and left it on the counter by the cash register for others to read. He walked a few steps across the sticky linoleum floor, put his hands in his pockets, bracing himself against the weather outside as he pushed open the door, knowing he was free.

Free of the deafening sound of jet airplanes taking off every few minutes from Reagan Airport. Free of pollution from vehicles choking too few traffic arteries flowing in and out of the District. Free of sidewalks so overcrowded a person couldn't get from one place to another without elbowing others aside. Free of every sight and sound and smell that would remind him of a life he no longer had and one he no longer wanted.

Despite the loving embrace of his grandparents, Daniel grew up a loner. He mostly kept to himself in school, lettering in tennis because it wasn't a team sport. When he had the choice, he practiced law alone. Only his grandparents and Mallory had been able to penetrate his defenses. Now that was all behind him.

Daniel didn't mind the Colorado winters he knew lay ahead of him. He minded being there without her. It hadn't been their plan. His and Mallory's. Now he was alone. All alone.

Head down into the wind, walking toward his Jeep, Daniel had no way of knowing that in less than two years, he would experience not annus mirabilis, rather a *week* of miracles with a woman from Tennessee who would have met with Mallory's approval.

Six

1998
Three Oaks
Thursday, Day Three

P aula and Daniel shared a leisurely breakfast in his kitchen before
she departed for the seminar's second day. Roads had partially
cleared and she insisted on driving herself. He protested, but to
no avail.

"I can't persuade you to come along?" She pulled her coat over a
third stylish outfit and flipped her hair over the collar. "Might brighten
those ladies' day. A handsome poet in their midst. Would mine."

"Nah." Jeans and flannel shirt, both well-worn and entirely suitable
for The Diner, would normally have been his selection from his meager

post-D.C. wardrobe. The presence of his guest had caused him to step up his game as best he could, without overdoing it, to newer jeans and a newer flannel shirt.

"Nah? Now that's a change. And here I'd gotten so accustomed to no."

"Broadening myself."

"A worthy pursuit, and one you can rest assured I applaud." She tucked a silk-lined wool scarf around her neck. "And there's something else I would applaud."

She wanted him to take the bait, and after their brief time together, wasn't surprised he didn't.

"Mr. Collins, can you remember back to a time when your half of a conversation was more than just a word or two?"

"I can."

"Do you think you could do it with me? You know, I say something, then you say something that's at least a whole sentence. We'll go back and forth. One, then the other. It'll be really easy, once you get the hang of it again."

"Are you upset with me?"

She couldn't yet read him well enough to know when he was being serious, or jousting.

"Oh, no! My goodness, no. I was only trying to be helpful."

"I'm glad. Afraid my day was beginning badly. And did I hear an offer to tutor me?"

Jousting. That's a relief!

"I don't know what I'm going to do with you. But, yes, I'd love to! That'll be great! The sooner the better, don't you think? We can begin class when I get back this afternoon."

She impulsively kissed him on the cheek, then hurried toward the door.

"Paula," he called after her.

She turned around. "Yes?"

"What was the other thing you were going to applaud?"

"I'm impressed. You really do listen to me."

"Doesn't everyone?"

Hardly. Especially men.

"Not always. Where were we?"

"Applauding, I believe."

"Right. There's a standing ovation waiting when you tell me the rest of your story."

"We'll see. No promises."

Frustrated, she turned again to leave.

The voice behind her said, "The front desk asked me to ask how long you want to extend your reservation?"

He'd spiked the verbal volleyball over the net. She'd been with him in his home for two nights, and he'd made her time there so easy, so enjoyable. But her reason for being in Three Oaks would end the next evening, and at that moment, she realized she'd been allowing herself to imagine staying longer. How long she didn't know. Just longer. He waited patiently, but an answer couldn't find its way through her jumble of thoughts. She stared at him in silence. He cleared a path.

"Paula, Blue and I are happy for you to stay on as long as you wish."

"Thank you." Not knowing what else to say, she added. "I need to get going. Still in the running for teacher's pet."

After she left, Daniel returned to a morning routine Paula's arrival had disrupted. In the corner booth at The Diner, after his friend had departed to open his clinic, Daniel finished reading the paper and stared at a third cup of coffee growing cold as he pondered the uncertainty her captivating presence had brought to his small and otherwise certain world. Was there more than casual flirtation as she passed ever-so-briefly through his life on her way back to her husband? Had her arrival changed anything?

He went to the counter to freshen his coffee, and by the time he sat back down he'd satisfied himself that loneliness had given way to foolishness. She was literally here today, gone tomorrow. And he knew what the future held in store for him. Or thought he did. He stretched his legs to rest his boot heels on the edge of the bench across from him and looked out the window to Manor House across the street. He pushed thoughts of Paula aside and began thinking about the only promise he'd made to Mallory that he'd kept.

Back home, skipping lunch, he headed to his study to read poetry he'd written over the years, trying for inspiration. New words wouldn't come this day, and he returned the notebooks and loose papers to their bookcase resting place. Thoughts of Paula crowded back in and stayed with him the rest of the afternoon until he and Blue, waiting on the porch, saw her car pull up around four o'clock. The winter cold Paula felt when she stepped out and closed the door vanished when she saw them. Daniel had added an insulated ski jacket as a concession to the falling temperature.

"How nice," she called out. "Sitting there, just like before. With Blue by you." She climbed the steps. "Say, isn't that the name of a song?"

"It is. Spelled differently, of course."

She settled into the empty rocking chair. "Linda Ronstadt, right?"

"And Roy Orbison. He wrote Blue Bayou."

"Which is your favorite?"

Daniel read somewhere there were two kinds of men. Those who had a crush on Linda Ronstadt, and those who didn't know who she was. He knew who she was.

"Ronstadt."

"What was it that delightful waitress said yesterday? Oh, yes. *Figures.*"

Daniel smiled appreciatively at Paula's playful recollection, then asked about her day.

"First things first. I could tell Blue missed me, but you didn't wag your tail. This morning we agreed I'd be your conversation tutor. So, here goes. Daniel, I don't mind one bit saying I missed you. Thought about you. You know, being with you." He remained mute. "And you?"

"Me what?"

"Damn it, Daniel! I mean, darn it. Here I am, being all vulnerable with you, telling you that I missed you while I ..."

"Paula."

"Yes?"

"Do you remember a moment ago when I asked about your day?"

"I do," she answered, hesitantly.

"Well, doesn't that count as conversation?"

She crossed her arms, her effort at pouting a quick and dismal failure before graciously surrendering with a gloved two-thumbs-up gesture and radiant smile.

"Touche!"

He correctly anticipated the recounting of her day would be both detailed and lengthy. When he thought she'd finished several minutes later, and with dinner preparation in mind, he asked, "Lunch at The Diner?"

An unexpected reaction sailed his way. "Are you kidding me? Not on your life! Had all of Miss Congeniality I care to put up with yesterday, thank you very much. And you? Did you return to your morning coffee and newspaper there?"

"I did."

"Bet she was happy to see you -- without me."

Daniel felt he knew men. Women, including at times his beloved Mallory, were often a puzzle. He wasn't expecting either Paula's jealousy or that it would so quickly travel to her lips.

"Wouldn't know." He crossed one leg over the other as a distraction to move his eyes away from hers. "She wasn't there."

"Okay, sorry. None of my business." She knew she'd overstepped and changed course. "Say, I got to thinking on the drive back. How'd you and Blue come to be a twosome?"

"Never had a dog," he answered, grateful for the redirection from his tutor, hoping it was a lasting one. "I knew older dogs, especially black ones, are difficult to find homes for. They said years ago he'd come from a reputable breeder, but he got sick and was abandoned at the clinic. Kinda like leaving a baby at a fire station, I guess. Doc called me, and we took to each other right away."

"I'm glad you did. You seem perfectly matched."

"But don't worry. He's not the jealous type."

Was I being that obvious?

"Paula, we've still got a half-hour before nightfall. If you can stand the cold a bit longer, how 'bout a glass of wine and a change of venue?"

"Of course. You're the innkeeper, so I place myself in your capable hands. Speaking of which, I didn't give you an answer this morning. May I extend my reservation one more night? The seminar ends mid-day tomorrow and I can make my way out to an interstate hotel before dark."

Hearing Paula talk about her departure, Daniel struggled against a sinking feeling but managed to glibly reply, "I'll alert housekeeping."

Daniel returned with a bottle and wine glasses, holding all three in one hand. With the other, he touched Paula's elbow as they led Blue along the extension of the cobblestone pathway from the front porch around the side of the house to an area in back sheltered by a stand of towering juniper trees. Memories of his Arlington home had inspired him to install a large wooden swing firmly implanted in the ground with inlaid bricks beneath it. He steadied the swing for Paula to sit, then joined her. She swirled the wine in her glass and extended her long legs inches above the bricks as he created a slow back-and-forth glide. He tried to imagine the shapeliness of the legs beneath her tailored slacks.

"I'm guessing none of those bags I lugged up to your room had sensible shoes."

She moved her feet from side to side. "These are sensible shoes. Just not for here it turns out."

"Unfortunately, here is where we are."

"True. Since they seem to be troubling you, any chance you can drive me to Denver to shop for sensible ones? We should be able to make it there and back in a day. Unless it snows again."

Remembering her comment about his home field advantage, he said, "Score one for the visiting team."

Paula lifted her glass and tilted it in his direction to accept the accolade.

"Speaking of driving," he continued, "it's got to be, what, a thousand miles or so from here to Nashville. Why'd you drive all this way? Wouldn't it have been much easier to fly, then rent a car?"

"Easier? Yeah. But I wanted the extra time alone. To think. To try to clear my mind about some things. And besides, I love to drive. And I've got just the car for the open road."

"Unless there's snow."

"Well, there is that. But now that I'm here, I have to say, it's simply beautiful. And everything about your home is wonderful. All of it. How'd you find it?"

"Built it."

"You did? Tell me about that," she coaxed. "And this isn't tutoring. I really wanna know."

"There's that really word again."

"True. But that doesn't give you the right to say no."

"Okay. Mallory and I were childhood friends. We were together nearly every day for years, in school and out. The sister I never had. The brother she never had. Went our separate ways after college, then ran into each other years later. Began dating, for the first time I might add. Came to Three Oaks on a hiking trip. This swing is right about where I proposed. Before we got married, we decided to buy the D.C. townhouse she rented. I sold my home, and we used that money here."

"You knew back then you wanted a house here? What was the attraction?"

"The vibrant nighttime restaurant scene," he answered, straight-faced.

"I thought we were having a serious conversation," she said. "At least, I was."

"Okay, seriously. We planned it as a vacation home, thinking maybe one day we might move here for good. An architect finished the plans and we'd gotten as far as Mallory and a Denver decorator picking out all the furniture. Or almost all of it. I built it after she died."

"Anyone can see the woman's touch, and her taste was exquisite." Paula knew she had him on a roll. "I know about yours. Career, that is. What was hers?"

"A friend of my grandfather was a congressman from Kentucky where Mallory's parents met in college. I got her the introduction and she wowed him in her interview. She began as a staffer doing different things, but quickly became his legislative aide and most trusted advisor. She told anyone who'd listen she was happy to be the congressman's number two and even happier to be my number one." After a sip of wine, he added, "She often said things like that."

Paula noticed the animation in his face and in his voice when Daniel spoke about his wife.

"I understand why you came here after she died. Because of the plans you made together. But to build a home and live in a place so isolated, so different from everything you'd known before. Other than maybe George, Washington, when you were much younger. I mean, let's be honest. This place is isolated."

This wouldn't be the first or the last time his answer would be slow in coming.

"At the time, I wanted to live where weather would be the only authority in my life."

"What about God?"

He looked toward the canvass of mountains and sky off in the distance thinking, as he often did, that different artists or sculptors were at work with the changing seasons. He was lost in thought so long Paula thought he wouldn't answer.

"He was there for Mallory," he finally said. "I do believe that. Especially at the end. But not for me." Empty watering cans and barren gardens clouded his mind. "Not then. Not now."

Paula sensed him retreating, the roll coming to an end.

"Daniel, are you uncomfortable talking about Mallory?"

Whenever Daniel thought about Mallory, her memory wrapped around his heart like a protective shield. A few months after his arrival in Three Oaks, when he spoke about her for the first time with his only friend, a fellow widower, he did so hoping the man could understand the depth of his pain and suffering. Turned out, Doc could. At this moment, Daniel hoped he was right a second time when he answered Paula's question.

"I don't know. I still think about her often. And before meeting you, until now, there's only been one other person I've trusted enough to talk about her."

With those words, he opened a door. Not for the first time, or the last, she spoke without thinking.

"Miss Congeniality?"

OMG! I can't believe I said that.

"Paula, I'm not totally clueless." Testiness in his voice, his defenses returning much faster than they'd collapsed. "I can appreciate how women are curious about such things. A few nights together. Two lonely people in a lonely place."

In for a penny, in for a pound.

"What ended it? Sorry, sometimes I just can't help myself."

"Something we both know." An edge to his voice. "It ended after a couple of weeks when I learned she had children. Guess I understand why she didn't tell me at first. Nothing against her. Just not something I wanted."

The sudden onset of Mallory's illness made their decision to delay having children especially painful. Mallory had told Daniel she needed to work through issues she was still having with her own mother before she'd be ready to become a mother herself. He'd reluctantly agreed. During his darkest moments at her bedside, Daniel tortured himself over Mallory not living on in their child, and hated himself for the occasional times when his thoughts turned to anger, an emotion he kept to himself. After she was gone, being involved with a woman with children by another man held no interest.

"Ever? Never? About children, I mean?" Paula asked.

Her blunt words bounced off the heart shield. He closed and locked the door he'd opened, keeping Paula on the other side. He ended their conversation without answering. If only he *had* answered. If only Paula would remember this moment differently a few months later. Both of their worlds would have turned out differently.

Barely a glint of sunlight remained, and the air was growing colder by the minute. He stopped the swing, stood, and reached out his hand. "Time to go in. Blue has a dinner bell in his head, and I try not to disappoint him."

Daniel held on to her hand after she was out of the swing. Despite what had just happened, when she squeezed his hand and their eyes met, both sensed they were heading to a place on both of their minds ever since Daniel rescued her from hunger and homelessness a few hours after her arrival at his front porch asking directions. Blue led the way to the much-closer back door that opened to a mud room off the kitchen.

That evening, after another gourmet fish delicacy, Daniel gathered up a bottle of brandy and two snifter glasses before showing Paula to his study. A large bay window offered a spectacular sunrise view over the mountain peaks most mornings when the winds kept the low-hanging clouds aloft. He'd sparingly furnished the room without Mallory's influence, and it showed. A few wall hangings, a bookcase with only a smattering of books, a chair on rollers flush against the desk, a chestnut brown leather sofa long enough for him to fully stretch out for the occasional afternoon nap.

Paula sat halfway down the sofa. Daniel sat beside her and poured the brandy. In front of them was an irregular-shaped coffee table carved by the same local craftsman who'd made the kitchen stools. The long single piece of gnarled wood came from a tree downed on Daniel's property during a storm. He handed her a glass as he lifted his.

"To our guest. May our humble Western hospitality meet her Southern expectations."

Their glasses touched.

"Not met. Exceeded. Thank you. And you, too, Blue."

Blue was already asleep in a soft bed with his name on it beneath the window. He napped there whenever Daniel was in the room, and had a matching bed in the master suite. Indoors or out, Daniel's ever-present shadow, seldom more than a few feet away.

Paula's request for Daniel to read some of his poetry was met with a frown.

"All right, how 'bout this? You told me sometimes you read to Blue. You can pretend he's awake and I'm not here."

"If I thought you wouldn't give up until you got your way, would I be mistaken?"

"What's your favorite word?"

I do like this woman.

Daniel lifted a file folder from a bookcase shelf with one hand while reaching for his reading glasses with the other. He stood by his desk for a few minutes sifting through the folder, leaving it on the desk when he returned to sit beside her, a few sheets of paper in hand.

"Private readings limited to three selections. House rules."

Paula tried to concentrate on his words as he read, but the brandy warming her, and the richness in his voice, stimulated poetic thoughts of her own about the handsome man at her side, the one who had cast a spell over her. Finished, the poet innkeeper crossed the room to refile the papers.

"Daniel, those were beautiful. Simply beautiful. And now that I've had a drop, I'm thirsty for more."

Walking back, he asked, "Did that come from your writing class?"

"Don't make fun of me. Please don't. What I'm asking is if you'll let me read more. That is, if you don't want to continue. And I think it's obvious you don't."

"Like I said, house rules are house rules."

"Well, sometimes rules should be broken. Believe me, I should know." She left her words to float in the air. "I don't want to beg. I'm not very good at it. Put it down to lack of experience. But I will if I have to. Do I have to?"

After saying good night an hour later, Paula carried his file under her arm as she climbed the stairs. Reaching the bedroom, she remembered encouragement from one of the instructors to get started writing before leaving for home.

Months before arriving in Colorado, Paula had been inspired reading *My Way*, a book that passionately advocated the practice of journaling. It was co-written by a friend of hers, Marla Jo Taylor, and

Josephine "Jo" Gilpin Taylor, two women related by marriage. Unfortunately, Jo succumbed to effects of sickle cell anemia and didn't live to see it published. When Paula learned her friend would be an instructor at a Colorado gathering for aspiring writers, an opportunity to escape her troubled home life for a few days presented itself.

Paula arranged pillows against the headboard, re-read a few *My Way* chapters she'd remembered, then picked up the journal and began writing. Leaving several empty pages at the front, the recording of her life's journey began with Winston's marriage proposal -- the same place her storytelling to Daniel had ended the night before. The words flowed as if the events had just happened.

****

Months before proposing, Winston had shared his desire to go to New York City after Ole Miss law school. The two had been childhood friends, dated off and on in high school and college, and the meshing of shared future plans enabled Paula's head to prevail over her hesitant heart when she committed to marriage and a three-year delay pursuing her own dreams.

Paula accepted a graduate school scholarship, but as has often been said, life happens while you're busy making other plans. Winston came home after a year in law school and told her his heart wasn't in it. He blindsided her, saying he now felt a call to the ministry. Had she known a year earlier, she'd have taken off for New York, alone and unmarried.

She remained quiet as he told her his wealthy aunt, not a person of faith, wouldn't be paying for seminary as she had law school. Paula kept her emotions in check until she was alone in her car that night, driving aimlessly around town. She made no effort to hold back tears as her mind fast-forwarded to a future of lowered expectations and abandoned dreams.

After a lot of prayer and listening to her mother's relentless pleading, Paula decided to stay in the marriage. Her sisters openly delighted in her change of circumstance, leading already-fragile family dynamics to fray to the point she took herself out of the picture once and for all. Following graduate school, she got a job at the Oxford newspaper to help pay the bills but grew increasingly distressed her life would never be what she wanted. The loss of a career in New York came on top of an even greater one discovered after her wedding.

Paula was a virgin on her wedding night and was certain Winston was, as well. But her inexperience hadn't prepared her for his lack of passion, his lack of desire for her sexually. She knew there could be more, much more, between married couples, especially newlyweds. She wanted it, and its absence despite her best efforts to encourage it, created an ever-growing emptiness and desire. He deflected all her efforts to talk about it, blaming pressures of first-year law school. Later, once he entered the seminary, Winston closed off completely and refused Paula's pleas for marriage counseling.

Paula increasingly doubted her upbringing and church teachings, especially anything about a woman's place in relationships, at work, in life. Thoughts of infidelity and divorce haunted her. With so much standing in the way of her happiness, she convinced herself that many women, perhaps some she knew, were similarly conflicted. But, unlike her, lacked the courage to act. She sought counseling on her own.

In their fourth year of marriage, Paula had had enough. She agreed with her therapist that she and Winston were living together not as husband and wife, rather as lifelong friends, though she did accommodate his rare sexual urges despite the absence of romance. Because of their long history together, their friendship, and his need for her income, Paula decided to wait to divorce him until he finished seminary. She felt she owed him that much.

A week before his graduation, she discovered she was pregnant. Her early months were difficult, compounded by Winston's first church calling moving them from Oxford to Nashville. It was there, in a modest, sparsely furnished parsonage, she miscarried. Paula omitted details while writing in her journal, saying only that the doctor told the young couple their future life together would be one without children.

She wrote sparingly, just a few sentences, about her family. Her sisters stayed in Oxford, married willingly into subservient domestic lives with men they met at church, and produced nieces and nephews from whose lives Paula chose to exclude herself. Contact with her parents, whose world centered around being doting grandparents, also ended years earlier.

In touch with the needs of his flock but not those of his wife, Paula begrudgingly acknowledged Reverend Chandler excelled at his long-hours, low-paying profession, and allowed herself to be paraded out to complete the picture of a happily married pastor and his devoted wife. But regarding him as a good and decent man had to co-exist with the marital hypocrisy that ate away at her, a trickle becoming a stream becoming a river flooding its banks. Her emotional ebb and flow caused bouts of depression during which she came to believe her inability to have children meant she wasn't marriage material for another man. She was trapped.

While Paula bitterly settled into a marriage without love or passion, she never let her physical appearance suffer because of it. If anything, she grew more beautiful with each passing year. She prospered professionally, finding happiness and fulfillment outside her home, her fashionable "nice but not necessary" wardrobe a veritable finger in her mother's certain-to-be disapproving eye were she to see her prodigal daughter again. She never did.

Paula nurtured her dream of becoming a successful writer and found a best friend in Marla Jo Taylor, a university professor and author living nearby in Kentucky. She trusted Marla Jo, and during long talks confided that she thought about filling voids in her life in the arms of other men. Her friend listened without judging or encouraging her one way or the other. Paula's fear of rejection, more than being a pastor's wife, kept her from initiating anything, resulting in emotional solitary confinement in a prison without bars.

✳✳✳✳✳✳✳✳✳✳✳✳

Paula closed the journal and reached for Daniel's folder. Long past midnight, she fell asleep reading the poetry of the man lying in a bed one floor below. But not before an idea came to her.

Seven

1998
Three Oaks
Friday, Day Four

Paula was a whirlwind of motion and words preparing to leave for her last day at Manor House. She put her hands on Daniel's shoulders to help pull herself up slowly to kiss the cheek of a disappointed chef after apologizing for skipping the breakfast he'd prepared because she'd fallen back asleep after answering his rap on her door. She again insisted on driving, telling him he could put the time to better use.

"Writing poetry, for instance."

Standing alone in the kitchen after she left, her enticing perfume still fresh in the air, Daniel decided against going to town, finished his second cup of coffee and poured a third to take to his study. Looking at the bookcase, he remembered she'd taken the file to her room. He set the coffee cup next to the computer, and with Blue at his heels, found the object of his search lying on a carefully made bed. Next to it, a leather journal. He moved the file aside and opened the journal.

He turned the pages, but found nothing. He started to close what appeared to be a brand-new journal when the last page he turned revealed the first page of writing. After a few sentences, he knew he should end his intrusion, but it felt as if the book had him in its grasp rather than the other way around. He moved to the small swivel chair by the window. As Paula's words pulled him into her life, he felt more and more like an opposing coach reading the other team's stolen playbook. When he finished, he sat silently for several minutes, then returned the journal to the place he found it, scooped up his file and left the room.

Slowly descending the stairs, he knew what he'd done was wrong, a terrible invasion of privacy. Guilt weighed heavily on him throughout the day, disrupting his concentration as he sat at his computer, unable to write. He returned his poetry file to the guest room where Paula had left it, smoothing the Navaho-design wool blanket covering the bed as if wiping away crime scene fingerprints.

A few miles away, thoughts of Daniel caused Paula's classroom attention to plummet, the voices around her melding into just so much chatter. Sitting on an uncomfortable folding chair, she felt a warmth come over her as she imagined being with him in a few hours. The day before, she'd told him she planned to leave the next afternoon, but he'd offered no encouragement for her to extend, so the warmth began to cool with the realization her rapidly approaching departure from Three Oaks meant something she thought she badly wanted might never happen.

When she walked out of Manor House, she was surprised to find over an inch of mid-afternoon snow had already fallen and was growing in intensity. The woman clearing the car next to hers was a Colorado native and offered her an essential winter tool.

"I keep an extra in my car – just in case."

When they finished, the woman insisted Paula keep the long handle with a brush on one end and an ice scraper on the other. Paula regifted a box of homemade Kentucky bourbon-ball candy Marla Jo had given her, fibbing that she always kept one in her car. Just in case.

"A fair exchange," the woman said, as she opened her car door. "Snow's supposed to keep up 'till early morning. Travel safely."

"You, too," Paula replied, before saying a quick prayer under her breath.

Years could go by between measurable snowfalls in Nashville, accounting for Paula's white-knuckle grip on the steering wheel of a car without winter tires as she slowly navigated the few miles back to Casa d' Collins. The front of Daniel's house, encircled by snow-capped sugar maple trees, came into view and she saw a man and his dog waiting for her. Blue jumped down and ran as fast as unsteady legs could carry him over patches of ice to eagerly greet her as she trudged her way in wholly unsuitable shoes up the path Daniel had cleared.

No porch sitting this day as Paula shed her coat, scarf and gloves before being led by the hand to the living room sofa. Daniel knelt in front of her, holding first one ankle then the other to pull off her ruined shoes, setting them aside before gently massaging her feet with a thick towel to dry and warm them. The experience eclipsed any foreplay she'd ever imagined reading romance novels.

"Up to you, but I hope you'll think about not leaving tonight." He rested his weight on one knee while looking up at her. "If you try, you may not make it. And the world won't end if you wait a couple of days, will it?"

Paula's heart pounded. Two more nights with Daniel, maybe more! A weather delay was something Winston would have to understand when she called him. If he didn't, she didn't care. She didn't even want to think about him. She struggled to slow her racing pulse.

"I guess you're saying you don't want to follow me down wintery roads in case I need to be rescued. Again."

"Hadn't looked at it that way. But yeah, that doesn't sound like a fun evening for either of us."

"And am I to assume you didn't pull a Manor House and give my room away to someone else?"

"Paula …"

"What?"

"There is no someone else. Hasn't been. Until now."

Growing up, Paula had often been told proper Southern women occasionally perspired but never sweated. Nervous driving, and her temperature rising with Daniel's words and touch, blurred any distinction between the two. She felt her blouse sticking to her skin, and much as she didn't want the experience to end, excused herself to go freshen-up.

Blue had waited his turn patiently, then buried his head in his favorite towel. After drying him, Daniel dropped all the towels in the laundry room before heading to the first-floor master suite. Hearing the shower directly above him, he visualized Paula soapy-wet and naked, an image he found pleasantly unsettling.

Hot water cascading over her, Paula recalled all the time she'd spent over the years wondering what it would be like to stray from her marriage vows. Now, far from home, her mind's eye painted a picture so vivid it created a lustful stirring she hadn't felt for years, if ever. She wondered if Daniel desired her in the same way. Despite his flirtations, she was certain she'd have to take the lead in lovemaking as she had in conversation, though she felt far more confident with the latter.

Especially since she knew she'd have to chase away the ghost of Mallory.

Cloaked only in apprehension and rationalizations, she admired her nude reflection in the full-length mirror. As she slowly dressed, she gave herself permission to cross over a bridge to intimacy with a virtual stranger, knowing her first foray into unfaithfulness, if it happened, would end in a few days.

When Daniel no longer heard the upstairs shower, he turned on his. Looking in the mirror as he undressed, his eyes went to where they always seemed to go. To Mallory's cross. He'd wanted to take it off countless times because he'd lost all faith in what it represented, but couldn't bring himself to no longer have something Mallory had touched – touch him. Until now. He grappled with the stubborn clasp until it came loose and placed the cross and necklace on a shelf inside the medicine cabinet above the sink. He'd find a more appropriate place of safekeeping later.

Half an hour later, make-up in place and shoulder-length hair partially towel-dried, Paula entered the kitchen in a white silk blouse with nothing underneath, sleeves rolled up to her elbows, tucked into her tight designer jeans. Seeing his reaction, she felt confident she'd achieved her desired result. To at least bring the stranger to the other side of the bridge.

"You look stunning!"

"Who, little ole me?"

Daniel had arrived in the kitchen a few minutes ahead of her, dressed for the evening in newer jeans and a Black Watch tartan flannel shirt, open at the collar three buttons down. The same button-count opened Paula's blouse, offering him a glimpse of her ample cleavage, more than a glimpse when she moved a certain way. Their efforts at nonchalance a few days earlier had been replaced by a sense of inevitability that permeated the room as palpable as springtime Rocky Mountain air foretelling rain.

"Let's mix things up," Daniel said, intoxicated by her appearance and perfume. And he noticed she wasn't wearing her wedding ring.

"And just what do you have in mind?" she asked, anticipation in every word.

Daniel's home had a beautifully appointed formal dining room, but Paula shared his preference for the kitchen's informal ambiance. She got her answer when he returned with sterling silver candleholders and dimmed the overhead lighting. Music to make love by began playing in their heads, but neither made a move to lead the other to the metaphorical dance floor. Unspoken thoughts accompanied the touching of raised wine glasses. The coming downpour loomed all around them.

Minutes into their candlelight meal, Daniel asked Paula if she'd finishing telling him her story. The freshness of her lengthy journal entry the night before caused everything to spill out succinctly (for her) and chronologically. Despite her teasing, she thought Daniel wonderful company because he listened attentively, something missing in her relationship with her husband and encounters with other men. Paula hated the second Winston intrusion into her thoughts in as many hours.

Daniel tried unsuccessfully not to stare at nipples pressing against silk while listening to her share what she had no idea he mostly already knew. He immediately regretted his first interruption. It came when she spoke about not feeling she was marriage material for anyone else.

"Any man would be lucky to have you."

Her reply came instantly.

"You, for instance?"

His answer came slowly.

"Well, there are complications."

"Does that mean your answer would be different if I weren't married?"

He tugged nervously at his collar. "Given time, I'd say most likely yes."

"How different? How much time?"

"Can I get back to you after dessert?"

Paula wasn't surprised when Daniel didn't offer dessert. She followed him to sit on the thick woven wool rug he'd had custom-made that extended out and away from the fireplace in the living room. He poured the Port wine before they both reclined to lean against the sofa, the only sound the crackling fire he'd lit before preparing their dinner.

"Oh, I almost forgot. Your file is still upstairs. I'll go get it before anything can happen to it."

He started to protest, but she'd already covered half the distance across the room. He watched every sensuous movement. She returned a minute or two later, and the sight of her walking toward him caused a stirring against his tight jeans. She handed him the file before sitting. He set it aside.

"Did you get around to reading any of them?"

"Several. Easy to tell so many are about Mallory. Are they the older ones, or newer ones?"

He didn't answer.

"Do you have a picture you can show me?"

Daniel thought it an odd request, certainly at this moment, and Paula regretted asking the second the question escaped her lips. When he returned from his bedroom, he handed her a framed picture taken on their wedding day. Of the few pictures he had of Mallory, it was his favorite, occasionally moving it back and forth from the top of the dresser to the nightstand by his bed.

"She's beautiful! Not that I'm the least bit surprised, of course." She handed the picture back to him. "Do you think you'll ever marry again?"

Daniel stared into the fire.

"I won't say I haven't thought about it. Thing is, I know I'll never have another like the one I had. She often told me, and anyone else who'd listen, that she was the best thing that ever happened to me. She was right."

How can any woman ever compete with that? Oh, well.

Paula reached for the bottle and refilled their glasses, thinking if she changed the subject, the night still held promise for intimacy.

"Reading some of your poems last night, I came up with an idea. I think it's a good one, and I hope I don't offend you."

"I doubt that's possible."

"Oh, I think I've already been there and done that. And you've been quite the gentleman about it. Anyway, with this, only one way to find out. Okay, here goes. I didn't read all of them. But of those I did read, I didn't particularly care for the ones that didn't easily rhyme. But true confession, I've never had much interest in poetry. Of any kind."

Daniel had never deluded himself. He was his own harshest critic and didn't think his poetry all that good. And certainly not great. Together with no vision of a life beyond Blue's passing, it explained his lack of interest in being published again.

"And your idea is …?"

"This may sound crazy, totally off-the-wall, but remember me telling you I love country music?"

"I do. Something we share."

"And where my home is?" He nodded. "And what my job is?"

"I remember all of that, yes," he said, impatiently. "Where are you going with this?"

"Well, I think some of your poems, ones that rhyme, would make wonderful country music songs."

Tempted as she was to keep talking, to fill the emptiness of a few seconds, she waited.

"To borrow your favorite word, really?"

"Yes. Absolutely. Want me to show you?"

"Sure."

She finger-gestured for the file. He handed it to her and she leafed through the loose papers, withdrawing several, not realizing her actions and words were taking her further and further away from what she'd fanaticized while showering.

"Here. Look at these. And when you do, imagine someone singing."

Paula had been right. Several had been written with Mallory in mind, and as her picture lay beside him on the floor, they flooded Daniel with her memory.

"Now, remember, you have to imagine someone singing, not reading. Could be a man, could be a woman. Maybe even a duet. Doesn't matter. Think about that beautiful Glen Campbell song, you know, the one that goes like this." She sang the first verse. "It's one of my absolute favorites. And I bet if we had the lyrics in front of us, we'd agree it's a wonderful rhyming poem. Just like some of yours. Whatta ya think?"

"Intriguing." He tried his best to appear interested in her idea while thoughts of another woman were gentle on *his* mind. "And you thought this up while reading them?"

"I did."

As her few days with Daniel revealed, Paula seldom had unspoken thoughts, to the point of sometimes talking out loud when she was alone. Good friends told her it was part of her charm. Forgetting what she'd asked him just moments ago, and he hadn't answered, she went on.

"And like I said, I could tell many of them were about Mallory. Or must have been inspired by her."

Paula's words caused Daniel to recall Mallory's hospice-bed admonishment: "Danny, after I'm gone, don't let your sweetest music go un-played."

This isn't what she had in mind, he thought. *Or did she -- without knowing?*

Paula's attire had been intentional and unmistakable. But seeing him lost in thought, she now knew for a third time in as many days, Daniel had gone to that faraway place without her. And for the third time, she realized her words had sent him there, turning out the lights on the evening she'd wanted, their intimate time together ending with the songwriting idea. At the bottom of the stairway, she initiated a tentative good-night kiss. She could taste the wine on his lips, and they lingered uneasily before parting.

Lying in bed, Paula felt lonely, confused, and most of all, vulnerable. A vulnerability enhanced by always sleeping nude regardless of season. She fixated on her life before Three Oaks, one without the romance and passion she desperately craved. And especially on the night's missed opportunity. She knew Daniel was everything Winston wasn't. And more. So much more. More than any man she'd ever known and may ever meet. She knew he could fill the empty places in her life. She was confident of one thing. Fate *had* tipped him into her life. But even if he'd have her, and she now doubted more than ever he would, she wondered after such a brief time together if she could be in love with him?

"I'm tormented by my present," she announced to the ceiling as she hugged a pillow instead of Daniel, "and that man downstairs is shackled to his past. What a pair we are."

Without hope for anything more than the evening had brought, Paula resolved not to succumb again to lustful temptation during the remainder of her stay. She'd exposed herself to him in so many ways and wanted to hang on to what little remained of her pride. Her resolve didn't last. She didn't know how much time had passed and wondered if she might be dreaming when she rose, threw back the bed linens and blanket, and dangled her legs over the side of the bed. She took a few steps over to the swivel chair by the window where she'd let the partially buttoned blouse fall and slipped it on before opening the door and entering the hallway.

In the light of a full moon shining through the skylight, even before she could take the first downward step, Paula saw Daniel at the foot of the stairway, his hand on the railing, looking up at her. Her eyes adjusted to the dim light, and a second look confirmed that compared to him, she was overdressed. She slowly undid the remaining buttons and her blouse slid off. Her tasteful clothes hadn't concealed her shape, yet Daniel found himself unprepared for the sight of her now, his eyes quickly closing the gap between his imagination and her reality. The stirring returned.

"Your place or mine?" She pinched herself to make certain it wasn't a dream.

"Let's not disturb Blue," he answered, and began the seventeen-step climb. She met him half-way.

The first time, their lovemaking was almost primal in its rushed intensity. A Rocky Mountain downpour of feelings and emotions too long suppressed before they met, willingly by him, unwilling by her. The second time, when Paula's lips aroused him awake, they slowly explored each other. His touch coursed throughout her body as she trembled with a sensation she'd read about, heard others talk about, but until then, a place she'd never been. With Daniel, she came to that place several times. Both of them spent, she lay at his side with her back to him, her breathing rapid and shallow. His hand traced from the womanly roundness of her hip to the firmness of her breast, up her neck, then back again. And again. And again.

"I'll give you until tomorrow to stop that."

"It's already tomorrow," he said into the darkness.

"Day after tomorrow, then." She exhaled slowly. "I'm not in any hurry."

Eight

1998
The Weekend, Days Five and Six

Paula responded as Daniel hoped when he awakened her before the Saturday morning sunrise, then spooned tightly in his embrace. Her all-over glow vanished, as did any thoughts of sleeping late, when she heard breathing not coming from her lover. The room was ripening with sunlight peeking through the blinds, and when she opened her eyes, she saw Blue staring back at her.

"Did you come to see what the fuss was all about?"

"Huh?" Daniel asked, sleepily.

"Not you. Your companion. The one before me."

"What?" Still barely awake.

"Blue's over here."

"Not enough to steal my heart," he said, stretching his arms above his head. "You want my dog, too?"

'Steal my heart' brought back her glow.

"Isn't he old enough to make his own decisions?"

"Well, in that case, *you* can go outside with him."

Paula turned toward Daniel and propped herself up on one elbow. "I'd never dream of getting between a man and his dog. Especially at a time like this. In weather like this."

"Okay. Okay. It'll give me time to try and win him back. I'll shower downstairs and meet you in the kitchen. Take your time."

"You certainly did. Do. I should be able to find just the right words to describe last night. And this morning. But I can't. Too many superlatives to choose from. At least that's my excuse."

"Too bad your seminar's over. Could've been a class project."

"Oh, I doubt that! And aren't you the confident one?"

"Brimming over." He kissed her, then climbed out of bed, offering an au naturel departure.

"As well you should be. Though I'm not sharing you with anyone." But she knew she was.

Blue followed Daniel, and Paula joined them in the kitchen a half-hour later.

"I've answered the question, haven't I" she asked, reaching to accept her first cup of creamed coffee.

"Which one?"

"The one about what I'm going to do with you."

"I agree."

"Hope you don't mind if I answer again."

"I'd be disappointed if you didn't."

Their familiar, at times provocatively intimate, exchanges continued over breakfast. Paula said she hadn't packed for the extra days and hoped he didn't mind she was wearing her prior evening's dinner attire.

"Doesn't trouble me, and shouldn't you. I did notice you found the buttons this morning."

The scarlet coloring returned as her mind began churning other thoughts best left for later. Or not at all. But Paula was Paula.

"No, that doesn't trouble me. But I can't help wondering if something else might be troubling you."

"Nothing I can think of. Apart from you leaving us."

Paula was keenly aware Daniel had built a wall to hold Mallory in and keep others out. She'd fretted about the doors he closed, yet tumbled clumsily through the ones he opened. This held promise if only she'd wait a thoughtful moment before speaking. She didn't.

"Well, that troubles me, too. But I was thinking more along the lines of having an affair with a married woman. A minister's wife, at that."

"We're both adults," he said, evenly, shivering as a sudden chill entered the room. "And I seem to remember us meeting in the middle of the staircase last night."

Leaving well-enough alone was another of the things Paula knew deep down she needed to work on. Down too deep to be helpful at this moment.

"And my husband being a minister?"

Even though she'd dreamed for years about her experiences in bed with Daniel, she was feeling guilty the morning after and her thinking out loud unsettled him. He'd given no thought to her husband or his profession. Since Mallory's death, and until a few days ago, he'd cared about only himself and a dog. He'd followed Paula's flirtatious lead more slowly than he'd sensed she'd wanted. True, he'd had the unfair advantage of reading her journal before his naked climb up the stairs, but she'd made her decisions and should live with them. His reservoir of guilt was already filled to overflowing before her "I'm lost" entry into his life.

"Paula, stop! You're not being fair. I don't know what's gotten into you. A clerical collar didn't stop you last night. Is it stopping you now?"

"No," she answered, feeling her way through competing emotions.

"Is anything stopping you?"

"Stopping me from what?" she asked quietly, averting her eyes.

A skilled trial attorney never asks a question without already knowing the answer. Long absent from a courtroom, Daniel had done just that. Paula remembered their first day together when he threw her a lifeline when she needed one. Looking his way, she returned the favor.

"Don't worry, Daniel. I don't know where we are either. Or where this is going. I don't know what I'd be stopping."

Breakfast over, they both lamented what had befallen them so quickly and each felt the need to be alone. Paula retreated to her bedroom, Daniel to his study, which is where she found him an hour or so later. She stopped in the doorway, giving a physical dimension to the distance she felt separating them. Distance she'd created.

"I have a question."

"Okay."

"Apart from sweating together between the sheets again," she said, smiling nervously. "Something I'm eagerly anticipating and hope you are, too. What *does* one do when one is snowed-in, as we are?"

He knew she'd extended an olive branch, an act he'd intended to initiate but she'd gotten there first. As she would the next day with something far more profound.

"We're not."

"We're not what?"

"Snowed-in. At least I don't think we are. Saw it when Blue and I went out earlier. Look for yourself."

Paula went to the living room window and pulled back the curtains. Despite the morning sun, the windows were still mostly frosted-over. She fumbled around trying to open the front door until Daniel reached in and turned the latch. She felt the rush of cold, evergreen-fragranced air when she stepped out onto the porch, leaving the door open behind her.

"What happened?"

"It's what didn't happen." He threaded his arms around her from behind, holding her tightly. "Weather guys got it wrong. They often do."

Neither of them had noticed, and wouldn't have cared, that moonlight coming through the skylight the night before and illuminating them on the staircase signaled clear skies long before midnight.

"If it's okay with you," she said, shivering, "I'd still like to wait and leave on Monday. No sense rushing away."

"No sense at all." He kissed the back of her neck. "The roads should be clear by then."

Back inside, with the relationship road between them having been quickly cleared, Paula said, "I haven't seen anything of your Three Oaks except for what's between here and the little town. Since you've got that four-wheel thingy, can we go for a drive?"

"Doubt we should try today. Roads could be tricky. But tomorrow should be okay. Blue will want to go, too."

"Wouldn't dream of excluding him. But let's try, can we? Never been one for putting things off until tomorrow if today might be just as good. Maybe even better. And, of course, you have winter tires."

They got less than a quarter-mile down the uncleared road before drifting snow forced them to turn back.

"Oh, well, you know what they say," she said, looking at the road no other vehicles had dared travel. "Nothing ventured, nothing gained."

"Who might they be?"

"You're not upset with me, are you?" Concern in her voice as she thought back to their troubled waters earlier.

"Not at all. Just makin' conversation like you've been teaching me. Or tryin' to."

She reached to put her hand on his knee as the Jeep slowly carried them back home.

"Daniel, I was thinking back to something you said."

"What was that?"

"Very good. Much improved. I say, then you say. Fewer words, of course. Took a while, but that's what makes you so irresistible."

"Less is more. That's what won you over?"

"And everything else about you."

"Flattery will get you anywhere you want with us." He could see a dog's head in his rear-view mirror. "Right, Blue?"

"Where I want to go with you when we get back to your house, I'd rather you were alone. Find something else to entertain Blue."

"Done." When she didn't speak, he said, "You were thinking about something."

"I was." She reached from his knee to his hand. "You said this is a place where weather is an authority in your life."

"I believe I said the *only* authority."

"Then that's another conversation I'd like to have with you sometime. But for now, the weather. Is it like this for a long time?"

"Can be. Sometimes snows in early October. And Mother's Day is almost a given."

Paula began counting on her fingers.

"That's well over half the year. I don't think a Southern Belle like me could ever get used to it."

A casual comment, but Daniel turned those words over in his mind and would return to them later.

Back home safe and warm, Daniel told Paula he didn't want to be an ungracious host but would like to spend some time looking at his poetry file with her songwriting idea in mind.

"Thought maybe we could talk about it later."

Paula told him she was happy, indeed "flattered" he was pursuing her idea, and she'd keep herself busy reading. But she had something else in mind. Back in her bedroom, she returned to her journal. Blue wandered in and jumped up on the bed, prompting her to write about him as he nestled by her side. When her thoughts shifted to Daniel, her seminar-inspired writing became rich with intimate detail as she recounted their lovemaking. Aroused reading what she'd written, and attired only in the blouse that had served her so well the night before, early in the afternoon she made her way down to his study. He didn't hear her bare feet on the hardwood floor, but turned toward the doorway as Blue entered and headed toward his bed beneath the window.

"I ask the poet's pardon for the interruption. I thought perhaps he might like to take a break for lunch." After a seductively slow unbuttoning, she dangled the blouse on her finger. "You once told me you had a hunger for my voice. Anything else?"

Lunch was forgotten.

Daniel stretched out on the sofa, Paula lay in front of him, both facing the door to the study. In the sunlight flooding the room, he could see a scattering of freckles between her shoulders and began touching them one at a time.

"Too much sun when I was younger."

"I could take a pen and connect them."

"And why would you want to do that?"

"I don't know. Maybe create a constellation."

"Hmm. What would it look like?"

"An object of some sort. Doesn't really matter."

"Constellations all have names."

"True."

"What would you name this one?"

He didn't have a ready answer. Finally, one came to him.

"How 'bout Southern Belle?"

"Perfect."

Instead of lunch, they decided on one meal late in the afternoon. Paula followed the chef's patient lead and helped prepare a bouillabaisse.

"Pescatarian," Daniel said, as he cut the halibut.

She pretended to hear another word.

"Presbyterian? No, I'm Southern Baptist. Always have been, probably always will be." Winston started to creep into her thoughts, but she quickly forced out his unwanted presence. "Back home, Presbyterians are so stuffy. You know, about church. We sometimes make fun of them behind their backs. Awful, aren't we?"

"Don't know. Ever thought about saying it to their fronts?"

"Oh, that would never happen! But I understand what you're saying." She began setting the plates and flatware on the island. "Where were we before we got off onto that?"

"Pescatarian."

"Okay, unlike you, I will pose the question we both know you're dying for me to ask. What's pescatarian?"

"Someone like me."

"That's not very helpful."

"Someone like me" covers a lot of ground. Impossibly handsome. Sexy in so many ways. Gifted lover. Kind. Gentle. Great listener. Gourmet cook. Dog lover. Poet. An endless list.

Paula's back was to him when Daniel said, "Didn't mean to put you in a stupor."

"Oh, I'm sorry." She turned around. "You were saying?"

"Only that pescatarian means someone who eats fish and seafood. No other kind of meat."

"Well, I couldn't help noticing. I mean, the food has all been wonderful. You'll get no complaints from me. And I certainly wasn't going to ask. But for a Southern gal ..."

"Belle."

"Right. For either one, breakfast without bacon *is* a new experience."

"An unpleasant one?"

"Not in the least. And you know I'm now going to ask. Why?"

"Personal preference. I think it makes for a healthier life."

"That's it?"

"There's more. But not dinnertime conversation."

Later, Paula spoke over the faint sound of dishes being scrubbed in the dishwasher.

"Dinner's over."

"It is," Daniel confirmed, sensing the verbal volleyball net had been strung across the kitchen.

"And?"

"And what?"

"And you said there was more to you being a Presbyterian." Her word play rewarded with the smile and appreciation she'd hoped for.

"M' lady's wit is both sharp and quick this evening. All I wanna say is I'm troubled by how animals in the commercial food chain are treated. Rather, mis-treated."

"Fair enough. You don't need to paint me that picture. How long have you felt this way?"

"Oh, I'd have to stop and think."

He gave her the year. Paula did the math. His coffee shop reunion with Mallory. *Her influence, no doubt.*

"Well, it might be easier for me to become a Presbyterian than a pescatarian. But if it means being with you, I'd give it all I've got."

Sunday morning, Paula and Daniel were grateful Blue slept in as they lay together in tangled sheets. Good to his word, after breakfast Daniel drove the three of them slowly on the roads surrounding Three Oaks, looping around to recross a rushing river for their return.

The passing weather front left behind a mostly cloudless blue sky, but Paula thought there wasn't much to see on the ground. Fences that seemed to go on forever. Snow-covered pastures dotted with a scattering of trees. Mile after mile without a single structure of any kind, then a small cluster of farm homes and outbuildings before more miles of rolling terrain unblemished by stop-lights or grocery stores or gas stations.

"Pretty out here. Beautiful, in fact. But as my grandpa woulda said, as a daily diet, it's more like a whole buncha nothin." Seeing his silent reaction, Paula said, "Oh, I'm sorry. I didn't mean to hurt your feelings. I'm not being critical, Daniel, really, I'm not. I only meant there doesn't seem to be much to do out here." The verbal tap-dancing continued. "Outdoors, I mean. We've certainly figured out what to do indoors, haven't we?"

He smiled but didn't answer. Otherwise, Paula might have realized the still waters of his unspoken thoughts not only ran deep, but in the opposite direction she wanted.

During their evening meal, she told him she'd noticed *The New Yorker* magazines in his study.

"Seems like quite a contrast. You know, Manhattan and Three Oaks."

"Provides a splendid intellectual balance to *Garden & Gun* and *Outdoor Colorado*. Gives me an occasional taste of the Northern charm from whence I came."

"From whence I came, folks would say Northern charm is an oxymoron. Not me, mind you," she said, smiling. "Other folks."

"I see. Other folks. Well, since you brought it up, are you disappointed you didn't get to New York?"

"At times. Not so much, anymore. Who knows, it might still happen. Probably only to visit."

"I can see why." He got up off his stool. "Do you want to stay with chardonnay or switch to a red?"

"Chardonnay. Thanks."

He headed toward the refrigerator.

"And just how is it you're so certain I'd only visit New York and not move there?"

"Not just me," he said, returning with the bottle after opening it. "Anyone who has spent any time there, and knows you well, would know."

Here we go.

"Pray tell, Mr. Collins. Pray tell."

"Simple, really." His second word elicited the faux smile he was hoping for. "And intuitive."

"Because ..."

"Because everyone who's been there knows that while New Yorkers may be tolerant of Paula Chandler's beliefs, her lovable, quirky ways, even her accent, ..." His voice trailed off intentionally.

"Yes?" Asked impatiently.

"They'll be judgmental of her shoes."

"Well, I never! My last night here, and yer still makin' fun a me, Dan-yul!"

"No, ma'am. Tryn' ta have fun *with* ya."

They laughed together and then grew quiet, each dreading the reality it *was* their last night together.

"I have an idea." Daniel rose from his stool. "It's not too cold and there's still a full moon out. What say we take Blue for a stroll down the lane and back?"

Holding hands as they walked, Paula reached again into her writing seminar, this time for conversation.

"At Manor House, we studied differences in writing styles. Talked about Hemingway and Faulkner. Their writing is quite different, you know."

"Honestly, I don't. Read both a long time ago. I remember liking Hemingway. The other guy, not so much."

"Well, I'm not surprised. The instructor said Faulkner wrote longer sentences, more elaborate descriptions. You know, people, places, things. Used a lot of words to describe everything he wanted readers to imagine. And he had no problem repeating himself."

"And Hemingway?" At that moment, Daniel remembered the author had ended his life with a shotgun.

"Fewer words. No fluff."

His mind had careened elsewhere, and when he didn't respond, she squeezed his hand. "Still with me?"

"I'm sorry. Yes." He thought for a moment. "Would I be correct this is your way of using literature to describe our differences?"

"Very good, Daniel. But conversation is just one of our differences. We're different in many other ways. Wouldn't you agree?"

"I agree."

"That's it?"

"If you'd been just a little more patient I …"

"Not one of my strengths." When he didn't continue, she said, "Sorry."

"As I was saying, or about to say, I'm thinking about how the big difference we got at birth has proven to be, dare I say, splendid."

"Mr. Collins, now you're repeating your words. Just like Faulkner."

"Am I?"

"You know you are. But about the thinking behind them. Are those thoughts romantic or, can a girl hope, drifting more to the obscene?"

"Uhhhhhh... both."

"Well, in that case." She clutched his arm as Blue stopped when the lane reached the road. "We could all run back to the house and ..."

"Or," he said, wrapping his arm around her, "we could walk back and ..."

After their first intimacy that evening, she asked, "Have you always been Daniel?"

"Danny until high school, then Dan. My grandmother suggested I change to Daniel when I went away to law school. She said it sounded more lawyer-like. From then on, everyone called me Daniel." With the one notable exception of Mallory he chose not to mention.

"I like Daniel best of all."

After their second time hours later, Paula lay perfectly still beside him. "Have a question for you. One you'll like. Well, maybe not."

"Why will I like it?"

"You can get by with a one-word answer."

"And why might I not like it?"

She told him she'd fallen in love with him and asked if the feeling was mutual.

"A simple yes or no will do."

A question he hadn't anticipated from a married woman with a life and career far from the Three Oaks fortress he'd created to insulate himself from the world he'd planned on leaving, as had Hemingway, while she seemed to savor life despite all the setbacks she'd endured.

"I wanna be truthful," he answered, slowly. "And I know you want me to be. Truth is, not yet. But getting there." He knew he wasn't being truthful. He felt the same way, or thought he did, but something was keeping him from saying the same words she had.

"Well, that's much better than hearing your favorite word, that's for sure. What will get you there?"

"Time," he answered, playing for time. *Maybe I'll get there before she leaves.*

Daniel reminded her that in the morning she'd be leaving him, going home to her husband. Paula thought she had an answer but chose to wait. Lying in his strong embrace, a feeling of contentment she'd never known enveloped her as they nestled together tightly beneath a soft down comforter. It was a feeling she never wanted to surrender, but knew she'd have to. In a few hours. With Daniel asleep at her side in the master bedroom, and Blue in his bed in the corner, Paula thought about what he'd said.

A mere half-dozen days of happiness after years of misery allowed her to come to an easy decision. With Winston finally relegated to past tense, she focused on a future with Daniel. She could become a pescatarian. In a heartbeat. His aversion to children? No choice but to easily check that box. Living the rest of her life in Three Oaks? Questionable. Living in Three Oaks with both Daniel *and* the ghost? Not a chance.

Memories are okay, she thought, but the apparition of Mallory would have to go. And she'd do everything she could to make it happen. Would it be possible? Only one way to find out. Come back; stay longer.

If he'll have me.

Nine

1998
Monday, Day Seven

After making love at sunrise, Paula and Daniel showered together. She wrapped herself in a towel and headed upstairs to begin packing while he prepared breakfast. Folding her clothes, a question came to mind. Inescapably obvious, yet only now occurring. For her departure, she chose the same clothes she'd worn the day she arrived.

Anxiety over her leaving dampened their appetites, both picking at spinach omelets and French toast, each thinking about their time together coming to an end.

"May I ask you something?"

From the way she'd been looking at him, he didn't think she wanted one of his recipes.

"About me?"

She nodded.

"Ask away. After all, you know what I look like with my clothes off."

"Believe me, that's a memory that'll be travelling with me. Anyway, you've got this weather authority thing that keeps you close to home. At least part of the year. Other than sometimes writing poetry, what do you do when you're here all alone? Except for Blue, of course."

He knew she wasn't finished.

"I mean, you've told me you quit working before you moved here. And that was quite some time ago. You don't watch television. At least I didn't see one anywhere in the house. Your bookshelves aren't exactly overflowing. You haven't mentioned hobbies or spoken about any friends. While I'm away from you, when I think about you, I also wanna think about what you'll be doing. So, Daniel Collins, what *do* you do with yourself?"

Knowing that they weren't going to eat, he carried their plates to the sink and sat back down.

"You were wondering, and so was I."

"Wondering about what?"

"Wondering if you'd ever get around to asking."

"And ..."

"I'll answer about the books first. There's a used bookstore here and a library in a nearby town. I frequent both. Never saw the sense in hoarding books so others can't read them."

"Didn't think about that. Okay, makes sense. What about the rest?"

"The vet is not only Blue's friend, but mine, as well. We often meet at The Diner for breakfast. He and his daughter come here a couple of

Saturday nights a month for dinner. He's a widower, like me. Comes for the beer, and food that's a few notches up from The Diner or his own cooking. His daughter calls me Uncle Dan. She comes to play with Blue, and brings a book to read."

"How old is she?"

"Fourteen. Her name is Annie."

"That all sounds great. And I'm happy for you. What else?"

"I own a ranch."

"Where?"

"Here."

"We're back to one-word answers, are we? Okay, I'll ask. How can you have a ranch with no fences?"

"The front you've seen isn't fenced. Don't want to discourage people from stopping by and saying, oh, I don't know, saying something like, 'I'm lost.'"

She reached across the island to hold his hand. "And for that I'll be eternally grateful."

"As will I."

"Now," she said, "back to the fences."

"The fence line is over the hill behind the house."

"Is it a big ranch?"

"Folks in Colorado wouldn't think so. A few hundred acres, give or take. We drove past some of it on our outing yesterday."

The newness, and the sameness, meant Paula didn't realize one of the roads they'd traveled ran behind the hill where she'd found his log cabin home a few days earlier.

"Why didn't you say something?"

"Well, I was about to when you said it all looked like a whole bunch of nothing. Or something like that. My little place can't change what's here. You know, to make it more interesting to an outsider."

She pulled back her hand. "Is that what you think of me? That I'm just an outsider?"

"Paula, let's not parse words. Not now. I didn't mean anything other than a few days won't change what anyone would think about what they find here. Or don't find here."

"Fair enough." She thought for a moment. "What does it take to become an insider?"

"Same as it did for me. Staying. Or coming back."

"Is that an invitation?"

"It is. Either one."

"Then I accept. Not staying. I can't do that. Coming back. We'll talk more about that in a minute. Back to you. Do you have the same crops you remembered from George? The ones you so eloquently described to put me in my place."

"That would make me a farmer. I'm a rancher."

"Alrighty, then. What do you *ranch*?"

Daniel recalled one of his first impressions of Paula. *This woman sure does have a way about her.*

"I mean I didn't see any animals on our drive. Have you hidden them away?"

"Nothing yet. I plan to have a haven for abused or abandoned animals. Large animals. Mostly horses, I guess. The rescue shelter where Blue and I adopted each other gave me the inspiration."

"Sounds like a lot of work. Who's going to do it?"

"At the beginning, just me. Pretty good on horseback. If I do say so myself. And I do …

Paula knew where he was going and good-naturedly finished his sentence. "Say so myself."

Time wasn't on her side to keep peeling away. She now believed his roots into Three Oaks ran far deeper than just memories of Mallory, and those alone were daunting. She now felt he'd never leave. And for her part, she'd made no effort to change what she twice told him. That she didn't think she could ever live there because of the weather.

Paula had no way of knowing what Daniel had just told her wasn't true. The refuge had been Mallory's idea, not something inspired by Blue's adoption. He never had any intention of going through with it, and now he had no idea why he'd just lied. But he was too embarrassed to walk it back when he heard her say, "That sounds wonderful. It really does. And as soon as I get back, I'll get Blue to introduce me to his new friends if any arrived while I'm gone."

"Sounds good to me," he said, half-heartedly.

"And when I'm back, we can talk about that only authority in your life. There's more. So much more. But I want to say just one thing before I go. Okay?"

"Okay."

"We haven't talked about religion at all."

"Been kinda sorta busy with other things," he said, uncertain where she was headed.

"That we have. And no regrets."

"Me, neither."

"Good. Now, here's the thought I want to leave you with. You've been richly blessed in your life. Loving grandparents. Wonderful education. Wealth. Mallory. And now, dare I hope, me. But I believe with all my heart those blessing came from God. And He is, or should be, *the* authority in your life. Above the weather. Above everything else."

She wanted him to respond. He didn't.

"You have a comfortable life here. Anyone can see it, and from what you've told me, you've earned it. Every bit of it. But I hope you'll accept that the fruits of your labor are also God-given, and there's no assurance what's been given can't be taken away."

"Anything else?"

"Only this. I'm concerned your wealth may have robbed you of a purpose in life. A purpose that involves people, not just animals. You have so much to give to others, and I hope and pray some day you will."

"Paula."

"What?" she asked, tentatively.

"If you promise to come back, and soon, while you're gone, I promise to think about all of what you just said. And talk about it when you return. Deal?"

"Deal!"

Daniel went upstairs for her luggage, and when he returned from her car, found Paula sitting on the sofa in his study. He joined her, putting his arm around her, pulling her close. Looking to where his file rested on the bookcase, he thanked her again for encouraging his poetry.

"And my song-writing idea. Let's not forget about that. I'm looking forward to you being indebted to me when you become a huge success. In my town, I might add."

"Been thinking about that." He hadn't, but was grasping at a way to prolong her departure. "A great idea, but I feel stymied. Like a car that can't get into first gear. Guess I feel I'm not worthy. That my writing doesn't measure up."

"You know that stuff bulls leave behind in pastures like yours? That's what I think of what you just said. And I'm having none of it."

"I can't seem to put the pieces together. Turning a poem into a song."

"Of course, you can't. There's a piece missing. Two, actually."

"And they are …"

"Someone to work with. A composer to write the music to go along with your words."

"Where will I find such a person?"

"Nashville, silly."

What she said made sense, and he told her.

"Duh." Accented with her smile.

"What's the other?" he asked.

"Other what?"

"Missing piece."

"Oh, you need a muse. Someone to inspire you. Blue can fill in until I come back. But not in the same way, of course."

"Of course."

The room became quiet, each trying to find the right words to say before she left. Paula told him again she knows she's "there." In love with him. And she understands he's not yet there. He was there, but wouldn't say the words.

"What happens now?" she asked. "Tell me what to do."

"I can't. That's about your life. A life apart from me. I don't even know if I'll ever see you again."

"But you did invite me to come back. Or weren't you serious?"

"Never been more serious about anything."

Paula told him her marriage ended, for her, a long time ago, and that she'd been making plans to divorce her husband. Plans she'd now go through with when she got home.

"Because of me?"

"No, because of me. I can't possibly have the life I want until I'm free of the one I have. But about you. When I come back, will it be to someone who'll commit to seeing if he can get there with me? To fall in love with me as I have with him?"

Daniel had loved Mallory with all his heart, yet broke every one of his deathbed, birthday-present promises except for his poetry, and that was something that didn't involve another human being. At this moment, he didn't think he was worthy of any woman's love. And there was so much darkness about him Paula didn't know. If she did, he was certain her feelings would change. That she wouldn't want him. Maybe that's why he lied. But he also couldn't bring himself to discourage her. To give her up.

"Do you know what you're asking?" he finally said.

"Of you, or of me?"

"Both."

"I do," she answered. "I know exactly what I'm asking."

"Then, yes. I want you to come back with that expectation. Of me."

"You're not just saying it because I'm leaving? You'll really be waiting for me, open heart and open mind?"

When he saw her tears, and knew she'd be gone in a few minutes, he wanted to make things easier. For both of them. "Yes, really. I make you that promise. And now I want one from you."

"Anything. Anything at all."

"Bring sensible shoes. Not being judgmental, mind you. This isn't New York City."

An understated comparison of epic proportions, but I know what's he's doing.

"I'll make certain to remember that. And you. No waitresses while I'm gone?"

"No waitresses."

"But you'll still go to The Diner every morning?"

"Have to. Gets me out of the house and in tune with town gossip."

Paula learned Daniel had neither email nor cell phone. She asked him to write his PO Box and landline number on the back of an envelope she pulled from her purse. As he was writing, she laid her business card with her mobile number on the gnarly table in front of him.

"I hope you understand I'm going to need time to do things right. I have no idea how Winston will react, and I don't want to needlessly hurt him. Or his ministry. He really is a fine man. Just not the man for me. You must let me be the one to contact you. You can't contact me. You just can't. There'd be no way to explain. Okay?"

"I understand. Completely."

"Thank you. It really does have to be this way."

"Any idea when you'll be back? Don't want to give your room to someone else."

"I thought you said there wouldn't be a someone else while I'm gone," she said, a catch in her voice.

"And there won't. For me. But Blue's shown himself to be a sucker for beautiful Southern women who've lost their way."

She sat down on the floor and put her arms around his dog.

"It's not Blue I'd be worried about. Anyway, Christmas is right around the corner and I can't dump this on Winston right away. Most likely it'll be February at the earliest before I can come back. Might take even longer. But please, please trust me, and don't try to contact me."

"Whenever it is, we'll be waiting. If you call ahead, we'll be on the porch when you arrive."

"Draggin' my feet isn't makin' this any easier. I need to be on my way. But first, a pitstop."

Paula found them on the porch, sitting where they were when she arrived a week earlier.

"Until we meet again, my lasting memory will be this one. Blue by you. We can even make *Blue Bayou* our song. Playing it until we meet again."

Daniel leaned against the porch post and watched her car grow ever smaller. The week had flown by, and things were different now. If she'd been truthful. Truthful about being in love, about ending her marriage, about coming back to him. For the first time since arriving in Colorado, he got down on his knees and reached for his metaphorical watering can now covered with rust. He prayed, awkwardly, for Paula's safe journeys away from him and back again. And for Blue to be with him for as long as possible. Life looked differently to him now, and he knew the reason why. That afternoon, he found his best friend curled up on the bed in the guest suite, something he'd never seen before.

"I know, fella. I miss her, too. Worked some real magic on us while she was here. Now it's just you and me. Until she comes back."

Replaying those seven days over and over in his mind had taken on a life of its own, like an unfinished movie with the heroine's departure leaving the ending unknown. In his first waking moments each day, he wondered if had all been a dream. She'd swept into his life like trade winds he recalled from his trip to the Hawaiian Islands, blowing incessantly for days, then stilled without warning. Before getting out of bed, he'd remember a neatly folded silk blouse, open three buttons down, left on the guest room pillow beside her copy of *My Way* open to a page with an underlined passage. A passage he would read over and over again. Both were affirmation of her promise to return. It wasn't a dream. It was tangible. It was real. Paula Chandler from Tennessee had heightened in him all the senses that lovers experience. She would return. Of that he was certain.

And when she does, I'll tell her that I'm in love with her, and I'll go anywhere she wants to go.

Instead of flying, Paula had chosen to drive across portions of six states to reach Colorado because she wanted the added time to be alone. To think. To pray. Seven days after her arrival, her mind was free of any uncertainty about what she now wanted, and her return home had not been an arduous one, her car a magic carpet swept along by westerly winds of Three Oaks memories. She sang familiar country music songs while searching radio channels, and sobbed happily when a station in Missouri played the Ronstadt version of "their song."

She relived every moment of her time with Daniel Collins as the asphalt of so many highways passed beneath her, and arrived in Nashville early-evening of the third day a changed woman. Anyone who knew her well, as Daniel had teased her about New York, would have noticed. Winston thought her happiness came from being with him again after their time apart, and completely surprised her by initiating intimacy. One of his rare urges, but Paula didn't mind. She'd been to the mountain top, literally and figuratively, with another man. And would be returning, maybe forever.

The third week in December, Daniel's post office box yielded a square envelope with a Nashville postmark but no return address. He recognized the handwriting from her journal and used the dull edge of a stainless-steel restaurant knife to ease the envelope open without damaging the gold seal on the back. At the top of the pre-printed message inside the religious-themed Christmas card, Paula had written "To *D* and *B*." Below the message, "Coming back soon. All my love. *P*."

Ten

1999
Things happen in threes.

Paula's Christmas card filled Daniel with confidence she'd make good on her promise and he stood it upright on the kitchen island by the left-handed stool. Beside it, he laid the envelope in her handwriting and her business card, removing them when Doc and his daughter came for dinner, then putting them back after they left. Paula's blouse and the book remained untouched on the guest room pillow where she'd laid her head. When Daniel wandered the house, Blue at his side, he remembered each time they were in a room together, seeing her face there and feeling her presence. He missed her touch, her scent, her speaking in paragraphs, their dueling repartee. Neither of them had thought to ask the other for a photograph. What he wouldn't give for a few seconds of "southerness" he could replay on his answering machine.

Long before Paula's arrival, Daniel's declining mental health had tied his longevity to his dog's. He'd made peace with his death coming after Blue's, as he'd remembered Mallory making peace with hers. Differences, though. They'd been helpless to prevent Mallory's, and she'd slipped away with her grandmother's Bible open at her bedside. If he went the way of Hemingway, he'd die a non-believer by his own hand. His passing would go unnoticed until days or weeks later when his only friend in the world became curious. But apart from one man and his teenage daughter, Daniel Collins would be neither genuinely mourned nor long remembered.

Then a Southern Belle from Mississippi by way of Tennessee with a purposeful stride approached the front porch where he and his dog were sitting and began the unwinding of his twisted plan by giving him something to live for. He'd fallen in love with a woman he knew Mallory would approve of, setting the stage for delivery of the *Twilight* promise. Daniel knew even before Paula left how he wanted the movie to end. All he needed was for the heroine to return.

Because of what she'd said, he didn't expect anything else from her in December and kept to his routine. The Diner in the morning, dinner with Blue in the evening, his occasional father-daughter Saturday evening dinner guests. As the calendar turned to the new year, Daniel hunkered down for his second mountain winter alone, each day anticipating a phone call or letter, each evening setting a place for two. When the roads were clear, his daily drive to the post office filled with anticipation, the return journey darkened with disappointment. A sense of longing growing with each passing day. In the solitude of his home, he imagined the phone ringing with a call from Nashville. It never did.

Daniel's lawyer mind struggled with the absence of facts, with thoughts shaped by guessing and colored by emotion. Distraught, he turned himself inside out, tormented by the silence, but honored Paula's insistence not to contact her. He began talking out loud to Blue, sometimes sitting, sometimes pacing. During their walks, Blue would occasionally look up as if he were listening, but couldn't help falling asleep indoors.

For a Southern woman still thinking of New York City, had the remoteness of Three Oaks become an insurmountable hurdle? He remembered her twice saying as much even before he lied about the animal refuge and the untrue depth of roots it implied. He never told her he'd often thought about moving away, and now he'd go anywhere with her.

Christian guilt too heavy a burden for her? People behave differently in different surroundings. A married person who'd never think of straying might give in to temptation far from home. Was that it? Had he only been a release, and once it happened, she could go back to her life without him?

He regretted not sharing more about what he'd been thinking and feeling. Not his dark side. He felt he'd done a masterful job hiding that. No, his feelings about her. About them. But why should it matter? She said she was coming back. Promised she was coming back.

Any one of these, or somehow in combination, or something else, could be the reason. An abundance of questions without answers, and he was too embarrassed to confide in his friend. February came and went, and with the arrival of March, he feared it had all come undone but didn't know why. His inner darkness crept back, he remained in bed later and later in the morning, and one evening he stopped setting a symbolic place for her before sitting down to eat alone. A loaded revolver replaced the Christmas card for a few days before he put it away ahead of Doc and Annie's arrival for Saturday night dinner.

The first day of the year warm enough not to always need layered clothing came in early April. In Daniel's stack of mail on the bench beside him at The Diner was a letter forwarded by a company that had published a few of his poems. An inquiry from a Nashville composer, Paul Dean, seeking an introduction to Daniel. Before folding the letter and stuffing it into his back pocket, he remembered Paula saying there were two things he'd need to become a successful songwriter. This was one of them, but because he felt abandoned by her, he didn't make the connection.

Paula's absence had returned Daniel and the waitress to cordiality, and he nodded to her when she looked his way as he left. Back home, he dropped down in the rocking chair next to Blue who was waiting on the porch for his return. He reached into his pocket, welcoming anything that might momentarily keep the darkness at bay.

"You know, Blue," he said, flicking the letter with his finger, "there may be something to Paula's idea. I mean, no sense me contacting this Dean fella now. But if I try my hand at it on my own, one thing's for sure. I'll be doing something I haven't been very good at. You didn't know Mel, but before she died, I promised her I'd keep writing. Same thing I promised Paula, and you did know her."

Blue exhaled deeply, twitched, but didn't wake. Their normal conversation.

"But not here. Nope. Been thinking about that. I no longer belong here. We'll go someplace else."

A real estate firm next door to the library he frequented two counties over advised it could take a long time to find a buyer for his unique home and small acreage. Daniel signed the papers and left their office feeling no sense of urgency. Blue seemed healthy enough, and what Daniel did feel was the darkness beginning to dissipate as he thought about both leaving Three Oaks and returning to writing. But this time writing with an eye toward rhyming lyrics that might find a home in country music. Thinking about both gave him something to live for.

On their drive back to Three Oaks, his thoughts turned to Mallory and Paula, women of faith, and he decided to give the watering can another try. Blue jumped down from the Jeep and followed Daniel up the front porch steps to stand beside him as he knelt and prayed for clear skies and smooth sailing into an uncertain future. When he finished, he went inside, unloaded the revolver and put it away.

After their meal that evening, Daniel dusted off his computer and placed it on the desk now flush against the wall beneath the bay window in his study. Beginning the next morning, he awakened with the birds to start each new day looking east while the sun was still low in its ascent, and learned his writing sweet spot came around nine. He listened to country music songs, but differently. For the story in the rhyme. He'd had a long dry spell, and his own words didn't come easily. Occasionally, both versions of *their song* wafted throughout the house, as did "Gentle on My Mind," the one Paula sang to him not so long ago.

What finally enabled him to begin thinking as a lyricist, and not as a poet, was re-reading the page she'd marked in her copy of *My Way* she'd left behind, where the author, Josephine Gilpin Taylor, had written:

"I believe country music songwriters are some of the world's greatest poets and storytellers. Their few words can capture a listener in seconds, and unfold an entire story of wonderous joy or painful heartbreak in less than three minutes."

After several weeks, Daniel was pleased with how his songwriting was slowly evolving with thoughts of Paula woven throughout. But he longed for her to be there, as the muse she'd once described, and to share in his journey, wherever his journey would take him. When he read his work aloud to Blue, he often thought back with regret to the evening he'd denied her request in the very same room.

His writing regimen meant a change to his morning routine, and after placing his lunch order at The Diner one Thursday in May, he opened the Washington Post. The lead story above the front-page fold, a newspaper's most valuable real estate, banished his appetite and turned disbelief into anger as he read about the magnitude of fraud perpetrated by Timothy Allen Dalton, the East Coast financial advisor in whom he'd entrusted almost all his wealth. Now he knew why his recent calls to Dalton had gone unreturned.

After taking millions in commissions, Dalton vanished without a trace, leaving behind dozens of wealthy clients whose money had also vanished into a sewer of risky financial investments. Daniel knew with certainty he was one of the defrauded investors and banged his fist on the table so loudly the small restaurant became as still as a church sanctuary during silent prayer. He gathered up the rest of his mail, threw money on the table before his meal arrived, and stormed out.

Back home, sitting in the swing, he kept looking at the newspaper, hoping somehow the next reading would have different words. Daniel's writing kept Paula constantly on his mind, as she was now, and he remembered her telling him that things God-given can be taken away. God-given or not, he thought, his wealth *had* been taken away. He became despondent, his personal darkness returning as the sun dropped slowly toward the horizon behind him.

But years of being surprised in courtrooms had blessed Daniel with a knack to quickly recover his bearings. When Blue approached, tail wagging, a reminder supper time was upon them, Daniel remembered the door he was about to open was to a home he'd paid cash for, as he had for the acres of prime ranch land. Once they sell, he told himself as he followed his dog inside, I'll have plenty of money. *Not as much as before, certainly, but enough. More than enough.*

A week or so after Daniel did the simple math and was satisfied he could sleep that night and the ones following, he looked up from his newspaper when he heard, "That seat taken?"

"It is," he answered. "I'm waiting for a beautiful, wealthy businesswoman to join me for lunch."

"Well, she ain't coming. I ain't a beauty, and I ain't wealthy, but I'm here, so give it a shove."

Daniel smiled as he slid around the circular booth to make room for Marlene McKenzie, the childless widow who'd owned Manor House as long as anyone could remember. Without knowing it, her mistake in giving away a reserved room a few months earlier meant she was responsible for Daniel's week with Paula.

After they placed their breakfast-for-lunch orders, Marlene said, "Can you keep a secret?"

"In this town? Who would I tell?"

"You've got a point," she whispered, "now that you're not pillow-talking with waitresses anymore."

"You knew about that! How?"

"Darling, I know everything that happens in Three Oaks. Including how long your little fling lasted. Or didn't last. But if you don't keep your voice down, so will everyone else."

"Marlene," his voice lowered, "is my disappointing love life the secret you wanted to share? In which case, I already know all about it. Sorry."

Marlene was an attractive, college-educated woman approaching seventy, but looked and acted well over a decade younger. She took pride in her appearance and had both the figure and the money to dress in the latest Colorado desert fashion. But she did so only occasionally, and with style, thereby incurring neither the animosity of other women nor the unwanted attention of their menfolk. After he changed from morning to mid-day at The Diner, Daniel often found himself in her delightful company.

"Enough about you," she said, leaning forward, "let's talk about me."

"Love to. What's new in your world?"

"I sold Manor House. Got a pretty penny for it. You're the first person I've told, so don't say anything."

Almost nothing new of any significance ever happened in Three Oaks, especially real estate. Daniel listing his property fostered plenty of conversation, but there hadn't been a word about this.

"I won't. I didn't know it was for sale."

"It wasn't. An investor from California with more money than good sense who'd stayed here once called one day and made me a Godfather offer. You know, one I couldn't refuse."

"Well, I'm happy for you, I guess. If you're happy."

"I am. Made my new beginning all that much easier."

Daniel recalled Paula mentioning her love of new beginnings the afternoon they met. Lunches arrived and the waitress departed.

"This new beginning. Will it be here?"

"Lord, no. Denver. And it's the second secret for you to keep."

Daniel's hand closed his lips like a zipper. When she hesitated saying more, he whispered, "Marlene."

"What?"

"You're blushing."

"I am? Well, maybe I've got a good reason."

She looked around to be certain no one was eavesdropping, then reached for the salt and pepper shakers. Instead of sprinkling her omelet, she clicked them together as she held them side-by-side in front of her as if they were the bride and groom on top of a wedding cake.

"And ...?" he prompted.

"I'm getting married."

"You are? That's wonderful!"

"Shh. After I'm gone, gossips around here'll say at my age I married for money. Truth is, I'll have more than him."

"Pay them no mind. Tell me about him."

"Widower, seventy-five, retired shyster like you. And almost as handsome. What can I say? Kept putting him off, but couldn't keep him from falling in love with me."

"And you with him. Good for you."

"Well, Daniel," she said, carefully choosing her words, "truth is, not really."

"Meaning?"

"Meaning I'm not in love with Michael. I'm *in like* with him."

"If you don't mind me saying, that's quite a difference."

"It is. I know that. And I think he does, too. We adore each other, and he's a perfect gentleman, to me and everyone else. He's what I've always wanted and well-worth the wait. I get along just dandy with his children and grandchildren, and they bring me those things missing in my life."

"Sounds perfect."

"And that's not all."

"What else?"

She looked around before saying, "I can still curl his toes in the bedroom, if you catch my drift."

"Marlene, if you don't stop, I'll be the one blushing."

A wink and smile as she set the salt and pepper shakers aside.

"Anyway, I wish you the very best."

"And you, Sir Daniel, what about you? Selling out must mean a new beginning for you. Tell. Tell."

"Nothing to tell. Haven't got it all figured out like you. Not yet. But I will. In time."

Marlene waited until the waitress refilled their coffee and was out of earshot.

"Praying about it? We can all use that kind of help, you know."

"I am. Not certain anyone's listening."

"What makes you say that?"

"Experience."

"Well, keep at it. As I heard a preacher once say, prayer is like a muscle. The more you exercise it, the stronger it becomes."

"Wise words."

"And here's my two cents' worth. We believe in the sun even when it doesn't shine. Right? That's easy. It's the other times, the times when we think God is silent, that believing in Him is not so easy. He hears us and will answer. In time, as you just said, and in His way. I hope you'll believe that. What's easy is to give up. Don't do that. Listen to an old lady and do what she says. Don't give up."

"Okay, I will. If I ever encounter an old lady, I'll listen and try to do what she says."

"You, Daniel Collins, could charm the devil himself. But you're still gonna have to buy your own lunch like always. I'm not *that* susceptible to your charms."

Marlene said she was leaving for good in a few weeks. They said their final good-byes, promised to stay in touch, knowing they wouldn't.

Back home, Daniel began thinking that without at least one child, he had no chance of ever rounding out his life in the way Marlene now would. It became an emptiness he hadn't given much thought to before, making him even more anxious for his own property to sell. A restlessness to get on with his new beginning.

Daniel had waited months for something that never happened. The phone in his kitchen ringing with Paula on the other end. But two calls he wished had never happened did, one he received, one he placed.

Sitting on the front porch, Blue at his side, he replayed both in his mind as if he were sitting in his D.C. office, feet up on his desk, recalling the day's testimony in court. Testimony that hadn't gone his client's way. Searching for weaknesses to find a better outcome when none was apparent. This time, none was.

The first call came the previous evening while he was scraping Blue's dinner into his dish.

"Daniel, sorry to bother you this late," the Realtor said, "but we're confused. I told the others in the office I'd call you."

"Happens to the best of us. What is it?"

"Well, we remembered you told us you paid cash for the house. And for the ranch."

"I did. Both of them."

"That's why we saw no reason to check courthouse records."

"And?"

"Well, sir, another agent with an interested client discovered a lien on both properties totaling more than the price we're asking."

"That's impossible!" Daniel said, walking in circles around the kitchen island, holding the cordless phone. "Must be some mistake."

"That's what we thought. But we checked, and that's what the records show."

"I'm telling you, it's some kind of mistake. You guys are the pros. You fix it."

"We tried. We can't do anything. The bank will only talk with you. If you've got something to write with, I can give you the name and number of the person in Denver. But it's after banking hours now."

"Of course, it is," Daniel replied, sarcastically, reaching for pen and paper. "Those clowns are probably gone by mid-afternoon anyway. I'll call in the morning and get this straightened out."

"Thank you, sir. Sorry to have troubled you."

"Don't worry. Trouble is what this guy whose number you gave me is in for tomorrow morning."

It would be the last good night's sleep Daniel Collins would have for a long time. He called Denver first thing the following morning.

"How is this possible?" Daniel asked, hard-pressed to control his temper.

"Mr. Collins, I'm going to have to insist that you calm down. A raised voice will get us nowhere."

"Thank you for that scolding. Now, tell me what the hell is going on with your bank and my property. Property I purchased with cash. My cash. My hard-earned cash."

"We have all of that information here in the file, Mr. Collins. You are correct. When the deeds were first recorded, there were no encumbrances. But a question for you. Do you know a Timothy Dalton of Washington, D.C.?"

Daniel's knuckles whitened as his grip on the phone tightened when he heard the name. He conjured up all manner of vile thoughts about another human being, but only managed to spit out, "I do."

"Then do you now recall that after you took out a second mortgage on both the residence and the land, you instructed us to wire transfer all the funds to an account in your name managed by Mr. Dalton?"

A thick wave of nausea swept over him as something Daniel had only given passing thought to a couple of years earlier came rushing back. The banker's words were a reminder he'd agreed, in one brief phone call, to Dalton's suggestion of the low-interest mortgage to free up the equity in his real estate to invest elsewhere. Daniel now remembered not worrying about repaying a loan on illiquid real estate because there would always be plenty of money in his investment portfolio. Liquidity he'd learned weeks earlier no longer existed.

"Mr. Collins, at the risk of upsetting you even more, I'm afraid the news is a little bleaker than you might realize. Real estate values have declined somewhat, so the amount of the loans owed actually exceeds what we understand you're asking for the properties."

He'd heard that the night before.

"Mr. Collins, are you still with me?"

"I am."

"Now, I think I may have good news for you."

"Oh, joy," he said, with unmistakable sarcasm. "And that would be?"

"Well, I'm looking at the financial statement you provided when the loans were granted. If you'll update that for us, I'm sure they'll be no problem waiting until your property sells. Sound good to you?"

"Wonderful."

But it wasn't.

Before he disappeared, Timothy Dalton made the same thing happen to all of Daniels' holdings, so there was nothing to update on a financial statement. Daniel had relied entirely on earnings from his investments, and when the bank learned those funds no longer existed, and that he had no other source of income, the loan would be called and the property foreclosed. The breathtaking speed at which he'd plummeted from wealthy to broke was daunting, and almost impossible for him to get his mind around. The night they met, Paula had joked about her being homeless. In a few weeks, a few months at the outside, Daniel knew homelessness would become his new beginning.

Pithy wisdom on a little piece of paper baked inside a cookie served with Chinese food says:

"Misfortune comes in threes."

Lost love. Lost wealth. For Daniel Collins, the third lay ahead for him in Colorado.

He had no idea Paula's life was also unraveling for her a thousand miles away.

Eleven

Nashville
Life happens

On the long drive home from Three Oaks in early December 1998, Paula knew the coming Nashville Christmas season would be her last as a pastor's wife, but chose to wait until the first week in January to talk with her husband. Her plan went awry when Winston threw her a curve. With only a day's notice, he left for Florida to fill in for a friend from seminary days who had a family emergency. He told her not to expect him back until the end of the month at the earliest.

Weeks later, with Winston still away, Paula learned for a second time, and unexpectedly in the same way, life had intervened while she was making other plans. She desperately needed to talk with someone, and that someone was Marla Jo Taylor, an hour up the road in Kentucky.

"I need a friend in the worst way. Please call me as soon as you can."

Both Marla Jo and her husband Ben heard the desperation in Paula's voice as they listened to the message. When Marla Jo returned the call, Paula begged her to meet in Bowling Green as soon as possible.

A few hours later, Marla Jo greeted Paula at the door of their stately home on Park Row, a restored historic residence on one of four downtown streets configured around the town square. Sitting at opposite ends of a couch in the Taylor's spacious living room, coffee cups and saucers on the table in front of them and niceties out of the way, each woman awkwardly anticipated the other would speak next.

"Let me guess," Marla Jo said. "You finally got up the courage to have the talk with Winston."

"Good guess, but you're a few steps ahead of me." Paula reached into the oversized purse at her feet and pulled out her journal. "I need you to read this. I'll just sit here and say nothing."

Minutes ticked by, the only sounds coming from pages being turned as Paula tried to read her friend's expressions and body language. When she finished reading, Marla Jo closed the journal and set it on the couch between them. Both women were wearing the expensive slacks and cashmere sweater combinations they could easily afford. Seeing the agony on Paula's face, Marla Jo tried for levity.

"Well, I'll say this. You certainly had a lot more going on in Colorado than the rest of us. And now I know why you missed those less-than-delicious evening meals catered by that diner across the street."

Paula opened her mouth to speak, then her eyes shifted to look out the large picture window, at oak trees winter had stripped of their leaves.

"I can tell you're in pain. Please tell me what's wrong. Why did you need to see me today? Why did you want me to read your journal?"

Paula turned to look at her friend, then back to the window. "I'm pregnant. I just found out."

Although she'd only met Winston briefly on one occasion, her friendship with Paula had made Marla Jo aware of the most intimate details of her friend's unhappy marriage, including the long-ago prognosis the Chandlers could never have children.

"Because of what that doctor told me years ago after I miscarried, I had no reason to be cautious. You know that. And Daniel is the only man I've ever been with other than Winston."

"Are you saying Daniel is the father?"

"That's the problem! I don't know. Winston and I were intimate the night I returned. Not something I wanted. He did, and it was only three days after my last time with Daniel."

"What a hell of a time for Winston to have his semi-annual awakening!" Marla Jo blurted out.

Paula's effort at a wan smile failed as her eyes filled.

"I'm so sorry. I don't mean to make light of things. But I do think we need something stronger than coffee."

Marla Jo returned and extended a wine bottle. "I believe this brand is perfect for the occasion."

"You got that right," Paula said, reading the Conundrum by Camus label before handing the bottle back. "And I have no idea what to do. That's why I'm here."

"What about this?" Marla Jo asked, while pouring. "Let's imagine how each man will react when he hears the news. Which one first?"

"I guess the man I no longer want to be with. Marla Jo, he'd be over the moon to be a father. He'll think it's some kind of Christmas miracle." She paused, then exclaimed, "And I'd like to wring that doctor's neck!"

"Let's slow down. How do *you* feel about having a baby?"

"If not for the, the conundrum," she said, lifting her glass and staring at it, "I can honestly say I'm thrilled. I really am! It's all this other crap that's got me so messed up."

"That's wonderful! And I'm so glad to hear it. Now, you've had much more time to think about this than I have, so let's talk about options."

"It's all I've been thinking about. Tried counting them on one hand and had fingers to spare. Now I don't know if I have any. You know, options."

Marla Jo remained silent.

"For some women, ending it would be one. Not for me."

"I'm with you and understand completely. But don't you have at least two with Winston?"

"Don't know what you mean."

Marla Jo took a second sip of wine, setting the glass back on the coffee table. "I mean, you can stay with him and tell him nothing about Daniel."

"That would be safest. And I think I know where you're going with the other."

"Divorce," Marla Jo said, firmly.

"Oh, trust me, I've thought about that one. A lot. You and I talked so many times about me leaving him, long before going to Colorado. But let him believe a child is his without knowing for certain, then divorcing him? Couldn't do that. Unfair, and cruel. Unhappy as I am, I'm not willing to ruin his life that way."

"Like he ruined yours? Dropping out of law school. Becoming a minister. Taking your New York dreams away. Like that?"

"Marla Jo, I'm surprised at you! I thought you were my friend."

"I am. Or trying to be. It just that ... "

"I know. I'm sorry I said that." She reached across to hold her friend's hand. "I apologize."

"Not necessary," Marla Jo answered, hurriedly, patting the back of Paula's hand. "Let me ask this. Are you thinking at all of confessing your affair?"

"Maybe. Would you?"

"Oh, that's not a fair question. Only you can decide that. But even though I barely know your husband, which is why I can call you Paula instead of Arlette when we're together, if you do fess up, things will change. You know that."

"I do. But what are you thinking?"

"I think any husband would use it to gain the upper hand."

"In what ways?"

"Oh, certainly the two big ones. In your marriage, and as parents."

"Saint over sinner?"

"Something like that."

Paula shuddered at the troubling imagery. "What about asking Winston for a paternity test after the baby's born?"

"Well, it'll be a two for the price of one. You'll get your answer, and he'll get your confession. And if Winston isn't the father, then what?"

Paula was subdued. "I guess that brings us to Daniel, doesn't it?"

"It does." Marla Jo placed her hand on the journal. "In here, you said you told him you'd divorce your husband and come running back. If Winston takes the test, and he isn't the father, what then? Would you call Daniel, or just show up on his doorstep with a tiny package?"

"That's why I wanted so badly to talk to you. I can't figure things out. I told him I had no children, could never have children. We had no reason to be careful when we slept together. Now, he'll think I wasn't being truthful."

"Okay, there's that. And it's a big that." Marla Jo picked up the journal without opening. "What about those other things?"

"What things? I wrote about a lot."

"You did." Marla Jo smiled as she refilled their glasses. "Really took my class on journaling to heart, didn't you? And you left little to one's imagination, I might add."

"Well," Paula said, twisting a handkerchief, "I never intended anyone else to read it. Even you."

"I'm sure you didn't. Here, put this away," she said, handing the journal to Paula. "I was trying for a compliment and missed the mark. I'm sorry. Anyway, about what you wrote. You said Daniel didn't want children. Did he really say that?"

"I'm not sure," Paula said, dropping the journal into her bag. "It all happened so fast, that conversation on the backyard swing. And we never talked about it again. No reason to. I do know he didn't want a woman who had children. The whole waitress thing. I guess I didn't pay it any mind later since it would never be an issue between us."

"And now?"

"Before I left, I knew I was in love and told him. He said he was getting there with me. Those were his words. Getting there. I knew we both had baggage, and I left hoping that when I came back there'd be enough love between us to smooth out any rough edges."

"Did you think the edges might be this rough?"

"Of course not. But I can't help believing he'd accept me with a baby."

"Don't know if you meant to, but you said accept, not love. Isn't it possible you'd be trading one friendship for another?"

"I hate to think that way, but I guess maybe that's true."

"You've been doing a lot of guessing, a lot of maybes. That's understandable. But you also wrote you didn't think you could live your life in a place that remote. Could you raise a child there? What about schools? Other children for friends? Medical care? Have you thought about any of that?"

"What a lovely picture you've painted."

"Paula, I'm not trying to be unkind. All I know is what you've told me. And what I read a little while ago."

"Anything else?" Wondering what her friend was thinking but not saying, the suspense became too much. "Well, anything else?"

"There's the little matter of the ghost you wrote about. I believe her name is Mallory. Wouldn't there be four of you living there?"

"Marla Jo."

"What?"

"Please pass the arsenic."

Ben had left on a business trip before Paula arrived, and with evening upon them, Marla Jo insisted her friend spend the night.

"I'd like that. Thank you."

"More wine?

"No. I've had plenty. And it'll have to be my last for the next several months."

"Oh, my goodness! I'm sorry. What was I thinking? Or not thinking?"

"Nothing to worry about. But food would certainly be welcome. Haven't eaten today. May I take you out for dinner?"

"How 'bout we stay in and I fix something. May not be at the level of Daniel's cooking you wrote about. Since Ben isn't here for you to see his growing waistline, you'll just have to trust me."

Dinner conversation, and talking afterward before they called it a night, found them covering old ground but with no new insights. Circles they couldn't square no matter how hard they tried. They agreed to sleep on it, but for Paula, it was a long and restless night. At breakfast the next morning, she said she'd made her decision.

"And?" Marla Jo asked, as she poured their first cup of coffee. The breakfast nook and kitchen were bathed in winter sunshine, unlike the conversation that followed.

"The only one I *can* make. Stay with Winston. Tell him nothing about Colorado."

"You know I'll help any way I can."

Paula reached for her friend's hand. "I know. I don't see how I can get through this without you."

"I'll be there. But please do something. And soon."

"What's that?"

"Destroy that journal before it can cause problems. I'll even do it for you, if you want."

"I've thought about that, and I will."

"Promise?"

"I promise."

Back home in Nashville later that morning, Paula poured a glass of iced tea at her kitchen table and began to write in the journal about her heartbreaking conundrum. In a perfect world, she and her child would be with Daniel Collins. In her imperfect world, it would have to be with Winston Chandler. Despite her promise a few hours earlier, she tucked the tattered envelope containing an address and phone number back inside the journal, then hid it away. After years of fantasizing about what had finally come true for her in Three Oaks, she convinced herself she needed the journal to help re-color those precious memories when they began to fade. Memories were all she would ever have of Daniel Collins.

Days later, Winston learned the news as soon as he unpacked his suitcase. As Paula predicted, he became ecstatic, rushing to the phone to tell his mother about the Christmas miracle.

Her pregnancy mood swings caused Paula to occasionally think about telling Winston the truth, but she never did, finding ways to peacefully co-exist while hiding her secret. Despite escaping a Scarlet Letter fate, and being tormented by shame and secrecy, she told Marla Jo she wanted her child to be Daniel or Danielle. When a daughter was born on September 1st, Winston insisted on his mother's name.

"Don't push your luck," Marla Jo advised when she visited Paula in the hospital.

Although her lover remained ever-present in thoughts and daydreams, bolstered by reading her journal and frequent playing of Ronstadt's version of Blue Bayou when Winston wasn't around, Paula never contacted Daniel. Instead, she asked her friend Paul Dean, a Nashville composer, to reach out to him. Paul promised he would, indirectly and without ever mentioning her.

Twelve

1999
Daniel's third misfortune

Blue's slowing with age became a descent into lethargy. He seldom ate, and when Daniel took him outdoors, he'd lie down near the house and stare off into the distance. After a few days of Blue struggling to walk more than a few feet, Daniel lovingly carried him to the Jeep for the short trip to the Hayworth Clinic.

Daniel looked at Blue cradled in his lap and remembered back to the day they first laid eyes on each other in the very same room. Now those bright blue eyes had a vacant look about them. The wait for the verdict wasn't a long one.

"We're at the end."

Daniel turned toward the sound of his friend's voice as the man entered the room and closed the door. Doc Hayworth had been a long-distance runner since his high school days, and even sitting in a chair his presence gave others the sense he was tightly-coiled, anxious to be out on the back country roads instead of in a small, windowless room. Despite his many efforts to encourage Daniel, the escapee from D.C. never laced up and joined him.

"Days? Weeks?" Daniel asked.

"A few days, maybe," Doc said, leaning against the wall, arms folded in front of him. "Impossible to tell for certain."

"Is he in pain?"

"He is."

"A lot?"

"Not unbearable. If he's not moving. Or being moved. Otherwise, there's pain he shouldn't have to endure."

Daniel sat motionless. "What are you saying?"

"It's your decision, Daniel. But if he were mine, I wouldn't move him again. He's comfortable now. Why not remember him that way?"

Daniel felt the walls of the already small room close in on him, and thought the air had taken on an unpleasant staleness as he drew deep breaths.

"I should let you put him down. Is that what you're saying, Doc?"

"That's what I'm saying."

Blue lifted his head, and Daniel's body tensed as the harsh reality sank in.

"Doesn't sound like there's any choice."

Doc Hayworth shook his head.

"I want some time alone with him."

"Certainly."

Doc dimmed the lights as he left.

Tears flowed as Daniel remembered all that Blue had meant to him in their few years together. Time that passed all too quickly. Best friend. Most of the time, his only friend. Couldn't imagine a life without him, and there wouldn't be one for very long after today. When the door opened ten minutes later, Daniel didn't bother to look up.

"Hi, Uncle Dan," the soft voice said. "My dad told me. May I sit with you?"

A thin, almost waif-like girl, clad in bib overalls and an ill-fitting Denver Broncos sweatshirt, closed the door and silently pulled up a metal chair on plastic casters to sit beside him. She removed a red and white bandana she'd tied loosely around her neck. He mouthed "thank you," and she sat quietly as he wiped his tears before handing it back. She put the handkerchief in her pocket before brushing away a tangle of red hair to reveal jade green eyes framing a slightly upturned nose.

"Annie, why are you here?"

"Because I don't want you to be alone, that's why."

"And you know what's going to happen?"

She gently touched the back of Blue's neck.

"I do."

"You're sure you want to be here for this?"

"I am."

"Why?"

"Like I said. You shouldn't be alone."

They both looked toward the door as her father entered. He had one hand behind his back as he sat on a stool and slowly rolled over to where one of his knees touched one of Daniel's.

"Ready?"

Daniel nodded. When he saw the syringe, he averted his eyes, then closed them. He opened them a few seconds later when he felt a small hand reach to hold his.

Doc Hayworth left, leaving Daniel and Annie to watch as Blue slowly closed his eyes for the last time. Still holding his hand, with her other Annie gave Daniel a card on which she'd written in teenage cursive:

Psalm 36:6: You, Lord, preserve both people and animals.

"What does this mean?"

"It means Blue's gone to heaven. Or on his way. Says so in the Bible."

He held the card for a moment before putting it in his shirt pocket.

"A long time ago, I was maybe four or five, when one of my Dad's patients died, my mother helped me write a letter to God tellin' him to watch out for Rusty. That was the dog's name. I thought it would help to put Rusty's picture in, too. So we did. He was a Lab. Anyway, later on, after my mother went away, my Sunday School teacher told me God always knows and will be waiting for our pets. She wrote down that Bible verse for me. I wrote more letters for other dogs. I stopped when I got older and got busy with other things helpin' my dad."

Daniel reached his hand to his shirt pocket, slipping one finger inside to touch the top of the card.

"May I ask you something, Uncle Dan?"

"Sure."

"Do you know where you're gonna bury him?"

Her question jolted him, and he held Blue even tighter.

"No idea. Hadn't planned for this to happen today."

Squeezing his hand, she asked, "May I help?"

He nodded.

"What's the most special place for the two of you at your home?"

He took some time answering.

"The front porch, I guess."

"Well, that won't work. Second most?"

"Kitchen."

"No. Try again."

He finally understood her question.

"The swing behind the house."

"I think that's where he belongs. Don't you?"

"I guess. Yeah, that'll be fine."

She released his hand as he started to get up.

"May I go with you?"

"Why?"

"If you'll let me," she answered, standing, "I want to finish Blue's journey with you. Or would you rather be alone?"

"No, I don't think I would."

"Okay, then. I'll get a blanket for him. One of mine."

Annie sat on the swing, holding Blue wrapped in her blanket, while Daniel dug a grave just outside the edge of the inlaid bricks. He stopped to rest and asked if she really believed what she wrote on the card.

"I do. Don't you?"

"Hadn't thought about it."

"Well, I don't know how long it takes, but it's been long enough. He's there by now. You know, in heaven."

"You sound very certain."

"Well, it's what I believe." Her best grownup voice. "And who's to say otherwise?"

Who, indeed?

"Say, do you know who Mark Twain is?"

Daniel leaned against the shovel, taking in her schoolgirl's innocence.

"Yes, Annie, I do. Why?"

"Well, he once wrote that if dogs don't go to heaven, he wants to go where they go. Or something like that." She paused. "I just thought you might like to know that, too."

Despite the day, and the task at hand, Daniel couldn't suppress his smile as he resumed digging. When he finished, he asked, "Do you want to keep your blanket?"

"No. I want it to stay with him."

"That's very kind. Thank you."

After Blue was laid to rest, and he listened to the prayer she offered while holding his hand, Daniel drove Annie back to the clinic. When she opened the Jeep door, he thanked her for helping him.

"That's what I'm here for, Uncle Dan." Before she closed the door, she added, "See you again soon."

Nice of her to say, he thought, as he drove away. *My business with them, and everyone else, is done.*

Daniel parked the Jeep in the garage, went briefly into the house, then returned to the swing. Looking at the mound of freshly turned dirt, thoughts of self-pity and loathing of the world around him spread through his mind like thorny vines. They pricked his memory as he bitterly recalled praying for Mallory to be spared. Praying for Paula's return. Praying for clear skies and smooth sailing into a new life. All for naught. Now, Blue's gone. That's it, he thought, the revolver resting in his lap. Nothing left. Nothing and no one to live for.

Daniel had been born in October. Listening to him share his courtroom adventures, Mallory told him more than once he was ideally suited to be a lawyer because the zodiac scales of his Libra mind were forever balancing, seeking truth, seeing both sides. He couldn't stop those scales now as he kicked the ground, propelling the swing higher.

He also remembered Mallory telling him, when they first learned of her cancer, "Danny, God doesn't give us more than we can handle."

Is that a message for me now? Can't be.

He recalled how Mallory dealt valiantly with her tragedy, and knew his sorry life after her passing spoke for itself. His mind kept churning, the scales going back and forth. He recalled Paula's prayer before their second meal together when she thanked God for putting people in the path of others. After she was gone, her songwriting idea moved him from breakfast to lunch at The Diner, putting Marlene in his path. Marlene. The woman who not so long ago told him, difficult as it may be, to keep believing in God when He is silent.

"Okay, God, let's you and me have a conversation about this. Is that how it's going to be? This watering can thing. Me doing all the talking, the praying, and nothing back from you? Never getting anything I ask for? Nothing, and I do mean nothing, in my garden?"

Long, familiar shadows began falling across the ground in front of him. Exhausted by confused thoughts tipping the scales, and emotionally drained by Blue's passing, Daniel trudged back into the house, set the gun on the center island as he passed by and drifted into the study where he collapsed onto the couch. Sleep lasted until he was awakened by the sound of the phone ringing, and he listened to the answering machine engage as he stumbled still half-asleep into the kitchen.

"Daniel, Doc here. We've got some unfinished paperwork from yesterday. It'll only take a few minutes, and you'd be doing us a great favor if you could come by today since we'll close tomorrow for a two-week vacation." The message ended with the "please come today" request repeated and sounding more urgent.

Why today, Daniel thought? Do them a favor? Sure, why the hell not. Probably want me to pay the bill right away for killing my best friend. He pushed the delete button. He looked at the revolver on the island, picked it up and returned it to the nightstand next to his bed. This time he left it loaded. With no appetitive for food or human contact, he avoided The Diner and waited until early afternoon before deciding to drive to the clinic. What's the hurry, anyway?

Annie had been watching for him out the clinic's front window all day. When he arrived, instead of the business office, Daniel was shown to the same room as the day before. When he opened the door, he saw Annie sitting in a corner with a tiny puppy in her lap. Before he could say anything, or retreat, her father gently nudged him from behind and they entered the room together and the door closed behind them.

"What's this all about?" Daniel asked.

"You might say history repeating itself," Doc answered.

"Explain."

"Another Aussie orphan, like Blue. Same breeder, but much different."

"Different how?"

"Six months old, but from its size, you'd think it's half that. Needs a lot of care every day. Feeding, medicine, even confidence being with people. Won't survive without it."

"And I'm here because …?"

"We've tried every other possibility. You know. Adoption. Even offering our services for free. Came up empty. No takers. It's you, or … "

"Or what?"

"Or we'll have to put her down."

Daniel backed away, reaching for the door.

"Doc, I can't do it. I feel bad for the dog, for you …" He saw the tears in Annie's eyes. "For Annie. Really, I do. But I can't. I just can't. You should've told me what this was about when you called. Before you got me here. I'm sorry. But this isn't going to happen. Not with me." He pushed Doc Hayworth's lean, muscular body aside, opened the door and fled the room.

Daniel sat on the steps leading upstairs, nursing a second glass of bourbon, tormented by thoughts of what he'd done and hadn't done. An image of a bearded Hemingway formed in his mind. The knock on the front door so soft he thought he'd imagined it. He heard it again, this time louder, more persistent. The last thing he wanted to see was standing on the other side of the screen door.

"Oh, no. No way." He started to close the door on Annie, holding the puppy. "Not gonna happen."

"Please. Please Uncle Dan," she pleaded. "Let me talk with you. Just for a minute. Then I'll leave. Promise I will."

He hesitated, then slowly pulled on the wooden door as if it were made of lead and motioned her to follow him into the study. Daniel sat on the sofa; Annie remained standing.

"I need to use the bathroom."

"Okay, you know where it is." She made no effort to move. "What?"

"I can't do that and hold her at the same time."

He had no choice but to accept the bundled blanket and was surprised to hear the back door open and close. What the …, he thought. When she didn't return, he walked through the kitchen and mud room, the puppy cradled in one arm still in the blanket, opened the back door, and found Annie sitting on the swing.

"What are you doing?" he asked, as he stepped into the backyard and approached the swing.

"Visiting Blue."

"I see. What about this one?"

"Oh, I wanted you to have some time with her. You know, get acquainted. You left in such a hurry."

"Annie, you know why I left. I made that very clear to you and to your father. Now you need to take it and go back." He thought for a moment. "Wait a minute. Where *is* your father?"

"At the clinic."

"Then how did you get here?"

"Rode my bike. I have a basket on the front for the puppy."

"But it's several miles."

"I know. But worth it. I hope."

Daniel was suddenly aware he was towering over the young girl as she sat in the swing, yet she seemed unintimidated by either that or his words. He stepped back and to the side, and softened his tone.

"You hope what?" he asked.

"That you'll change your mind."

"Not a chance, Annie, not a chance. And does your father know you're here?"

"He does."

"Okay, I'll call and tell him you're on your way home. Here, you take the puppy."

"Uncle Dan, before you do that, will you please just sit here with me for a few minutes. Then you can call my dad, and he'll come get me. Please?"

His effort to hand off the puppy rebuffed when she crossed her arms as he sat down. The left strap of her overalls caught his eye.

"What does your pin say?"

She reached to touch it. "I believe in angels."

A poignant, distant memory tugged at him, and he asked, "Do you?"

"Of course. Don't you?"

Those few words took him back to another time, another place. He sensed that in her own way, Annie's childish faith was as strong as Mallory's had been.

"Uncle Dan."

"What?"

"I helped you with Blue, didn't I?"

"Yes, you did. And I'll be forever grateful. I want you to know that."

"Then would you do me a favor?"

What happened next, he never saw coming.

"If I can. What is it?"

"Keep the puppy for just one night. If tomorrow morning you don't want her, I'll take her away."

Caught completely off-guard, he recovered quickly. Or thought he did.

"I wouldn't know how to take care of it. You know, all its problems your father talked about. There's no food here for a puppy, only what's left of Blue's senior citizen mix. And certainly no medicine. Otherwise, I would."

The last thing Daniel expected to see was a smile spreading across her face.

"No problem. I know how to take care of her. I'll stay with you. We'll call my dad and tell him."

"And the food? The medicine?"

"Brought them with me. I have a big basket on my bike."

"Well, I have to say, I'm impressed." And he was. "Thought of everything, have you?"

"Almost everything." The smile disappeared and she narrowed her eyes.

"What haven't you thought of?"

"You were my idea. My only one." Tears began streaking her cheeks. "She can't travel. If you don't adopt her, my dad will put her down when I get back home because we're leaving tomorrow and they'll be no one to take care of her. Like he said, we've tried everything else."

The teenager sitting beside him had pushed her way into his life much the same as Mallory had by helping with his school locker and Paula by asking directions. Three strong women, each one stronger than him. What are the odds, he thought? At that moment, he knew this was meant to be.

"Annie."

"What?"

"Please go in and call your father. By now he's probably worried about you. Tell him you and the puppy are staying the night." She jumped down from the swing. "If it's okay with him, of course."

"Oh, it will be!" She wiped her tears with the backs of her hands. "Believe me, it will be. He's used to me doing things like this."

"I'll just bet he is. Now go call him before I change my mind."

Alone with a tiny creature squirming in his lap, and before Annie returned, Daniel decided to round out this day as he had the one before, wondering if God would be surprised to hear from him again so soon.

"This is how it plays out?" he said, aloud. "A widow I barely know tells me, in a restaurant of all places, to keep praying even when I hear nothing back from you. My Mel, who you didn't spare despite me pleading with you, believed in angels. Now a girl named Annie, who believes in angels and whose young mother also died of cancer, forces a sick puppy on me to take Blue's place. One that just happens to be the same breed and will die without me living to take care of it for the next, what, ten or twelve years. That's the garden I get from my watering can? That's it? That's your plan to save my sorry life?"

That evening, Annie sat on Paula's stool at the kitchen island, holding the puppy while Daniel prepared dinner.

"Annie, it just occurred to me. You're leaving tomorrow for a couple of weeks. How am I going take care of things while you're gone?"

"Got that all figured out. My dad said I could spend the vacation time with you instead of going with them."

"I see. When did the two of you work all that out? When you called him?"

"No, sir. Before I left to come out here."

"You were that certain I'd go along?"

"No, but I hoped you would. And I got a lot of prayin' done riding my bike. Like you said, it's a long way."

She has quite the watering can.

"Okay, after we eat, I'll fix things for you and your little friend in the upstairs bedroom. You'll be comfortable there."

"I have a better idea."

By this time, Daniel had no doubt she did.

"And that would be …?"

"We all sleep in your den. Me on the sofa, and you on the floor beside her."

"Are you kidding?"

"No, sir. That's where she'll be, on the floor, and you need to be right there beside her. All night."

"Why?"

"Remember my dad telling you she needs help being with people?"

"I do."

"Well, you're her people now."

Daniel sought Annie's approval to name the puppy Baby Blue, BB for short, initials that also reminded him of Blue Bayou. It wasn't long before they knew she would grow to be much smaller than Blue, and weeks later, when all their sit-stay-come training efforts failed, realized she was deaf. Daniel offered to provide transportation, but Annie insisted on riding her bike the three-plus miles out and back at least twice a week to help him nurture Baby Blue to health. On their daily walks, Daniel often carried BB part of the way when she acted like her little legs couldn't keep up, all the while suspecting he was being conned much the same as Annie's clever plea for just one overnight stay.

When they sat in the swing during Annie's visits, BB always went to lay across Blue's grave. One afternoon, Annie talked about her plans for college in a few years before joining her father's clinic, and as he listened, Daniel knew he couldn't put off earning a living much longer. He mulled over which path to take. The uncertainty of songwriting or the certainty of law? He knew what Paula would say since one was her idea. And equally certain Mallory would send him to the watering can. Which is where he went after Annie left that afternoon, asking questions, seeking answers, as uncertain as always if he was being heard. But for the first time since Paula left him, he was once again wearing his wife's Jerusalem cross.

He knew the safe bet would be a move west to Denver and a return to law. Or he could roll the dice and move east to Nashville. And there was a third option. He could start east, then along the way decide to go north back to D.C. and the law, or south to Nashville and songwriting. Weeks later, Daniel knew the time had come to leave, to not wait for eviction from the dream home he and Mallory had envisioned and he had built, one now also holding memories of Paula and Blue. With the Three Oaks properties still unsold, Annie sat on the fence in front of the house, her arms around Baby Blue, keeping Daniel and Doc company during an auction that drew scores of people from miles around. When it was over, all the home's contents that belonged to Daniel were gone except for clothing and a few personal items he'd carefully packed in the back of his Jeep.

Daniel had loved two women. One was taken from him; the other left him. One wasn't his fault; he wasn't certain about the other. He was certain that whatever he decided to do now, wherever he decided to go, he wasn't running away from captive memories, rather running toward a new beginning he knew both women would have encouraged.

Daniel couldn't count the number of times he'd sat in the porch rocking chair, but knew this would be his last. Annie was in the other rocker, her feet dangling well above the wooden floor. Doc and Daniel had already said their good-bye's.

"Annie, thank you for coming today. It meant a lot to me."

"I'm going to miss you, Uncle Dan. And Baby Blue."

"We'll miss you, too. After all, if it weren't for you, she and I wouldn't be together, making this journey. And we have something for you to remember us by. But please don't open it until after we're gone."

An hour later, Annie waved to the disappearing cloud of dust. She sat on the porch, her feet resting on the steps as she unwrapped the package. She began to cry as she hugged the gift to her chest. Something Daniel had once shown her. Mallory's *I believe in angels* pillow.

When Daniel could no longer see the house in his rear-view mirror, he wondered if he'd ever have the same feeling about a home again. He reached the interstate an hour later and headed east without hesitation. Along the way, somewhere between Kansas and Missouri, with Baby Blue riding shotgun and country music playing on the radio, he made his gutsy decision.

As part of a new beginning where no one knew him, when he approached Music City, he decided to change to his middle name. Colin Collins had moved to Paula's hometown at her urging, but arrived intending to stay out of her life. She obviously wanted it that way, and he was humbled by his new beginning. But after renting an inexpensive downtown apartment, he searched for her byline in the newspaper and magazines. He didn't find it anywhere.

From time to time, he thought he'd caught a glimpse of her. Ahead of him on a busy street or quiet pathway in a park. A restaurant, a nightclub, a bookstore. Across the way at a table outside a coffee shop. A few rows in front of him in a movie theater or at a concert. Moments of eager anticipation quashed by disappointment. In time, he gave up, ignoring fleeting sightings, telling himself it simply wasn't meant to be. It had begun in Three Oaks … and ended there.

No do-overs in life. No second chances masquerading as firsts.

Thirteen

Long gone

Had Colin spent every waking hour of every day searching for Paula in Nashville, he'd have never found her. She was gone. Long gone. She left soon after he arrived, bound for the metropolis where he'd once told her inhabitants might be tolerant of her beliefs but judgmental of her shoes. Back when he was Daniel, Colin fled D.C. after the death of his spouse. Paula left Nashville after the death of hers.

****

Anticipation of childbirth and a shared love for a newborn brought change to the marriage of Paula and Winston Chandler, one still lacking romance but now filled with a renewed homage for two lives intertwined since childhood. The renewal was short-lived. Paula noticed in the months after their daughter's birth that Winston's joy of being a father was being pushed aside by melancholy he refused to discuss. She became alarmed the week before their daughter's first birthday when his moodiness reached new depths and his erratic behavior new heights. She was in the throes of putting last-minute touches on a party planned for later in the afternoon when she heard the doorbell ring.

A sheriff's deputy, standing on the front porch, nervously took off his hat when the door opened and he asked if he could come in. He followed Paula into the living room where, when they were seated, he informed her Winston had died in a one-car accident less than an hour earlier. She broke down and sobbed. Her tears were shed not for the loss of a husband she had never truly loved, rather for a man who, despite everything that had happened, and not happened, was a good and kind man, her friend, and possibly the father of her child.

She would later learn Winston's aging Toyota left the road at a high rate of speed, no evidence of braking or veering away to miss the solitary tree near the pavement's edge at a curve in the road where locals knew to slow down. Investigators could find no one, including Paula, who knew why he was driving that direction, on that stretch of familiar road, at that time, on that day. An unbuckled driver-side seat belt became the cornerstone of suspicion, yet his death was ruled an accident, preserving Winston Chandler in the memories of others as God's dutiful and faithful servant called home early. A few days after she closed the front door as the deputy stepped off her porch, Paula would become far less certain.

The day after the funeral, with Elizabeth down for an afternoon nap, Paula began to sort through the clutter in her husband's home office, a place she stayed away from while he was alive. Pushing aside some papers, she felt light-headed when she lifted a newspaper and underneath it saw her journal lying on his desk. Her hands shaking, she slowly picked it up and barely managed to keep it in her grasp before she collapsed into a chair. She opened the leatherbound book to where the envelope was sticking out, and realized it marked the place her writing had ended. The last page of her last entry.

The morning newspaper that had hidden it bore the date of Winston's death. Tears of anguish flowed as she cast her eyes on what Winston had read days earlier when his behavior changed so dramatically. Her love for a man other than her husband, and her regret she and her daughter could never be with him. Paula assumed Winston connected her lover to the middle name she'd insisted for a child her husband had no reason to doubt was his -- until he found the journal. The envelope dropped from her trembling hand, followed by the journal. She sat motionless, drained, unable to arrange an avalanche of troubling thoughts into anything that would enable her to regain her composure. She lost track of time and remained in the chair until a crying baby beckoned her.

Daniel had once kiddingly alluded to a cadre of folks who knew Paula so well. Yet those who actually did, especially Marla Jo, were at a loss to understand why her grief over the loss of a spouse who was more a friend than husband descended into a depression that went so deep and lasted so long. Paula refused to share the answer with anyone, and she alone bore the awful burden of doubt about Winston's death.

Remembering Daniel had sought a change of place after Mallory died, Paula entertained a passing thought of returning to Oxford where she spent the first twenty-four years of her life. But her parents had passed away and the Cinderella scenario with her sisters would be waiting there. Having no idea the man of her dreams was now living in Nashville, her success as a journalist gave Paula all the courage she needed to finally follow the dream she had before Three Oaks. She and Elizabeth left for New York City.

****

Colin couldn't help but remember little Annie Hayworth when he placed a cheap frame on the desk beside his computer in his tiny Nashville apartment. In it, a Mark Twain quote cut from a magazine he found while searching for Paula's byline.

"History doesn't repeat itself, but it does rhyme."

When the stars align perfectly, though they rarely do, Nashville is a place where dreams can come true.

Fourteen

Nashville
Twenty years later
A Friday in June

No do-overs in life. No second acts masquerading as firsts. Or so a country music lyricist from Three Oaks, Colorado believed until two words from an alluring young woman thoroughly rattled him.

"I'm lost."

Colin Collins looked her way, started to answer, then fell mute.

Despite a self-assured posture and womanly figure, he guessed her barely beyond teen years. Long auburn hair and hazel eyes, fair complexion dotted with a scattering of freckles across her nose and cheeks. Pink western-styled shirt with snap-button cuffs, form-fitting black designer jeans tucked into tan cowboy boots, an elaborately woven belt with ornate buckle cinched around her small waist.

Wearing dress blue jeans and a white long-sleeved shirt, lightly starched, Colin reached to touch the dog sitting at his side to keep from staring at the achingly young and beautiful incarnation of someone he'd recognize anywhere. In any setting. In any attire.

This can't be happening, he thought. *Or could it?*

His mind went into overdrive. Summer now; winter back then. Urban sidewalk coffee shop now; rural front porch decades ago. Early twenty-something here; late-thirty something there. The balancing scales of his Libra mind began restoring his equilibrium, but words still wouldn't come.

"Knock, knock. Anybody home?"

"I'm sorry," he finally said. "Say again."

"I said I think I'm lost."

Not fully in the moment, he struggled to answer. "Do you know where you're going?"

"Of course. I …" She frowned. "Never mind. Sorry to have troubled you." She began to walk away.

"Wait!" he hastily called after her. "It's me who's sorry. I apologize. Perhaps I can help."

"Hope so." Three steps and she was back at his table. "I'm looking for Adelaide. It's a recording studio. Supposed to be in this block, but I don't see it anywhere."

"It's just over there." He tilted his head. "Across the street."

"White building? The one with the blue awnings?" She pointed, and Colin's eyes followed.

"That's the one."

"Really? Wonder why there's no sign."

"There's lettering on the window. By the front door. Guess the sun's glare hides it from here. And besides …"

"Besides what?"

"We wouldn't be having this conversation." *Anything to keep her here.*

"Well, there's that. I suppose." *Is he flirting, or just being friendly?* "Anyway, thanks."

She started to leave. He couldn't let that happen.

"Might want to cross at the light a bit farther down. Drivers are almost as bad as Atlanta."

"I know. I live here. Thanks, again."

"Are you in a hurry? If not, may I buy you a cup of coffee?" She didn't answer. "To enhance my apology?"

She looked at him, and settled on *friendly.* "You know, that would be nice. I've got some time. You got a name?"

"I do." He stood and pulled back the chair next to his. "Colin."

She knew men were often intimidated when her boots made her as tall or taller. Standing next to him, she sensed this wouldn't be one of those times.

"Mine's Danielle."

"It is?" He asked, trying to absorb the coincidence.

"Yes, it is. Why would I say it was if it wasn't?"

"I don't know." He shrugged slightly, then signaled the waiter.

Danielle gently stroked the furry head now resting on her thigh, looking up at her.

"Who's your friend?"

"Oh, this is Blue."

"How'd you come up with the name? Wait, let me guess. Her eyes?"

"His eyes. My third Aussie Shepherd. Boy, girl, boy. Named 'em all Blue."

She began scratching behind the dog's ears and started to remark "what a strange coincidence" when the traffic light stopped an SUV with the windows rolled down and radio blaring directly in front of their sidewalk table. They both waited to speak, but the moment the car moved on, their waiter arrived. In the brief time it took to serve them, she decided not to mention the other dogs named Blue she'd heard about on a recent trip to Colorado. Instead, she said, "I'll tell you my story if you'll tell me yours."

Colin dropped his chin, slumped forward slightly and shook his head in disbelief. Surprised by his reaction, she added, "Oh, just something my mother taught me. To get conversation going with strangers who interest me."

"Did she now?" His mind in a memory-infused free fall.

"She did. And you interest me."

"I do?"

"You do."

"Tell me one thing that interests you."

"You're wearing very expensive leather shoes with no socks. What's up with that?"

"Nothing special. Habit, I guess."

"A non-answer answer. Okay. Now, Colin, about your story."

"Ladies first." *Can this really be happening?*

"Clever. Didn't see that coming. You a lawyer, or something?"

He hesitated before answering. "Was once. A long time ago."

"What happened?"

Not telling that story. Not now, anyway. "Packed my bags and left the zoo without saying good-bye to the animals."

"Sounds mysterious." She thought for a moment. "Talking like that, you must be … you must be some kinda writer."

"I'm confused," he answered, stroking his lower lip between his thumb and index finger.

"About what?"

"I thought you were going first."

"I am. I am. But it helps if I know my audience."

The radiant smile she cast his way was one he'd seen before, but never thought he'd see again.

"Fair enough. Yes, Danielle, I'm some kind of writer."

"Okay, Colin," she answered, playfully mocking his formality. "You're going to make me ask. What kind of writer are you?"

"Songs."

"Songs," she repeated, before sipping her coffee and setting the cup down. "Any good?"

He answered slowly. "Others think I am."

"I see. These others. Do their opinions really matter?"

"In this town, it seems they do."

"Does that mean you're a big deal? Have I stumbled my way into coffee with a big deal? Oh, boy!"

"No, truth is, I'm just a small-town country boy," he deadpanned, as he drained the last of his coffee, "tryin' ta find my way in tha big city."

"Yeah. Uh, huh. And I'm Patsy Cline."

Serve and volley with a worthy opponent. *Mother would be proud of me.*

"Okay, Patsy. I believe we were at that place where you were going to tell me your story."

She rested both forearms on the table and leaned toward him. "You know something. You've been looking at me as if you know me. Have we ever met?"

"I'm sorry," he answered, nervously picking at a fingernail, feeling his way from one word to the next, knowing he *had* been staring and couldn't help himself. "It's just that you do remind me of someone."

"A special someone, perhaps?" she asked, sitting back, her look unmistakably teasing.

"Are you flirting with me?"

"Second nature. Something else I learned from my mother. But don't worry. I'm harmless. Like she is." He remained silent, and she sensed his uneasiness. "Colin, I can assure you, nothing's going to happen."

"No, I'm the one who can assure *you* nothing's going to happen!" His voice nervously pitching higher.

"Ooh, we seem a bit touchy. Are you married? Or is it because you're old enough to be my father?"

"I'm not married. I am old enough to be your father. And we both know you're making fun of me."

"No," she said, retreating. "I'm trying to have fun with you. Big difference. But if I've upset you, it's my turn to apologize."

"No need. I overreacted. I was just trying to hold my own, and failing miserably." He looked at his watch, then over his shoulder to the building across the street. "Are you a singer?"

Growing up, Danielle shared her mother's love of country music. After graduating high school in Manhattan, one of five boroughs in the country's largest city, she enrolled at the Blair School of Music at Vanderbilt University across town from where she was sitting with Colin. During those four years, she immersed herself in the local music scene and stayed on to pursue her dream.

"I am. But that could be a lucky guess since about every third person in Nashville is. Or wants to be. Or maybe you guessed I wasn't just playing dress-up looking like this on a Friday afternoon."

"You're on your way to an audition, aren't you?"

"Wow! Are you clairvoyant or something?"

Another Three Oaks memory. "Something. And here's something I know about both of us."

"And that would be …?"

"We're late. I'm supposed to listen to someone named Danielle audition at Adelaide."

She hadn't been told specifics, but in addition to being a studio backup singer, she was also auditioning for the last opening to go on tour with one of county music's hottest new stars.

"Then why are we sitting here?" she asked, pushing her coffee cup away and reaching for her purse.

They waited for the light to turn green at the cross walk.

"Just so you know, Danielle's my middle name. My first name's Elizabeth. Like the queen."

Her words pried loose one more in what was becoming an endless stream of memories. A distracted Colin stumbled slightly as they began crossing the street.

"You okay?"

"I am," he answered, recovering his gait as he walked beside her. "What's your last name?"

"Keepin' it a secret."

"Why?"

"Don't want you to be confused if we meet again later on since I haven't decided on my professional name. You know, for when I become rich and famous." They reached the other side of the street. "And you still haven't told me your story."

"And you haven't told me yours." They arrived at the recording studio front door. "Danielle, we have two choices. You can tell me what I'm certain will be an interesting story. And I can tell you my boring one …"

"Or?"

"We go inside and you perform for the folks we've kept waiting. Who knows? Might get you on your way to a new name and becoming rich and famous."

"I'm not worried. Ya'll are gonna be so impressed you'll beg me to do whatever it is I'm auditioning for. And I bet I find out some of the songs are yours. Right?"

"Could be."

"Then let's get this outta tha way and we'll tell our stories some other time." He held the door open for her, and as she walked through, he heard, "And I doubt yours is boring."

****

Ten years of collaboration with composer Paul Dean allowed Colin to pay his bills and save some money before becoming an "overnight" industry sensation with lyrics inspired by Paula Chandler. The refrain came to him as he and Baby Blue journeyed from Three Oaks to Music City:

Doesn't she know / Oh why can't she see.
She means all the world to me.

The piece had been shopped around publishers and recording studios for several years before it became a mega-hit for the unknown singer who finally recorded it, also bringing accolades to the team of Collins and Dean, securing them a place on the short lists of top-tier producers and recording artists. The affable Dean eagerly went along with something close to Colin's heart. A desire to help talented but undiscovered singers as he'd been helped by those he believed God had placed in his poet-turned-lyricist path during his early years of struggle in Nashville.

****

From the moment they met, Colin had the eerie feeling he was in the presence of Paula's daughter. That feeling turned to certainty when he settled into the booth with others to hear her audition and was shown her profile sheet. What for so long he'd thought impossible could now be within reach as he listened to Elizabeth Danielle Chandler sing a selection of songs, some he'd written for the star performer preparing to go on tour. His thoughts took him ahead in time. Weeks, maybe months from now, when he and Paula Chandler might meet again.

Although made in jest, Colin felt Danielle's confident prediction would come true when he heard her sing and saw the others in the booth smiling and enthusiastically nodding approval. The audition over, she navigated around instruments, microphones and cables strewn across the room and walked up to where she found him sitting at a piano in the corner of the studio.

"I'm not going to embarrass you by asking what you thought. Wouldn't be fair." She tapped her rose-colored fingernails on the top of the piano while deciding what to say next. "Listen, if you don't have other plans, would you like to have dinner?"

"You don't already have your Friday night all planned out?"

"I do. But I can easily change."

"Why would you do that?" He slowly pushed the bench back as he stood.

"Just thought you might like to meet my mother. I know she'd love to meet you. She's pretty. Beautiful, actually. Your age. I think. She's unattached. Makes sense to me. Oh, unless you are."

"Are what?" Colin asked, trying to appear calm.

"Attached. You know. Significant other. Friend with benefits. Like that."

"No. In your words, nothing like that."

"Then is it a date?"

Not wanting to appear over-anxious, his answer came slowly. "Sounds like a great evening."

"Then you accept?"

"I do."

"Great! We already have a reservation. Now it'll be dinner for four."

The timeframe he'd envisioned while listening to her sing collapsed from weeks or months to within the hour when Danielle gave him the restaurant and time.

"Four?"

"Yeah. My mother's best friend. Lives up the road in Kentucky. They're like sisters."

He was apprehensive, and struggled not to let it show. "Hope I'm not at a disadvantage."

"In what way?

"Three against one."

"Oh, I have no doubt you can hold your own. You'll be with three demure Southern Christian ladies who'll be awed by your presence. Especially when I tell them you're a big deal and all. Even though you say you're not. Probably have to pry words out of each of us. Especially Mother."

That's not the Paula I remember.

Fifteen

~~~) (~~~

A memorable evening

Colin arrived early to sit at the restaurant's bar and slowly nurse a bourbon on the rocks. Having no idea how the evening might unfold, he knew what lay ahead would be memorable. Ten minutes before the time Danielle had given him, Colin saw men and women already seated in the restaurant cast admiring glances at two women who could almost pass for sisters being escorted to their table by the tuxedo-clad maître' d. Colin waited a few minutes to collect himself after seeing Paula Chandler from a distance for the first time in over twenty years. He finished his Maker's Mark, settled his check, and began making his way to their table.

"Mother, this is the man I told you about. Colin, this is my mother, Paula Chandler."

Colin thought Paula looked remarkably unchanged from the afternoon she strolled confidently up the Three Oaks cobblestone walk and into his life. Ageless beauty frozen in time. Yet he was taken aback, stunned, when she extended her hand the way she would to any man she was meeting for the first time.

"Here, Mr. Collins," she said, with a welcoming smile, "sit next to me."

Colin eased himself into the chair to Paula's right, and she reached across the table to pat her daughter's hand. "Dear, he's certainly handsome, just like you said. But isn't he a bit old for you?"

"Mother!" Danielle blushed with the scarlet coloring her mother's genes had passed on. "I told you. Colin is a songwriter. We met for the first time this afternoon. He doesn't know it yet, but I'm hoping he'll help me with my career. It's all professional."

"Oh."

Colin started to speak. Paula was quicker.

"Colin Collins. Do I have that right?"

"Yes, ma'am."

"Anyone ever tell you it sounds like an echo?"

"Mother!"

Despite feeling off-balance and beyond confused, Colin sent a discreet and reassuring wink Danielle's way, and said, "Not until now."

"Well, I know one thing about your mother." Paula tugged at the edge of her jacket sleeve.

"What's that?"

"The woman had a wicked sense of humor. She and I would've gotten along famously."

"From what I remember, she did. And I think you would."

"Oh, and by the way, Colin. I have trouble remembering things. Expensive doctors told me I'll just have to live with it. Pretty sure I'll remember that name of yours. But if I forget other things, and believe me, I've forgotten most of my life already, well, you've been warned. Only telling you so you don't get upset next time we meet." She looked across at Danielle. "Unless I'm too much of an embarrassment for my daughter tonight and she keeps me away from you."

"Paula, I promise you. I'll do all I can to keep that from happening."

"Good for you, Colin!" She turned to look at her daughter. "And I promise to behave myself. You'll forget I'm even here."

Not a chance, he thought. *The movie's missing reel.*

"All right then, with that all settled," Danielle interjected. "Colin, I have a confession to make."

"What would that be?"

"That I couldn't wait for you to tell me your story. After you left, I talked to some of the musicians."

"And?"

His eyes continued to dart back and forth between mother and daughter.

"You're not a big deal."

"I'm not?" His attempt to look dejected failed. "Well, that's disappointing to hear. I guess I'll ..."

"No, you're a really big deal! And you know it!"

It's the perception, not the person, people anticipate long before a luminary enters a room. When Danielle looked back on their sidewalk meeting, and this dinner, it would be his unassuming modesty and self-effacing charm she'd remember most. None of the arrogant demeanor, the trappings of celebrity she'd heard about in others far less deserving than the man she'd invited to meet her mother. Colin kept such a low profile it was his name and not his face that was recognized as, in Danielle's words, "a big deal" in the music industry. Few who knew his work doubted he would eventually be selected to more than one songwriter hall of fame.

Before he could answer, an attractive woman Colin guessed to be about the same age as Paula approached, also escorted by the maître' d who pulled back the chair opposite Colin.

"Colin, this is Marla Jo Taylor, Mother's best friend."

"Pleasure to meet you, ma'am," he said, standing.

"My pleasure, as well." She smiled and offered her hand in greeting. "If she hasn't already, I know Paula here is dying to jump in and tell you to please drop the ma'am business. Makes us feel older than we know we are. And look."

Marla Jo and Paula were dressed in classically tailored clothing perfect for Southern women of a certain age and social standing out for a casual evening on the town. Despite her mother's proffer of both money and encouragement, Danielle hadn't updated her wardrobe since graduation and usually dressed coed-casual in jeans and whatever. Tonight, she'd kept with her audition attire.

"Well, I can assure you, looks are deceiving. If I didn't know better, and I'm still not certain, I'd have thought Danielle invited me here tonight to meet her sisters."

"Danielle, dear. Forget what I said about his age. Grab this one before he gets away. He's so smooth a gal could ice skate on his back and not leave a mark."

"Mother!"

"Just sayin'."

Although her mother didn't recognize Danielle's new friend and possible mentor, Marla Jo had read the journal, was old enough to know who Steve McQueen was, and to see the resemblance. Older, of course, and graying at the temples, but Colin was the right height, same hair, same build, same eye color, same quietly confident demeanor. And Marla Jo thought she saw something each time Colin looked at Paula. For his part, early in the evening Colin remembered Marla Jo, recalling how Paula, while staying at Three Oaks, had described their close friendship.

Dessert finished, Paula, who had said very little as Danielle had predicted, folded her napkin, placed it on the table and told the others she'd grown tired. Colin would later learn it happens around nine almost every evening, caused by medicine to reduce the chance of another stroke.

"Between my daughter and my friend, I didn't get much of a chance to say anything tonight. I could tell they were really trying to impress you, so I let them. But I like to make a favorable impression, too. Have I, Mr. Collins?"

"You have, indeed. I only hope I have, as well."

Paula reached to place her hand on top of Colins'. "No question about that. Right, ladies?"

Danielle and Marla Jo smiled and nodded.

"Before we go, a question for you, Mr. Collins."

"May I answer as Colin and not as Mr. Collins?"

Paula blushed. "Of course, you may. So, Colin, have you ever known anyone like me before?"

Marla Jo gasped softly and Danielle reached for her mother's other hand.

"I believe I have. Once. A long time ago. And she was just as lovely as you are."

"Mother, it's time for us to go."

After giving her mother assurances she'd see Colin again, Danielle accompanied her on the short walk back to their hotel, leaving Marla Jo and Colin to finish their Port.

"Well, here's the thing." Marlo Jo rolled the tiny glass stem between her fingers. "Paula and I aren't merely friends. We've been like best-friend sisters since before Danielle was born."

"That's easy to see. And I'm happy for all of you. Especially Danielle."

"She's called me Miss Marla all her life. Except now and again she'll say Marla Jo when she wants to appear all grown up. Which, of course, she is. My, how time does fly."

She set her empty glass midway between them and clasped her hands together, resting them on the table's edge. He sat up straighter, and having been there countless times before, sensed his chair had become a witness stand and he was the one facing cross-examination.

"Colin, you seemed rather ill at ease tonight. Even confused." He looked away momentarily, then back. "Confused might not be strong enough. How about bewildered?"

"Did I?"

"You did. Thankfully, the others didn't notice. At least I don't think they did." She thought he'd say something. He didn't. "And we both know why. Don't we?"

"I'm listening."

"You recognized Paula, and it was a one-way street. As it were."

A sinking feeling in his stomach stopped his words, but not his expression. She had her answer.

"Thought so. Back then, in Three Oaks, did Paula ever mention me?"

"She did. You were the reason she came there. She left me a copy of your *My Way* book. I have it to this day."

"I'm flattered. I truly am. I'd like to talk with you about that sometime. But back to Paula. When you were together that week, and my goodness that was a long time ago, did you know she was keeping a journal?"

Colin felt a sudden dryness in his mouth. Not a question he wanted to answer truthfully.

"No."

"Well, she did. She insisted I read it when she got back. And you, sir, had a starring role. As I'm sure you can imagine."

Colin realized he'd read nothing in Paula's journal about their time together, only about her life before.

"When Danielle told me you'd be joining us tonight, I did an internet search from our hotel room. That's why I was late."

"I see."

"I read about your work with Paul Dean. But there's something you may not know."

"What?" Colin asked, unable to mask his puzzled look.

"It had its beginning when he was an up-and-coming composer in Nashville and you weren't yet a songwriter still living in boondocks Colorado. Did that ever strike you as odd?"

"How on earth did you know?" He shifted uncomfortably in his chair.

"Paula told me. A long time ago. She's the one who asked him to contact you. They were friends, and she swore him to secrecy. She's long forgotten Paul. Did he ever tell you?"

"No," he answered, shaking his head, "he didn't."

"Good for him. Class act." Marla Jo rearranged her hands on the table. "I think it's fair to say you owe some portion of all those Grammys and Dove Awards, and the money and everything else, including the idea to become a song-writer in the first place, to a woman who has no memory of you."

Colin looked vacantly over Marla Jo's shoulder, across several tables to the window behind and the darkness beyond, much as Blue had gazed across the grasslands toward the mountains in his final days. She couldn't help but notice.

"Colin, I'm afraid I've offended you. That certainly wasn't my intent. I apologize."

"There's no need. It's just a lot to take in all at once. And where are you going with this?"

"Truthfully, it was easier to begin than to find a way to end. I'll try. Paula's obviously comfortable with anyone and everyone knowing the reason she doesn't remember you and most of the rest of her life. In addition to reading the steamy prose in her journal, over the years I've listened to her talk, talk and talk, about you. And what might have been. Oh, and by the way, Danielle found the journal, and not too long ago took her mother to Colorado."

Sixteen

A memorable evening ... continued

A part from her diagnosis, Paula was in excellent health for a woman her age. Her physicians thought they knew what caused her memory loss -- silent strokes -- but only she knew of her feelings of guilt over the uncertainty of Winston's death that might have impacted her mental and physical well-being. The memory loss from her first stroke rendered her unable to tell her doctors, so no one would ever know if stress might have planted seeds from which decades later a bitter harvest would be reaped. She'd prayed about it, asked for God's forgiveness, but had never forgiven herself. And returning to the journal from time to time to relive memories of her brief time with Daniel only made matters worse, but it had become an addiction of sorts born out of her self-imposed loneliness.

Over time, Paula's memory loss became progressively worse, and when Danielle was home in Manhattan for spring break in her final year at Blair, she found the journal while looking for some papers her mother's lawyers had requested and her mother couldn't find. Danielle went through a predictable range of emotions sitting by herself in her bedroom. She wept as she turned the pages, heartbroken there was little chance her mother could ever remember the things she'd written. Over dinner that night, Danielle tip-toed through questions about Three Oaks, and wasn't at all surprised her mother had no recollection.

"It would've been a long time ago, Mother. He had a dog named Blue."

"No, honey, I don't remember a man named Daniel in that way. Don't think I've ever been to Colorado. Say, maybe you and I could go sometime."

Because she was mentioned in the journal, Danielle called the woman she'd grown up calling Miss Marla.

"Yes," Marla Jo admitted, reluctantly, "I've read the journal. Once. Years and years ago. Before you were born. Your mother insisted."

"All of it? You read all of it? Even the part about her wondering who my father was?"

"Yes. But Danielle, I thought your mother destroyed it. She said she would. Promised me she would. And she never talked to me about it again."

"This Daniel guy. Do you know if Mother ever contacted him again? Does he even know about me?"

"Your mother told me many times she never had anything to do with him after she came home. That it was her choice, not his." A long silence broken when Marla Jo asked, "Danielle, what are you going to do?"

An even longer silence.

"I'm going to go look for the man who might be my father. And take my mother with me."

Danielle Chandler and her mother came to the end of their westward journey more than twenty years after Daniel Collins left Colorado heading east. It was late spring, and the GPS voice in Danielle's cell phone said their exit off Interstate 70 was a thousand feet ahead. At the bottom of the ramp that emptied into a cluster of discount motels and fast-food restaurants, Danielle heeded the disembodied woman's voice and turned left. She noticed the tiny compass at the bottom of the rearview mirror in their rented Lexus hybrid sedan pointed them to the southeast. Only one more hour on a winding, two-lane road past arresting high-desert landscapes before they finally reached Three Oaks, a mountain hamlet far removed from anything Paula had ever known. Unless her memory returned.

Danielle arrived at their remote destination with the sole purpose of trying to find the man her mother had written about but couldn't remember. For Paula, it was a welcome change of pace and place, happy to be along for the ride for precious time travelling with her daughter. At Paula's urging, they'd driven rather than flown so they could spend more time together. It was still daylight when they pulled up at Manor House, their first night's accommodation. After depositing their luggage in a large, tastefully decorated room with two queen beds and adjoining bathroom, Paula accompanied Danielle to peer into each of the unoccupied first-floor meeting rooms before they ate their evening meal at a family-style restaurant down the street past the post office.

The next morning, they strolled arm-in-arm across the town's one main street for a comfort-food breakfast at The Diner. Less than an hour later, they began making the rounds, stopping people on the sidewalk, knocking on doors, seeking anyone who might still have contact with the object of Danielle's search. Or knew where he could be found. Everyone was friendly, a few thought they vaguely remembered Daniel Collins, but none had a clue where to find him.

"If he knew you pretty ladies were lookin' for him, betcha he'd wanna be found."

Both women smiled. Paula thanked the elderly man resting his chin on his cane as he sat on a bench in front of Manor House while Danielle lifted their suitcases into the car's trunk. Having scoured the town and come away empty, they stopped at a small country store to purchase a few groceries and ask directions before finding their way to the town's only animal clinic. A red-headed woman in her mid-thirties, *Doctor Annie* stitched in blue thread above the left pocket of her white scrub top, greeted them warmly.

"I sure do," she answered. "He brought his dogs here a long time ago, back when my father ran the clinic. He's now retired. My father, that is. Don't know about Mr. Collins."

"How long ago?" Danielle asked, thrilled at this glimmer of hope.

"Oh, I don't know. Gee, I might've been only thirteen or fourteen at the time. Twenty years maybe."

"How is it you remember?"

"Every one of our patients has a story, and so do their owners," Annie replied, bringing them coffee as they sat in her modest, cluttered office. "I remember there was an old dog named Blue. After he died, I kinda sorta tricked Mr. Collins into adopting a puppy we named Baby Blue. That's why I remember him and the dogs' names after all these years. I helped him take care of the puppy before he left a few months later."

"What else do you remember about him?" Danielle asked.

"He was such a nice man. I remember he wasn't like those of us born and raised out here. Different."

"Different how?"

"Oh, I don't know. Kinda like he was outta place living in Three Oaks. That he came from somewhere else. And needed to be somewhere else. Am I making any sense?"

"Of course, you are." Danielle looked at her mother stroking a tabby cat that had jumped into her lap. "Annie, do you have any records that might tell us where he went?"

"Let me check." She turned to her computer, and several keystrokes later, said, "No, I'm sorry. He didn't leave a forwarding address. And there would've been no need. Also doesn't look like we ever had a cell phone for him."

Annie had patients waiting, so Danielle thanked her, took one of her business cards and the two women left. Paula followed her daughter's directions and drove a few miles on a narrow dirt road to a luxury rental for their second evening's lodging. An imposing two-story log cabin home set back from the road, encircled by sugar maple trees.

Paula pulled up in front of the house and said she'd carry the groceries. Danielle followed up the porch steps, a suitcase in each hand. Paula placed the grocery bag on the kitchen's center island, Danielle set the suitcases by the staircase, and they held hands as they slowly walked throughout the spacious residence. Downstairs first, then upstairs, looking into every room. Danielle searched her mother's face for even the slightest inkling her memory was engaging, but like their brief time at Manor House, nothing.

"Let's see what's out back," Paula said, opening the mud room door and stepping out. "Look, a swing. Been a long time since I've been on one of those. Don't even remember when. Let's sit out here and have a glass of wine before starting dinner."

Paula's journal had led Danielle to bring Meiomi chardonnay with them from Tennessee, and to plan a pescatarian dinner for them to prepare together in the kitchen her mother once shared with Daniel. When her mother's medicine had its normal evening effect, Danielle insisted she sleep in the downstairs master bedroom.

Wide-awake, Danielle wandered the house again, taking in everything she'd imagined while reading her mother's journal. Her tour ended when she reached the front door and went out to sit in one of two sturdy, front-porch rocking chairs. Alone with her thoughts, she slowly finished what was left of the wine as a clear, star-filled night sky captivated her. It was well past midnight when she went back inside to climb the seventeen steps and enter the first door on the right.

They left for home the next morning.

****

"Please, Colin," Marla Jo said, "I've done all the talking. I want to know what you're thinking."

Colin clasped his hands together in front of him as they sat at the restaurant table.

"If I may be permitted a metaphor. Chalk it up to the writer in me. Anyway, what I hear you saying is that if our time together, Paula's and mine, was a book, it's one that'll never be finished. It's over. And it's not really a book, is it? It's just a short story."

"I'll answer your metaphor, and it was a good one, this way. A Three Oaks book might never be finished, but that doesn't mean there can't be a new beginning, does it? One for you and Paula, now that you've found each other again."

New beginning. But I'm the only one that's found the other.

One word in what he'd just heard stuck in Colin's mind.

"You said might."

"What?"

"You said a Three Oaks book *might* never be finished. What's left? What am I missing?"

Marla Jo reached across and took his hands in hers.

"You might be Danielle's father."

Seventeen

✦

Missing pieces.

The hour had grown late. Marla Jo and Colin had the dining room all to themselves. The maître d' approached with a request they move to the adjacent bar, assuring them it would stay open until at least two am. An emotionally exhausting day for Colin, but he knew the end was not yet in sight. Re-settled at a corner table by the street-level window, they silently watched the stream of late-night, bar-hopping revelers passing by. She broke the silence when their drinks arrived and the waiter departed.

"Shall I continue?"

He nodded.

Marla Jo told him about Paula's pregnancy, and her agonizing decisions to remain with Winston and have no further contact with a man she'd fallen in love with in Colorado. Marla Jo ended with Winston's death.

"Even though she didn't know which of you was Elizabeth's father, I urged Paula over and over again to contact you after Winston died. I never understood why she didn't. For the longest time, I thought it was the only big thing in her life she kept from me, though in recent years I came to doubt it. I had the sense she was carrying some awful burden, the kind only guilt could cause. I tried to get her to talk about it, but she'd have none of it. That's when I knew I was right, but I didn't know about what."

Colin leaned back in his chair, cast his eyes to the ceiling, then looked across at Marla Jo.

"I wish Paula *had* listened to you. Had talked with you. I wish even more I hadn't kept my promise not to contact her." He paused, then asked, "Anything else?"

"Well, I've gone back and forth in my mind about telling you, but there is something that happened the moment the two of you met. You see …."

The waiter interrupted to inquire about another round, Marla Jo shook her head and Daniel asked for the check. When they were alone again, she said, "The thing is, Paula isn't her birth name. It's Arlette. She changed it after Winston died. She never told Danielle, who was too young at the time. And as the years went by, well, I guess she saw no reason. And she made me promise not to tell her."

Even in the dim lighting, Marla Jo saw Colin's confused look.

"I don't understand. If I'm putting this all together right, we met a couple of years *before* her husband's death, and she introduced herself as Paula. Paula Chandler. Makes no sense."

"It *is* an interesting twist."

"Like all the other twists haven't been interesting?"

They looked at each other, then broke out in laughter, a much-needed release for both.

"Just hang in there with me, Colin. Other than my husband Ben more than twenty years ago, I'm telling this for the first time. And so that you know, only someone writing that book you mentioned could've thought this one up."

Colin buried his head in his hands, and Marlo Jo reached across reassuringly. He lifted his head.

"All right, go on. But please, please, don't start with once upon a time. That would do me in."

Hearing that, Marla Jo tried for her most pensive look before saying, "It was a dark and stormy night."

Their laughter returned.

"I can see why you and Paula have gotten along so well. Maybe you really *are* sisters and just don't know it. Twins even."

"Thank you for a wonderfully intriguing thought, but not a chance. And I'm a couple of years older. Anyway, let me get to the story. On her drive out to Colorado from Nashville, one evening she stopped in a small town along the way. Don't remember where. After checking into a motel and having dinner, she found herself in a local theater where they were featuring an old black and white movie. One from the early 1940s."

"Which one?"

"*Random Harvest.* She told me she was so taken with the movie that on the spur of the moment when she met you, she assumed the first name of the movie's heroine."

"Paula." He thought for a moment. "But why?"

"I knew for the longest time she was wanting a new start in life, and the name thing, well, you were the first person she met after seeing the movie. She told me she couldn't explain. Just something that happened. Anyway, on the off chance you and I might've met at Three Oaks, the next morning at the writer's conference she told me what she'd done. You know, spent the night at your house and told you her name was Paula Chandler. She asked me to play along. Of course, you and I never did. Meet, that is. A few years later, she legally changed her first name before moving to New York City. She knew there were only two people she'd ever expect to encounter in person again who would have known her as Arlette."

"You and Paul Dean."

"Right. Very good. By the way, have you ever seen the movie?"

"I haven't. Should I?"

Marla Jo nodded. "Greer Garson, the actress in the movie, and our Paula, look very much alike. Even their mannerisms are similar. And with what you now know about Paula's life, the plot will break your heart."

Marlo Jo looked at her watch. "Oh, my! It's almost two. We better get going." She paused, as though she were trying to decide about something.

"Please don't go. There's so much I want to ask. To know. Her life in New York. Her memory loss. I've waited over twenty years and …"

"And we both need to get some sleep," she answered, smiling.

Colin insisted on walking Marla Jo the few blocks to her hotel, one he remembered with an awning that extended from the front door across the sidewalk to the curb.

As they walked, Marla Jo asked, "Colin, if it turns out you're Danielle's father, and if you had known, you'd have moved heaven and earth to make a life with Paula and the child you had together. True?"

"True."

"Then I think you should be talking with Danielle, not me. And do it before she figures you out as I so easily did. In fact, why don't I tell her you and I've had a nice chat and ask her to call you?"

They arrived at the hotel. Standing underneath the dark green awning, Colin said, "I'm not sure I'd know what to say."

"Have confidence. You're the word guy. Lawyer. Poet. Songwriter. All that. You'll do just fine."

Marla Jo touched two fingers to her lips and then to his cheek before disappearing into the hotel.

It was two-thirty in the morning when Colin got home, but he was too wound-up to sleep, choosing instead to sit in his den and replay the day's events over and over again in his mind. At least an hour passed before he collapsed into bed and fell into an exhausted sleep. He always kept his cell phone on mute, and didn't hear the vibration on the nightstand at nine-thirty. He checked for messages an hour later after both he and Blue had seen to their morning health and grooming routines.

"Good Saturday morning." The voice both cheerful and familiar. "Danielle calling. Wakey, wakey. Please call when you get this message. Not a minute later. My number's right there in your phone. Bye."

Colin felt uneasy as he dialed, and when she answered, rushed a question. "How'd you get my number?"

"Well, a joyous good morning to you, too. Wanna try that again?"

"Sorry," he said, with genuine apology in his voice. "Good morning."

"Much better. Good morning to you."

"It's just that your call, well, it surprised me."

"I'll bet it did."

"How *did* you get my number?"

"I have my ways." A brief pause. "But to end the suspense, someone wrote a phone number next to the initials CC on my audition sheet. Being a recent college grad, with honors, I might add, I put one and one together and ..."

"Got me."

"And aren't we both glad. Especially since I'm calling to invite you for coffee. Same place as before. Say, in half an hour?"

"Why?"

"Do I need a reason?"

"No," he answered, hesitantly, "but I suspect maybe you have one."

"I do. Thought we might finish the conversation you had with Marla Jo last night after Mother and I left. The two of you must've really stayed up late. See ya in thirty. Bye." As he moved the phone away from his ear, he heard, "Oh, no need to dress up on my account. What with it Saturday morning, and all. Bye, again."

Colin left Blue sleeping soundly, turned the key to lock the door behind him and set off for a coffee shop rendezvous. Walking through familiar urban neighborhood surroundings, an alchemy of uncertainty mixed with trepidation made for an unsettling feeling on an empty stomach. As he approached his destination, Danielle smiled and waved him over to the same table where they first met.

"Where's Blue?"

"Sleeping in. Does that Saturday mornings. Actually, every morning."

She'd returned to her coed-casual attire with frayed jeans and a Vanderbilt University sweatshirt. She sensed tension and wanted to put him at ease. "That would make him the boss of you?"

"All day, every day." He also wore jeans, but of the dress variety with a pressed crease, and a light-weight dark blue cashmere sweater over a lighter blue button-down oxford shirt. "We have that understanding."

"I remembered from yesterday, so I ordered for you. Brewed drip. Black." The waiter appeared before they could sit down. "And here it is. Perfect timing."

They both watched as the waiter went back inside.

"First things first. Mother knows we're meeting and wanted me to say hello for her. She thinks you're…, what were her exact words…, oh yes, the living end. I guess that means something to people your age."

"It does. And coming from your mother, that's very flattering. Please thank her for me."

"Will do." Danielle took a sip of her creamed and sweetened coffee. "Miss Marla also knows we're meeting, of course. She set the whole thing up."

Colin watched the steam rising from his cup. "Am I to assume she shared chapter and verse?"

"She did! Got me out of bed early this morning. Much earlier than you. Obviously. But under the circumstances ..."

"About those circumstances. I ..."

"Wow, a lot sure has happened since the last time we sat here. And it was only yesterday."

Colin studied her. "You don't appear upset."

"You thought I would be?"

He nodded.

"Why? I've read Mother's journal. Several times. And Miss Marla only *thought* she was filling in missing pieces."

"Don't know what you mean."

"I didn't tell her, but I'd already figured out who you were." She raised her cup halfway to her lips. "Daniel."

He stiffened, pushing his shoulders back. "How? When?"

"Well, last night at dinner, while Miss Marla was doing most of the talking and you were politely answering her questions, I was listening. Carefully. And I remembered what you said when we first met. Right here." She tapped the table with her finger.

Colin had been resting his wrists, palms down, on the table's edge. He turned his palms up to gesture a question.

"About naming all your dogs Blue."

"Not following you."

"Sorry. Miss Marla said this morning she told you that Mother and I visited Three Oaks not too long ago, looking for you. Right?"

"She did. And?"

"And … we had a delightful time meeting with Doctor Annie. Said she remembered your dogs' names. First Blue, then Baby Blue. Oh, and she remembered Uncle Dan. Fondly, I might add."

Colin smiled. "So little Annie became a vet after all."

"She did. But back to yesterday. You and Mother found each other again, and we discovered each other. If not at the coffee shop, you'd have probably put the pieces together at the audition, wouldn't you?"

"Most likely. But about your mother. We both know that's only half-true. My half. I've found her again, thanks to you. But it appears she met me for the first-time last night."

"Not appears. Things being what they are, she really *did* meet you for the first time. It's just we know differently. And I should tell you Marla Jo went out of her way to assure me you knew nothing of what happened after Mother left Colorado. From the journal, and what Marla Jo told me, I know it was Mother's decision, not yours, that you never saw each other again. Or had any contact. Or knew anything about me."

He nodded, before saying, "I must say you're taking this remarkably well. Don't know that I would. If I were you."

"Well, here's the thing. I grew up never knowing the man everyone thinks is my father. Who knows? He might be. But don't worry. I don't need one now. Although I think as father's go, you might make a pretty good one."

"Quite an assessment in less than twenty-four hours."

"I'm a pretty good judge of people. No, actually, I'm really good. But my concern, my only concern, is my mother. That nothing bad happens to her."

"I don't see any way that can happen. Because of you. And me. And Marla Jo."

Tears welled up in Danielle's eyes. She reached for a handkerchief in the small, well-worn leather purse she'd hung on the back of her metal chair.

"Did Miss Marla tell you my mother never had anything to do with any other man after my father died?"

Not knowing what to make of that in the moment, he answered simply, "No, she left that part out."

"It's true. What about you? After Mother, that is. Yesterday you said no significant other. No friend with benefits. Has it always been like that since Mother left you?"

"It's been a long, long time since your mother and I were together. All I'll say is that relationships are one thing …"

"And?"

"Love is another."

"You were in love with my mother? I'm surprised."

"Why?"

"Because her journal says you told her you weren't."

"Danielle, she didn't give me a chance. A chance to tell her. I would have, but she didn't come back." He looked away to the traffic passing by. "I've never stopped loving her. Or maybe as the years went by, loving her memory."

"May I ask just one more question?"

"Of course," he said, looking back at her. "Not knowing what it is, I may not answer."

"That's fair. Mother wrote about your wife. Other than the two of them, have you ever loved anyone else?"

He shook his head.

Danielle asked about something her mother had written. His attitude back then about children. Colin reached to hold her hand.

"All I can say is that was a moment in time so long ago I can't recall what I said. I'll accept blame for any misunderstanding your mother may have taken away with her. What I can tell you, sitting here today, having a child with Paula Chandler would have been the greatest joy in my life. I hope and pray that in time you'll come to believe that."

Danielle appeared lost in thought. Colin waited several moments, then said, "My turn. A question for you. What about us?"

"Us? You mean are we okay?"

"That's exactly what I mean."

"Of course, we are." Her voice filled with reassurance. "We don't know if you're my father. And if you are, everything didn't turn out the way either of us would've wanted." She paused, a smile beginning to crease her lips, pushing her cheeks upward. "One thing, though."

"What's that?"

"Well, if you are, and even though we've just met, I sure do know a lot more about my father than probably any other girl ever would."

"That's quite a statement. Meaning?"

"*Meaning* … things were kinda smokin' hot between the two of you out there among the Juniper trees. What was it Mother wrote? Oh, yes. Sweating between the sheets. Or something like that."

He buried his head in his hands much as he had earlier in the morning when he was with Marla Jo.

"Oh, come on, Colin. Where's your sense of humor? Look on the bright side. There might even be a country music song in all of this. You know. Something with a blouse. Climbing a staircase. Maybe even throw in a constellation."

"Hmm."

"Yes?"

"If I'm going to live forever with what's in that journal, I think it only fair I read it."

"I dunno. Perhaps. Maybe when you're old enough for such grownup things."

"Don't worry," he said, leaning back, stretching his legs out, crossing his arms. "My memories of those days are still pretty vivid without it."

"Vivid, eh? Like what?"

He shook his head.

"Just one example. That's all I ask."

"One?"

She nodded.

"Think *you're* old enough?"

She nodded again, this time more eagerly.

"Okay." *Two can play this game.* "You mentioned a blouse, so your mother must have written about it."

"She did. In quite a bit of detail, I might add. Thought I was reading a trashy romance novel."

"That's descriptive. All right, then. If I am your father, you would know, of course …"

"Know what?"

"No blouse, no Danielle."

"Touché!" She smiled and clapped her hands. "Now, let's explore this a bit, shall we?"

"Let's not."

"Oh, let's. It was in the upstairs guest suite where the magic happened for the first time. Right?"

"You are your mother's daughter, that's for sure. But no."

"Then where? When?"

"The easiest question in the world to answer." He stopped talking when his mind brought forward the time and place, an indelible image he'd returned to thousands of times over the years.

"You know you're torturing me."

"Sorry. Don't mean to. It happened when your mother walked up to where Blue and I were sitting on the porch and said 'I'm lost.'"

"Wow! How romantic. And you know what? I believe you."

"Good. Because it's true."

"And that's exactly how you and I met yesterday. Me being lost. Even Blue sitting with you. That's bizarre!"

"I think it goes far beyond that. How far, and why, I don't yet understand. And may never."

Danielle waited for the traffic noise to subside. "Colin, do you still have Marla Jo's book, the one Mother wrote she left behind?"

"I do."

"What about the blouse?"

"That, too."

"Why? After all these years, why do you still have them?"

"I think you know the answer. I thought it was her way of letting me know she was coming back."

"But she didn't."

The sudden sting of his tears surprised him. "She still might." He dried the edges of his eyes with the paper napkin that accompanied his coffee.

Looking and listening, Danielle began to understand how her mother could have fallen so deeply in love with him so quickly.

"You mentioned Blue. By now, he'll be awake and need to go outside. Happy for you to join me. We don't live far."

Danielle begged off. "Thanks, but I probably should get back to the hotel. Please tell him hello for me."

"Will do. He thinks you're the living end."

"Cute. Mother's journal said you were a great listener. You really are."

"I remember your mother said really a lot."

"Still does."

"Not surprising."

She squeezed his hand.

"How does the rest of your day shape up?" he asked.

"Well, I have a date tonight. Nothing special. Just a friend from college. Mother and Miss Marla are out shopping and have dinner plans with friends." She read disappointment in his face. "But can you come by the hotel in the morning?"

"Certainly. Will you be there?"

"I will. I'm staying there for a few days while my house is being painted and some renovations finished. Mother just bought it for me."

They agreed on a time.

"Danielle, may I pay you for our coffee this morning?"

"You may not. Oh, Colin, when you get home ..."

"Yes?"

"Please give Blue a hug for me."

She kissed him on the cheek as she would at each greeting and good-bye, and he watched her walk away. He didn't move until she was out of sight. For the balance of the day and night, she was constantly on his mind. As was her mother.

Eighteen

More missing pieces

The next morning, Colin called the hotel to confirm what he thought he'd remembered. Despite its luxury rating and discerning clientele, it was pet-friendly. Accompanied by Blue, he arrived several minutes early and found Danielle already seated in the elegantly appointed atrium just off the lobby. He dropped the leash as she knelt down in front of her chair to hug the surprise visitor. She stood and kissed Colin on the cheek.

"Change in plans. Mother went to spend a few days with Miss Marla at her home in Kentucky. They left early this morning."

"Bowling Green, right?"

"Yep. About an hour up the interstate."

"Been there a few times," Colin said, taking in his surroundings, gathering his thoughts. "First time ages ago when my wife Mallory graduated from the university."

"I had a friend at Blair named Mallory. She moved back to California after graduation. We called her Mel."

Blue had Danielle's attention. Otherwise, she'd have noticed Colin's visible reaction the first time he heard his wife's nickname spoken by someone other than himself.

"Anyway, I'm happy to have you all to myself. But only for a few minutes. I've gotta leave soon, too."

She quickly answered when he didn't ask. She'd gotten the job she'd auditioned for.

"They called yesterday afternoon. Wanted to tell you when we were together this morning. Did you know?"

"I didn't. But was certain it would happen. Danielle, I've been meaning to ask. Before your years at Blair, were you performing anywhere?"

"Began at church choir when I was a little girl and kept at it. Sang in a local rock band when I was in high school. Other than my mother, not a lot of interest in country music where we lived."

Colin knew from her profile sheet at the recording studio, and from talking with Marla Jo, that "where we lived" was New York City.

"You have a remarkable voice."

"Thank you, for that. Means a lot, coming from you. Anyway, I have to be in Memphis this afternoon."

"Memphis?"

"Yeah. There's an outdoor concert stage for us to rehearse the show. We'll be leaving in less than a week."

"That all sounds wonderful. How long's the tour?"

"They tell me seven weeks. Don't think there'll be an opportunity to come home until it's over."

She answered his look of disappointment. "How sweet. Missin' me already."

"There is that, of course. And …"

"And what …?"

"I would've enjoyed seeing your mother again."

"Not a problem. Don't need me around. She'll be here while I'm gone."

"I thought she lives in New York."

"She does. But with her condition, she's agreed she needs to move near one of us. That's why Miss Marla kidnapped her. She's gonna try to persuade her to move to Bowling Green, but Mother thinks it's a distant second to Nashville. She'll come back to see me off, and stay in my house while I'm gone." Danielle saw Colin's face brighten. "Who knows? The two of you got a lot done in seven days. Imagine what can happen in seven weeks!"

"Okay, enough of that. But I am looking forward to spending time with her. If it's something she'd be open to, that is."

"Oh, I don't think there's any doubt about that. Here, I'll write down her number for you." She reached for a note pad and pen, each bearing the hotel's name, in a leather box on the small table separating their plush chairs.

"Is there any hope for recovery of some of her memory?"

"You won't be surprised Mother wrote in her journal she teased you about your favorite word. So, *no*, there isn't." She smiled as she handed him the paper. He folded it and tucked it into the front pocket of his dress blue jeans. "But if there's a silver lining, in a way, she's free. At least that's what she tells me."

"Free? I don't understand. In what way?"

Before he could ask more, Danielle went on without answering.

"I just wish it all happened differently for her a long time ago. But here's the thing. You and Mother are together again."

"Not yet, but hopefully." Talking with both Marla Jo and Danielle left Colin wondering what was around the next corner. "While you're gone, is there anyone I could talk with about her memory?"

"Oh, I don't know. I guess maybe Dr. McGinley in Bowling Green. He knows all about it."

"Any chance I could meet with him?"

"Don't know how that'd work. Probably best if you call him. Save you a trip. But why?"

"What I want, more than anything else in the world, is for her to recall some of my memories of our time together. Of me."

Danielle's eyes flashed and her expression soured, leading to an exchange of uncomfortable glances. They'd known each other less than forty-eight hours, yet he knew instantly he'd been the cause of the sudden chill but didn't know why.

"Your favorite word is no. Mine is really. Really? Really!"

"I don't know what you mean," he answered, cautiously. "But I can tell I've upset you."

"You have. Colin, you only had a week with her. Mother has lost all of my childhood. My teenage years. Almost everything up until I went off to college. And a lot of that's going away. You and I can't change any of this, so you need to get over it. And get over it now! I haven't completely, but at least I'm trying."

"But …"

"I'm not finished. You need to accept things, and her, for who and what they are. Obsessing about her memory of you will take you nowhere you wanna be. Or …"

He waited, but this time she didn't finish.

"Or what?" he gently asked.

"Mother is a different woman. Nobody's fault. Not yours. Not mine. And certainly not hers. Who knows? If you behave yourself, and play your cards right, the two of you might fall in love all over again.

And that would be a good thing for everyone, especially if it turns out you *are* my father."

Colin reached down to pat Blue on the head, and thought for a moment before clearing his throat. "You're right." He straightened up. "Right about all that you said. I'm sorry. Truly sorry."

Seconds passed in silence before Danielle said, "Done and done. Storm's passed. Movin' on."

Relieved, Colin asked, "May I still speak with Dr. McGinley? I don't wanna say or do anything stupid. Again."

"Tell ya what. I'll call and let him know you'll be calling. And why." She looked at her watch. "Oops. I need to get going. Still have to pack. Walk a girl to the door?"

"Don't see any girls around, but it would be my pleasure to walk a lady to the door."

They passed separately through the large revolving door. Blue chose to be at Danielle's side. Out on the street, she knelt down to hug him, then stood and kissed Colin on the cheek. She reached into her purse and retrieved a handkerchief to wipe off traces of lipstick.

"Travel safely," he said, as she stepped back. "Call me while you're gone?"

"You bet," she answered. "Got your number."

"Yes, you have. More than you know."

The next day, Colin had barely begun a phone introduction when Dr. McGinley stopped him.

"Pardon the interruption, Mr. Collins. I'll tell you what I told Danielle yesterday. I'm not her mother's doctor. Never was. And if I were, I wouldn't talk to anyone without Paula present. You understand why, of course."

"I do." Colin paused to think of another way forward. "I understand you can't talk about her. But may I ask a question or two about the kind of memory loss she has?"

"I'll answer if I can."

"Do people with this condition ever regain any of their lost memory?"

"I no longer practice medicine, but because of Paula, I've done a decent amount of reading lately. Couldn't find anything to make us hopeful. If regaining some of her memory was going to happen, it probably would have by now. Paula and Danielle know this. The doctors in Nashville told them."

****

On visits home during her second year of college, Danielle became aware of her mother's memory lapses. She called Marla Jo, who said she'd also noticed it during Paula's most recent Bowling Green visit and persuaded her friend to talk with Dr. Michael McGinley, a retired physician much beloved in town. When the three of them sat down together and talked openly, fear set in that it foretold early-onset of Alzheimer's disease. Known to almost everyone as simply Doc, McGinley arranged an appointment with renowned dementia specialists in Nashville.

A few weeks later, Danielle joined her mother and Marla Jo in a sparsely furnished clinic conference room, the kind where the plants in the corners are always green, never change size or shape, or need watering or pruning. They learned that if Paula was willing, a procedure with an off-putting name might reveal protein plaque, a potentially tell-tale indication of Alzheimer's. Saying she was always up for new experiences, and relishing spinal tap bragging rights to her friends, Paula consented. The test results were negative. But an MRI scan revealed the blood supply to her brain had been interrupted, confirming at least one silent stroke, maybe more. The doctor patiently answered their questions until he was called away for an emergency. Before he left, he told them there would be no way to know the number of strokes

Paula might have suffered, or predict future occurrences. There was no known treatment. And no cure.

Wanting more answers, the three women drove to Bowling Green later that day and gathered in Doc's living room at his residence on the town square a few minutes' walk from Marlo Jo and Ben's home. When everyone was comfortably seated, Danielle said, "Please tell us again why they call it a silent stroke."

Although in his early seventies, Doc McGinley had become accustomed over the years to people thinking him at least a decade younger. When he spoke, his manner, turn of phrase, and patrician Southern accent drew people to him like a magnet.

Doc straightened the corner of his hand-tied bow tie. "Because the damage occurs where the brain is silent."

"I've never been bothered being silent before."

"Mother, please. This is serious."

Paula's wrinkling of her nose gave way to a smile.

"Silent brain damage. Doc, what does that mean?" Marla Jo asked.

"It means it happens in a part of the brain that doesn't control any vital functions. Like walking or talking. Or vision."

"But what about mother's memory?"

"Silent strokes can have significant and lasting impact. Unfortunately, that's what the Nashville doctors are saying."

"Why didn't we know when this was happening to her?"

"Sweetie, you're talking about me as if I'm not still here."

"I'm sorry, Mother. My bad."

Paula reached to hold her daughter's hand. "Doc, I'd like to know that, too."

"Because there're no symptoms. Happens, as it did with you, without the person knowing. A diagnosis occurs only when after-effects become apparent." He paused. "Like memory loss."

"Is it a rare thing?"

"No, Paula, it isn't." Doc reached to hold her other hand. "In fact, it happens far more often than the kind that impairs speech or movement. Or causes facial paralysis."

"Will my mother get any of her memory back?"

"Family members always ask. The truthful answer is no one knows. Having said that, the brain does have a remarkable ability to heal itself. At times."

"How rare is it?" Marla Jo asked. "Getting memory back."

"From what I've read, extremely rare. Best not to hold out for any hope, and be delighted if any does happen."

"Anything we can do, Doc?" Danielle asked. "Besides pray, that is."

"Prayer never hurts. And in my experience, often heals. Any more questions?"

"Just one," Paula said. Everyone looked at her. "Where are we having lunch?"

****

"Dr. McGinley, just one other question."

"Mr. Collins, I'll answer if I can. Or should."

"Paula's memory about her daughter and her friend Marla Jo doesn't seem impaired. Yet she has no memory of her husband. Or of me."

"That's not altogether true. About Danielle and Marla Jo, that is." Colin then recalled what Danielle had told him when he'd upset her the day before. "Mr. Collins, how long did say you and Paula knew each other?"

"Seven days."

"And how long were you apart?"

"Twenty years. More, actually."

"There's your answer. Fleeting times, like yours, and traumatic events, like her husband's death, can be more easily purged by silent strokes. Danielle and Marla Jo have been a part of the very fabric of Paula's life. For now, she knows who they are and how they fit into her world. But that, too, will change."

"Is everyone so certain there's no hope? No cure? What about seeing more specialists?"

"Maybe if you can find one with a magic potion or elixir of some kind. And I think we better leave it at that."

"Thank you, Dr. McGinley."

"You're most welcome. And should we meet, which from Danielle I gather is highly likely, my friends call me Doc. I'd be honored if you would."

"Yes, sir. I will. I had a good friend once named Doc. But his patients were animals."

"Good day to you, son."

Colin hadn't heard that word since he was ten years old. As Marla Jo had said only a few days earlier, time really does fly.

"And to you. Good-bye, Doc."

Nineteen

Together, again.

Marla Jo drove Paula back to Nashville from Bowling Green in time for her to freshen up at Danielle's house before accompanying her daughter to the tour bus where her journey to follow her musical dreams was about to begin. Colin was also there, standing curbside, and they both waved as the bus pulled away. When it disappeared around a downtown corner, Paula turned to Colin.

"Sorry we rushed off last weekend without saying good-bye. Marla Jo was on a mission and wasn't going to be denied. Forgive me?"

"Nothing to forgive. I'll admit I was disappointed, but here we are. Together again. Anyway, it's only been a few days."

"Yep, here we are," she said, as they began walking toward the parking lot across the street. "Got plans for this evening?"

"I don't."

"Me neither. I'm staying at Danielle's house while she's gone. The pantry's bare. Refrigerator, too. Guess that's how she keeps that figure of hers. Any ideas?"

"Well …"

"My daughter tells me you're some kinda magician in tha kitchen." They reached the other side of the street. "Don't know how she knows, but that's what she says."

Colin assumed it came from Danielle reading her mother's journal.

"I can hold my own."

"Care to show me? It'll be supper time soon. Or at least mine. The medicine I take kicks my butt into bed pretty early."

Less than ten minutes later, Colin pulled his car into his driveway with Paula in Danielle's car behind him.

"Nice porch," Paula said, as they walked up the stone walkway. "All I've got back home is a stoop in front of my brownstone." As they approached the steps, she continued, "I think every Southern home should have one, don't you? They're so welcoming. And such a delightful place to sit a spell with friends or family. If your family are also your friends."

They climbed the six steps, and as they stood side by side at the front door, Paula in heels was taller but Colin gave it no notice as he inserted a key and stepped back.

"How nice of you to arrange a welcoming committee," Paula said, as she entered and knelt down. "My daughter told me she met you. Said if it weren't for her job, she'd run right out and get one just like you." She looked back at Colin. "What's his name?"

"Blue."

"May I pet him?"

"He'd be terribly disappointed if you didn't." Colin closed the door. "In fact, he won't leave you alone until you do."

After Paula and Blue became properly acquainted, she looked around. "I forget things. Told you that when we met. But this place feels awfully familiar. Have I been here before?"

As Colin's financial picture kept improving over time, he'd moved from apartment renting to purchasing an urban condo. Then he found a rare tear-down house in a highly desirable downtown Nashville neighborhood, and in its place built a smaller exact replica of his Three Oaks home, the one Paula and Danielle stayed in for one night only a few months earlier.

"No, you haven't. A lot of homes may look and feel similar the first time you're in them." Standing an arm's length apart, Colin remembered back to the winter evening of Paula's surprise return to his Three Oaks residence. "We hope your visit tonight won't be your last, so we'll try to be on our best behavior."

"I doubt that'll be a problem. I know you're not married, or I wouldn't have invited myself to dinner. The 'we' must mean you and the hound dog here."

"True."

"Just makin' sure. May I please have the grand tour? Don't be all worried about not havin' a woman's touch. You know. Everything all neat and tidy."

"Beautiful kitchen," Paula said, sitting on a stool she selected at end of the center island, watching Colin prepare grilled halibut and steamed vegetables. "And the wine is lovely. What is it?"

"Meomi. My favorite. It's a coastal California chardonnay."

"My. My. My. Quite a seduction thing you got goin' on here, Mr. Collins."

Startled, all Colin could stammer in reply was, "What?"

"Just kiddin' around. Something you'll learn about me. I'm a bit of a flirt. Harmless, though. Doubt I've ever had an affair. At least one to remember. Say, isn't that the name of a movie?"

"I believe it is. *An Affair to Remember.*"

"I like old movies. Don't remember who was in that one. Do you?"

"I think it was Cary Grant and Deborah Kerr."

"We'll say you're right. You ever have affairs?"

"I was married once. Had a few after she died."

"Any of 'em serious?"

"Well, I …"

"You know, like falling in love serious."

"Oh. In that case, just one."

"What happened?"

"Didn't work out."

"Why not? Oh, I'm sorry. Rather forward of me, wasn't it?"

"I don't mind. Guess at the time I wasn't what she wanted. Maybe if we'd had more time …"

"Dumb broad. You're quite the catch, if you don't mind me sayin'." She sipped her wine. "I was married once. Don't remember anything about it, though."

Struggling to come to grips with her memory loss, without thinking, Colin asked, "Then how do you know you were once married?"

"Well, Marla Jo keeps reminding me. Reminds me of a lot of things. Thinks of it as her job, and I'm glad she does. Anyway, probably so I won't think I was a naughty girl way back when. They don't sell daughters at the farmers market, you know. Means I've had sex ages ago. With a husband I don't remember."

At a loss to keep the conversation going, Colin asked to be excused to set the dining room table. Paula trailed behind.

"Any chance we could eat in your kitchen? Sit underneath those fancy copper pots? The stool is pretty comfy, and my butt's got some nice padding."

Colin followed Paula back into the kitchen, admiring her gravity-defying backside as she gracefully perched herself back on the comfy stool.

"Got any candles?"

Plates in front of them and candles burning, she asked if he was a Christian.

"I am. Better now than in times past."

"Then I'll let you say grace."

His brief prayer over, one in which he thanked God for putting people in each other's path, she asked, "Living near the buckle of the Bible belt, might you be Baptist?"

"No. Presbyterian."

"Isn't that what they call people who only eat fish. Like tonight." She answered his stunned look with, "I'm only messin' with you Colin. That would make you a pescatarian."

"Believe it or not, Paula," he said, smiling, "I'm both."

"Well, there you go." She began to cut her halibut. "Speaking of names, when that daughter of mine started college, Marla Jo told me she decided to start going by her middle name. And Marla Jo tells me you changed to your middle name when you moved here years ago."

"That's right."

"How 'bout that for coincidence? One changing to become Danielle, the other changing not to be Daniel anymore."

"Quite a coincidence. I realized it when we first met."

Paula told him Marla Jo said growing up Danielle's first name was Elizabeth.

"Did she ever go by Beth?" he asked.

"Not according to Marla Jo. Never Betsy or Lizzie or anything else. Always wanted to be Elizabeth."

"Did Marla Jo say why?"

"She liked having the same name as the Queen of England."

Memories of *annus horriblis* came flickering back into Colin's mind. When he remained quiet, so did Paula. He lifted the bottle to refresh her wine glass.

"May I call you Daniel, or do you prefer Colin?"

"If it's you, I'll happily answer to either."

"Mr. Collins, are you flirting with me?"

"Yes, ma'am, I guess I am."

She raised her replenished glass.

"I forget things, but you shouldn't."

"What do you mean?" he asked, concern in his voice.

"Remember our first night together when Marla Jo asked you to drop the ma'am business?"

"Done," he answered, raising his glass and returning her smile.

"Okay, then. And you get to be Daniel. Maybe it'll help me remember to call my daughter Danielle."

Though he anticipated her calling him Daniel, the name she'd told him she preferred over Danny or Dan when they were together in Colorado, after this one time, she never did.

"One thing about all this name stuff."

"What?"

"I'm going to stay Paula."

"And you should. It's a beautiful name." *I can't let this opportunity pass by.* "A moment ago, you mentioned liking old black and white movies. So do I. As a matter of fact, my favorite movie of all time is in black and white. Perhaps you know it. *Random Harvest.*"

"Don't seem to recall it," Paula answered, shaking her head. "Who was in it?"

"The leading lady was Greer Garson. The character she played was also named Paula."

"Another coincidence, huh? Maybe we could watch it together sometime."

"I'll see to it. And soon."

Despite striking out with the movie teaser, hearing Paula say her own name for the first time since they met on his Colorado porch, and despite what he'd promised her daughter just a few days ago, Colin would give all he had in the world to relive with her even a tiny portion of their *week mirabilis.* He had no idea it was only moments away.

Their meal finished, Colin told Paula that while he did have weekly visits from a housekeeping service, he was fully capable of cleaning up all by himself. And he reminded her she was their guest.

"You'd really be quite the catch for some lucky woman," she said, following him into the living room to sit in opposing chairs in front of a stone fireplace, its warmth unneeded for several months. Blue followed behind and sprawled in front of the hearth while Colin waited for Paula to settle into her chair.

"Colin, I know we've just met, but I want us to be completely truthful with each other. Would that be okay?"

Although her words unsettled him, he nodded as he sat.

"While the three of us were in that hotel suite, I overheard Marla Jo and Danielle talking. They thought I'd gone downstairs, but I was still in the bedroom. My cell phone rang, and they stopped talking. I didn't want them to think I was eavesdropping. I'd never do that. So I'll ask you."

He waited as long as he could. "Ask me what?"

"Did we know each other before that dinner?"

Colin licked his lips as he began to measure his words before speaking. Trapped, with no way out apart from telling a lie he didn't want to have to live with, he steadied his voice.

"Yes. Yes, we did."

"Are you the mystery man Danielle and I went looking for in Colorado?" she asked, looking straight ahead at the fireplace.

His pulse quickened. He hadn't expected to be where they are now. "I am."

"Thought so." She leaned forward, turned and asked, "Can we talk about it?"

"Now?"

Sitting back, she nodded.

As Colin had done in a bar with Marla Jo, Paula listened without interrupting. His recounting had been far briefer than Marla Jo's, and when she felt he was finished, Paula reached across for his hand.

"My, oh, my. A lot sure happened in a week."

"Yes, it did."

Colin could sense Paula had more to say, more to ask, but was struggling.

"Anything else?" he asked.

"Just one more teensy, tiny, itsy-bitsy thing I also heard Marla Jo tell Danielle."

"And that would be?" he asked hesitantly, thinking he knew the answer.

"That you might be her father."

There it was, he thought. *All the cards on the table.*

"Paula, from what Marla Jo and Danielle tell me," he said, gently squeezing her hand, "it is possible."

"Don't you want to know?"

"Sure, I do. I've had so little time with her, I don't know how she feels about it. And I certainly didn't anticipate you'd become aware so soon after Danielle and I stumbled into each other."

"Wanna know what I think?"

"Of course."

"Stumbling didn't have anything to do with it. I see God's hand in all this. Don't you?"

"I hadn't thought of it that way. But yes, I guess I do. Certainly about you and me finding each other again."

"Colin, I need something in the worst way." He saw the wetness in her eyes as she stood. "And I need it this very moment."

"Anything. Anything at all. Just tell me."

"I need a hug."

If asked to find the words to describe how it felt to have her in his arms again, he couldn't. At least not at that moment. Perhaps later, in the words of a song. A love song.

"Look what I've done," she said, stepping back. "Gone and gotten your shirt all wet. And smudged with makeup. I'm so embarrassed."

"Don't be."

The neatly pressed monogramed handkerchief from his hip pocket magically found its way into her hand.

"Tell me truthfully." She touched the linen to first one cheek and then the other. "Do I still look pretty much the same as when you knew me before?"

"It took less than a second for me to know it was you. And I recognized you in Danielle the moment I saw her."

He touched her elbow to gently guide her back to her chair before returning to his.

"Except older. Can't help that. I want you to know I'm perfectly healthy in every way but the one. And I think I've done a pretty good job accepting it. But what really upsets me is when people who should know better now think I've somehow become stupid because of it."

He had no idea how to respond.

"I'm sorry, Colin. That just slipped out. Forgive me."

Before he could say the words forming in his mind about an apology being unnecessary, she went a different direction.

"But promise me one thing. About Danielle."

"What's that?"

"She likes to have her own way. You'll learn that about her if you haven't already."

"I have. It took all of about five minutes when we first met."

"If it turns out you and I created her, don't let her call you Father. Mother works for her and me. The two of you figure something else out. Something that doesn't get people thinkin' you've got a stick up your butt. Or worse yet, a ... "

"What could be worse than ..."

"Yankee. I can say that 'cause even though I don't remember much about it, I've been livin' up North for a long time myself."

"But Paula ..."

"What?"

"Full confession. Like you, I was a Northerner for a good long while."

"Where?"

"Washington, D.C. Although technically I guess it's a Southern city."

"Not to me, it isn't. And that was before Colorado?"

"Before Colorado."

"That also makes it BP."

"BP?"

"Before Paula. The first time."

I was wrong, he thought. *This is no masquerade. There are do-overs in life.*

Colin was giving himself over to her again, falling in love, minute by minute, with the same woman twice, a stranger to her both times, decades apart.

He stood to stretch his legs, and she lifted her hand for him to assist her.

"You know," she said, "it's been fun being with you. Thank you for a wonderful evening."

"No, it's you I have to thank. I've enjoyed our time together immensely."

"Oh, my goodness! That makes you sound like a lawyer. Oh, that's right. You did fess up to being one when Marla Jo was givin' you the third degree at the restaurant."

"Third degree? I recall it differently."

"Really?"

"I recall a delightful evening in the company of three charming, sophisticated Southern women. Just as your daughter promised."

"She did? That's good. That's really good. Both of you."

Paula watched from the front porch as Blue took his time finding just the right spot and Colin performed clean-up duty. As the three of them walked back inside, she said, "I'm awfully tired, and even though it's not that far, I'd rather not make the drive to Danielle's house at night. Any chance I could sleep on your couch? No one needs to know, and I can leave early in the morning."

I could drive her, but this is too surreal.

Well, I ..."

Paula was dressed in a form-fitting pleated skirt and a tailored white shirt made of Sea Island cotton. She extended her arm. "I can use this as a nightgown. It's really long. Covers everything nicely."

"I have a better idea."

"I'll bet you do!" She smiled and touched her elbow to his.

"I didn't mean it the way it came out. I was simply going to suggest you avail yourself of the guest suite upstairs."

"Sounds like a plan." Remembering something from his narrative, the Three Oaks walk down memory lane, she touched her finger to her chin in a thoughtful pose. "Also sounds very familiar."

He returned her smile. "Want me to wake you, or let you sleep in?"

"Sleep in, if you don't mind. If anyone sees me leaving in the morning, it'll give any Presbyterians in your neighborhood something to talk about on their way to church. Think your dog might show me the way? We've taken a liking to each other. At least, I have."

"I know he has, too. But it'll be up to him."

"Come on, Blue. We might even make a night of it. Make ole Mr. Colin jealous."

Paula kissed Colin on the cheek, the same one favored by her daughter, and began to climb the stairs. Blue bounded up ahead of her.

Colin touched his hand to his cheek and watched them until they turned the corner toward the first door on the right, letting his thoughts wander to what the next day might bring. And the day after that. And the one after that.

Invigorated by his time with Paula, Colin felt not the first twinge of sleep beckoning. He turned on the television in his study and surfed aimlessly across the channels until he came upon a black-and-white image at the beginning of an early 1960s show. He settled back in his chair and heard the familiar voice of Rod Serling say, "*There is nothing in the dark that isn't there when the lights are on.*"

How appropriate, he thought, to end his day watching "The Twilight Zone."

Twenty

Living in the moment

Paula woke to the sun streaming through the bedroom window and noticed she wasn't alone. She propped herself up on an elbow, reached over with her other arm and stroked the dog's head facing her. He opened his eyes.

"I never asked, but I bet I know how you got your name."

She pulled back the covers on her side of the bed, swung her legs over, stood, and walked around to the other side.

"Do you need help?"

Unassisted, Blue jumped down and made straight for the door. She followed him out and watched him noisily tumble down the stairs. It was then she smelled the inviting breakfast aromas rising from the kitchen. She walked into the en suite bathroom, saw her reflection in the mirror, and exclaimed, "Heavens! I look a fright!"

Paula returned to the bedroom and realized her purse, with hairbrush and makeup, had been left downstairs the night before.

"Perfect," she said aloud. "Just perfect. Well, now he gets to see the real me."

With the wrinkled cotton shirt that served as a makeshift nightgown tucked into her skirt, she gathered enough courage to face her host. As she entered the kitchen, Colin's cheerful "good morning" was followed by, "I trust you slept well" before he motioned toward the stool. Her stool.

"I did. Didn't wake up once."

When she was seated, he asked how she took her coffee.

"Just bit of cream. Thanks."

"And your eggs?"

"After that wonderful meal last night, I'm certain any way you choose will be delicious. And Colin …"

"Yes?"

"I'm so embarrassed how I look. Wouldn't want anyone to see me this way. Especially you."

"Would you believe me if I said I think you look more beautiful now than any woman who goes to wherever it is they go and pay princely sums to be worked over for hours?"

Scarlett coloring began lightly shading her neck, working its way up as she answered softly while shaking her head. "No."

"Well, it's true."

"We'll agree to disagree." She reached to accept a coffee cup and held it in both hands. She lightly blew across the top and took a sip. "While you're doing things with eggs, may I excuse myself to find my purse and do what I can to make myself presentable?"

When she returned, Colin informed her three things had occurred during her absence. She raised her eyebrows and tilted her head slightly.

"First, as you can see, breakfast is served." She sat down on the stool to admire eggs artistically arranged with tomatoes, avocado and mixed fruit on the plate before her. "Second, I've freshened your coffee. And third, I've formulated a plan for us for today and hope you agree."

"If your plan is as good as your eggs and the coffee, count me in."

"Great! I was thinking we finish our breakfast, then you go to Danielle's house. Sundays Blue and I often go for a walk in Centennial Park. We come pick you up, say, about three or so. Have an early dinner at an outdoor café near Vanderbilt that allows dogs. After that, we'll call it a day." When Paula hesitated, he added, "Blue will be awfully disappointed if you don't say yes. After all, he did choose to spend the night with you, and the two of you had just met."

"How can I possibly say no?"

"We don't think you can."

Colin watched Paula rummage through her purse as she prepared to leave. She looked at the ceiling, then at him.

"I don't know what I've done with the keys to the house."

"No worries. It's Sunday, but tomorrow you can call Danielle to get the locks changed with new keys. Meantime, you and Blue can have another night together." He thought for a moment. "Although I am a bit lacking in ladies clothing for overnight guests. Since there haven't been any."

"If you say so," she said, smiling. "And no concern of mine, of course. But, as you said, no worries. Do you know how to get to Green Hills? Marla Jo and I were just there not too long ago."

"I do."

Although he only went there occasionally for the independent bookstore owned by a local resident who was a bestselling author, Colin knew Green Hills to be a Nashville mecca for upscale shopping and occasional celebrity sightings.

"You know the way and I have credit cards. A winning combination. Do you mind driving?"

As they made their way through traffic arriving for and departing from church services, Paula asked Colin if he'd be interested in hearing her view on the difference between shopping and buying.

"There's a difference?"

"There most certainly is. Buying is what men do. Find things quickly. Lay the card or money down." She patted the dash above the glovebox for emphasis. "Leave."

"Sounds familiar. And shopping?"

"Shopping is what ladies do. An experience. Sometimes an adventure. One best savored and not rushed. An opportunity to spend time with friends, and by that I mean other women. Men seldom add and often detract."

"You're telling me this because ..."

"Because you might want to think about dropping me off and coming back later. Hours later. I need to shop for things I'll need for the time Danielle's away."

Not a chance.

"I don't mind. I'll just fade into the background. And promise not to interfere."

"Promises, promises. But I will remind you."

She'd given him fair warning, yet it was Colin's choice to tag along for hours, watching her engage in lively small talk with sales clerks she'd just met as if they were lifelong friends. Her outgoing personality, her charm and sense of humor on full display just as he'd remembered. As her shopping was winding down at the first of many stores, Paula waved him over to the checkout counter.

"All of these things need to be delivered, but I can't remember Danielle's address. I know it's awfully presumptuous to ask, but can I have them sent to yours? I can come pick them up later."

His 'yes' was repeated several times before the afternoon was over, though they did load a few shopping bags she'd carefully selected into his aging Subaru for the trip back to his house.

Remembering her early bedtime, Colin prepared a light meal before they settled into matching rocking chairs on his front porch to enjoy a last glass of wine, Blue at Paula's feet. She wore a beige sweater and slacks combination purchased earlier in the day.

"Colin, it was really nice of you to put me up for another night. And to let the stores send things here."

"Delighted to help. No trouble at all. In fact, we'd like for you to stay on, at least until all your packages arrive. Just to make certain everything is okay. I'll give you a key so you can come and go."

"Are you sure?" she asked, a mischievous look forming. "We hardly know each other. You might come home and find the family silver missing."

"There isn't any. Besides, I know where you live. At least some of the time. How 'bout it?"

"You know, that's really very kind. I accept." She folded her hands in her lap. "Can I ask you something?"

"Of course."

"Do you think I say really too much? My daughter says we both do. That people probably think it's off-putting but won't tell us."

"Often, yes. Off-putting, no. How's that for honesty?"

Paula wasn't listening. She'd asked not seeking an answer, rather as a conversational bridge. "So, Colin, what are your intentions?"

Since she'd just mentioned her daughter, Colin assumed she was talking about him helping her career.

"Toward Danielle?"

"Who's Danielle?"

He couldn't mask the worried look on his face.

"Your daughter. The woman formally known as Elizabeth."

"I know," she said, laughing. "Just having some fun with you. Now, back to your intentions."

"About Danielle?"

"Heck, no. Toward me."

Her laughter had disarmed him, then her bluntness left him speechless. Dryness crept into his mouth, creating hesitation before he was able to say, "This is all so new, I'm still working things out in my mind. But whatever they turn out to be, you can be sure of one thing. They'll be honorable."

"I'm certain of that. And I'm also certain I was very forward in asking. Sorry."

"Nothing to be sorry about. As far as intentions go, for now, how about we honorably intend to be good friends and see where that takes us?"

"That would make me very happy."

"Me, too."

"Good." Paula sipped the last of her wine. "This has been a wonderful evening, Mr. Echo."

She'd stumped him until he remembered what she'd about his name the evening they met.

"Clever. Had to think about that one for a moment."

"I guess sometimes my memory is better than yours." She looked at her watch. "It's getting late, and I need to be turning in." She paused. "Before I do, any chance a gal could get a dance with a fella in this place?"

"No one's ever asked before, but it be would be my pleasure. What kind of music do you like?"

"In this town, I didn't know there was anything but country."

"Country, it is. The stereo's in the living room."

He held the door for her, and Blue wedged in between them. "Do you have a favorite song?"

"It's one by Glen Campbell. Something about being easy. Gentle. Gentle something."

"Gentle on my Mind?"

"That's it! But I don't think it'll be a good one to dance to. What's yours?"

He answered without hesitation.

"Who sang it?"

"Roy Orbison wrote and recorded it. Lots of other people covered it."

"Which is your favorite?"

"Linda Ronstadt."

Colin rifled through his collection of CDs until he found the one he was looking for and handed it to her. Eying the beautiful singer on the cover, Paula smiled. "Small wonder."

Blue Bayou filled the room as they slow danced on polished hardwood floors.

"One more time?" she asked.

Would that everything in life be as easy as how effortlessly I've fallen in love with her again. And I know now what my intentions are.

To never let this music stop.

To never let her go.

Twenty-one

A new beginning

The next morning, Paula found Colin sitting on his porch shortly after sunrise.

"You're up early," she said, closing the front door behind her. "And surprisingly, so am I."

Colin pointed to his sleeping companion. "His routine is our routine."

"May I join you?"

"Certainly. Coffee?"

"Love some."

When Colin returned, she held the cup to savor the inviting aroma.

"Is Blue's routine just his nature calls, going for walks and sleeping?"

"You got three out of four. He eats twice a day. In the morning, I mix his meds in with his food."

"Meds? Meds for what? Is he sick?"

"There can be problems with his breed. Congenital heart disease. And epilepsy is common in males. The meds are preventative. Hopefully. I could tell when my other two were approaching the end. But I'm told that's not always the case, so I don't know that I'll know about Blue."

"I'm sorry to hear that." She reached over to stroke Blue's back. "I'd have never suspected."

"Not to worry." He paused. "Paula, I want you to know how much I enjoyed being with you yesterday. Especially our dance at the end."

"Me, too. Helped me make my decision." She took her first sip. "Oh, this is delicious!"

"Decision?"

"Moving to Nashville. Gonna fly back to New York this week. Pack up what I want to bring with me. Sell or give away the rest. I'm told I won't have any difficulty selling my brownstone."

"Danielle told me you were thinking of here or Bowling Green. What tipped you this way?"

"You."

"Me?" His pulse quickened. "Really?"

"That's my word. And my daughter's. But, yes, really."

"I'm flattered. Really ... sorry, truly, I am. But I'd have thought it was Danielle."

"Nope. I expect she'll be gone a lot now, and I couldn't be happier for her. Has her own life to live. Truth is, you and I've got the makings of a new beginning. And if you're up for it, I wanna give it a chance. Question is -- are *you* up for it?

Colin struggled to control his emotions, hoping his voice sounded calm. "How does all-in, a hundred and ten percent sound to you?"

"Well, it's a start," she said, smiling. "And a good one, at that." She responded to his crestfallen look. "No, seriously, Colin, it's all a gal could hope for. And more. So much more."

"Any thoughts on how we should begin our new beginning?"

"One. Hope you agree."

"Anything."

"Tell me about you. Your life. All of it. Don't leave anything out. We know there'll come a time when I won't remember, but for today, I want to know everything about you."

"Here? Now?"

"Here and now. But with another cup. If it's not too much trouble."

Seated again, each with a fresh cup of coffee, Colin said, "Paula, I don't mean to be unkind, truly I don't. How will I ever be able to know your story after I tell you mine?"

"Don't think I didn't notice you slipped in *truly* instead of *really*. Smooth. Anyway, I can still remember bits and pieces, and I'll tell Marla Jo and Danielle to make me an open book any time you want. So, get to it. The life and times of Daniel Colin Collins and don't leave out any juicy parts. I'm a big girl, and we Christian women can handle hearing about an occasional slip and fall. From grace, that is."

With that assurance, Colin decided to tell her everything, including his depression both after Mallory's death and when Paula didn't return to Three Oaks. He told her about his legal success, how he fell on hard times with his financial collapse and his early struggles gaining a foothold in Nashville. Something stopped him from mentioning her friend Paul Dean and that debt he owed her. He ended recalling her prayer in Colorado when she thanked God for putting people in the paths of others, and how within a few minutes of their front porch meeting she talked about loving new beginnings.

"Colin," she said, reaching to hold his hand, "thank you for sharing. Now when you have time, go corral Marla Jo or my daughter to find out what you want to know about me. Though I don't think you'll find my life has been half as interesting as yours."

Seconds passed in silence as Colin thought of all the ways he could answer. He chose instead to offer a gentle reminder.

"Paula, don't forget to call Danielle. You know, lock and keys."

"Thanks. Got so wrapped up hearing about your life I forgot all about mine."

"Really, Mother, checking up on me so soon! I've only been gone a couple of days. Not even that."

"Hush. Believe it or not, I didn't call about you."

"What then?"

"Me."

"You? What about you?" Panic slipping into her voice. "What's happened? Is it serious?"

"Depends."

"Mother, stop tormenting me. Get to the point. What's going on?"

"Nothing much." Coyness in Paula's voice. "Apart from spending the last couple of nights with Daniel Collins. At his house."

"What!"

"Not what you might be thinking. Completely innocent. I invited myself for dinner the day you left and somehow managed to misplace the key to your house. What else could I do but invite myself to a sleepover until you could get the lock changed with new keys. That's why I called."

"All the hotel rooms in Nashville spoken for?" A tinge of sarcasm.

"Sweetie, let's remember a few things. Important things. I'm your mother. I'm old enough, and still sane enough, to make decisions for myself. And I paid for the house needing a new key. Please. Just make the call. Okay?"

"Yes, Mother. I'm sorry. Wait! You said Daniel! Not Colin. You said Daniel's house!"

"Yes, dear. It may have taken me a bit longer, but I figured out the big secret you and Marla Jo have been keepin' from me. Daniel and I've had some very long and intimate conversations since you've been gone. I know all about what happened in Colorado … with him."

"I don't know what to say."

"Just say you'll make the call, and that you'll go back and concentrate on your work. Mr. Collins and I can manage quite nicely all by ourselves until you get back. Will you do that? For all of us?"

"I will. And Mother."

"Yes?"

"I'm happy. For all of us."

Danielle called back thirty minutes later and Paula left to see about new locks and keys. Moments after her departure, Colin was on the phone with Marla Jo, explaining how he'd laid bare his life to Paula, who in turn had encouraged him to reach out to her or Danielle for her life story she was unable to tell.

"I'll do my best, with what I know. And …"

"And that would be a lot, of course."

"It would. And I'm sure Danielle would be happy to fill in anything I leave out or didn't know about."

After moving to New York, Paula divided her time between her career and the demands of single motherhood, demands she readily embraced. For a while, she freelanced for the Nashville publications, writing as Arlette Chandler, then quit to become a full-time editor for a Manhattan lifestyle magazine, using her new legal name. Years later, she became a syndicated columnist and then an author of several modestly successful non-fiction books in the Christian genre targeted at women. The guilt Paula carried with her over Winston's death enabled a heightened sense of compassion for others that found its way into her writing. All that, together with speaking engagements, gave her lifetime financial security while delivering the dream she first had while living in the Ole Miss sorority house.

Years of counseling and medication cleared away Paula's depression fog after Winston's death, but what Marla Jo had no way of knowing was that Paula prayed fervently that those seven days in Colorado would somehow be purged from her memory. Yet that would never be possible because she couldn't stop returning to the cold ashes of an old fire of passion and pain in a journal she kept hidden away.

Marla Jo told Colin that long past any reasonable mourning period, Paula continued to live her life as a celibate single mother, active in her church and civic activities but displaying no outward interest in romance. Marla Jo didn't know, because Paula never shared with anyone, that she'd convinced herself that remaining unmarried and denying herself that happiness was partial penance for her sins of infidelity, lies and deception, perhaps an out-of-wedlock daughter, and more than likely her husband's death. When asked, as she often was, she'd shut down romantic overtures. She would tell well-meaning match-making friends, "I'm not looking for a man to complete me. But if it happens, it happens." This denial became her way of life, and she convinced herself over time it was a life without regrets. But in truth, she hadn't forgiven herself and was forever running away, internalizing stress with no avenue of release. Until, perhaps, the silent strokes.

Paula's literary and speaking success, and her relationship with Marla Jo, led to a visiting professorship at Western Kentucky University, Mallory's alma mater, bringing Paula to Bowling Green twice each year. Thoughts of reconnecting with Daniel inevitably arose from time to time, but even if he would accept her and Elizabeth into his life, and she doubted he would, the uncertainty of both Winston's death and the identity of her daughter's father shut those thoughts down. That Southern novel of her life's memories going back to Oxford had taken on gothic proportions as she lived her life in Gotham City.

Colin continued to listen without interrupting as Marla Jo went on to say that Danielle had no memory of Reverend Chandler, but that she often said she regarded her childhood as idyllic, blessed with the parenting of a devoted single mother and her mother's best friend.

"We grew as close as any two sisters could ever be, and her daughter has matured into a younger mirror image of a woman whose beauty has defied her age. But trust me, Colin, when I say that Paula's inner beauty exceeds what the outside word sees. She is truly the kindest, sweetest, God-loving woman alive, and I'm honored to have her as my best friend."

Holding his phone, Colin was overcome by emotion listening to Marla Jo, and in a subdued voice said, "I'm so glad Paula has had you in her life for so many years, and I hope and pray for so many more years to come."

"Thank you, Colin."

Marla Jo went on to say that Paula's inner beauty had found its way into her daughter. Unlike her own mother, Paula encouraged Danielle's pursuit of things like homecoming queen and beauty contests, but Danielle never had the slightest interest. She chose to concentrate on music.

In New York, Paula took art classes for several years and became an accomplished sketch artist. Her works were occasionally shown anonymously in small local galleries to modest acclaim with only her daughter knowing the artist's true identity. Marla Jo had been wrong when talking with Colin. This was a second big thing Paula had kept from her. Mother and daughter with an abundance of talent – writing, art, music – had a fulfilling life together in the absence of a husband and father.

Before their call ended, Marlo Jo told Colin she would from time to time remind Paula that she was surprised when her daughter told her while filling out college applications that she wanted to change to her middle name. No reason given, only something she'd been thinking about and it seemed like a good time. Paula was speechless, but Danielle didn't think anything of it. And with all the outstanding music curriculums at colleges and universities in New York City and the Northeast, Paula was surprised when her daughter, Elizabeth at the time, decided on Nashville.

Colin thanked Marla Jo, hung up the phone, and thought about the last thing she said, remembering that Paula had told him she saw God's hand in his coffee shop encounter with Danielle that brought all of them to where they are at this moment in time. Not stumbling, or coincidence, or fate, but God's hand. And he remembered Mallory's encouragement to let prayer water his garden of life and be surprised at what would grow.

Colin offered to accompany Paula on her return trip to New York to begin closing out her life there. She told him she appreciated his thoughtful gesture and hoped he understood her choice of Marla Jo. Paula's lack of memories meant an absence of attachment to most of her possessions, and she wanted Marla Jo to help her make the decisions. The process took longer than anticipated, though Paula made a point of talking with Colin by phone every day. A week and a half later, Marla Jo's husband Ben flew to New York for a long theater weekend with his wife, and Colin greeted Paula's returning flight at the Nashville airport.

"Done and done," Paula said, as they drove the short distance to Danielle's downtown Hillsboro neighborhood. "Sold or consigned all my furniture. Consigned or gave away most of my clothes and household things. Shipped the rest here. Not a lot, though. Travellin' light into the future."

"Does it feel good? I mean, are you happy with all the changes?" Colin asked.

"You know, I am. I really am. I feel so … how shall I say it? So unburdened."

"Hope I'll never be a burden."

She reached over and squeezed his hand. "Not a chance." She held on to his hand. "And I hope, as time goes by, I'm never a burden to you." *Something I pray about every night.*

"Not within the realm of possibility."

"How lawyerly."

"Was once. Remember?"

"I do. Speaking of professions, I need to get back to mine."

"You do?

"Yep. I've got some deadlines. Still writing for periodicals. Say, could that be something we do together? You know. Writing. We could muse each other."

"Muse is a noun," Colin offered, but too quickly.

"Muse may only be a noun for songwriters or people from Colorado, but for the rest of us professional wordsmiths, it's also a verb. Look it up if you don't believe me."

"I believe you. Sorry. Anyway, I think it's worth trying. Musing together."

"Clever. I like how your mind works."

"Paula, do you need anything besides your computer?"

"Just my imagination. Which still works. And the internet."

"How about environment?" he asked, as he pulled into Danielle's driveway. "Anything special to get your creative juices flowing?"

"No. Not really. One thing remains to be seen," she said, as she opened the car door.

"What's that?" he asked, as he looked at her across the top of the car.

"How much a distraction your handsomeness creates."

Sometimes the lyricist and the columnist wrote in the same room in Colin's house, other times separately when Paula stayed at her daughter's house, both sharing a commitment to write each and every day. Although their writing was entirely different, they had one thing in common. They were inspiring each other, and the inspiration found its way into their words.

At the conclusion of their first full day at Colin's house, Paula said, "Let's enjoy an early dinner out. You pick one of those wonderful restaurants you know about and it'll be my treat. No argument. About who's paying, that is."

Neither of them felt like ordering dessert. As they were finishing their decaffeinated espressos, Colin asked, "Are there any extra copies of your books at Danielle's house? I'd love to read them."

"There are."

"May I buy them from you?"

"You may not."

He furrowed his brow.

"I'll give 'em to you."

"Will you autograph them?"

"You think I'm famous enough for you to sell them on one of those web sites to get enough money to pay for tonight's dinner?"

"It's a thought," he answered, going with the flow. "One that hadn't occurred to me until you suggested it. But I confess to being confused."

"Confused? About what?"

"On the way here, you reminded me you were paying for dinner and to not even think about creating a scene. Did you change your mind?"

"No."

"What then?"

She'd set him up, and it was time for the payoff.

"Something you'll learn about me. I don't change my mind. I make new decisions."

A month into Danielle's seven-week tour, Paula called Colin on a Sunday afternoon, inviting him to dinner.

"My cooking isn't on par with yours, but far as I know, no one's died."

"Love to. May I bring anything?"

"You may. In addition to your handsome self, wine."

As he stepped out of his car, Colin saw Paula walk around from the side of the house, a watering can in one hand.

"Welcome," she said, waving. As he approached, she added, "Been tending to the flowers."

The house Paula purchased for Danielle had been one her daughter selected, a small, two-bedroom with a living room, dining room, kitchen and breakfast nook, carefully restored to its original condition when it was new in the 1950s. Danielle had chosen it for its charm and location in a highly desirable, walkable urban Nashville neighborhood.

When they finished their meal, Paula asked, "Up for a walk? It's a beautiful night out."

"Absolutely."

She reached for his hand and off they went, walking past similar homes on small, manicured lawns.

"A real sense of community Danielle says is hard to find anywhere else in town. She loves it here, and I do, too. But the house isn't big enough for the both of us. I need to find something for myself."

Several minutes later, they reached a small park and Paula motioned to a bench. They sat quietly.

"Do you often think of your first wife? I believe her name was Mallory?"

"Not often, but sometimes. She's been gone a long time. Thought about her today, though, when I saw you with the watering can." Colin shared Mallory's prayer and garden analogy. "That stayed with me long after she was gone. Got me through some rough patches."

"That kind of symbolism. Has it been important in your life?"

"I'd have to say yes."

"Why?" she asked.

"Makes things memorable, I guess. To stay with me."

Thirty seconds of conversation that gave Paula an idea.

Standing in Danielle's living room, Colin said, "Paula, this has been a perfectly delightful evening."

"It has been, hasn't it?"

"May I be presumptuous?"

"Presume away."

The kind of banter he remembered from Three Oaks.

"May I come back and prepare breakfast in the morning? At an hour of your choosing, of course, and remembering Danielle's shopping habits, I can bring everything I need."

"Why, what a lovely idea. You know I go to bed early, as in right about now, so will around seven be okay with you? Or is that too early?"

"Perfect."

"Colin, before you go, will you do something for me."

"Anything."

"Take me in your arms and kiss me. Think you can do that?"

"If I can overcome the weakness in my knees."

Colin gently kissed her, then held her in his arms, her head resting against his chest. Several seconds passed before he relaxed. They held hands and gazed into each other's eyes before he pulled her toward him again. They kissed passionately, holding tighter. She eased out of his embrace and stepped back.

"Colin, I can't remember the last time I felt this way. No way of knowing. Only that it's been a long, long time. Too long."

"Paula."

She looked at him, waiting.

"I love you."

Moments passed.

"And I you, Colin. And I you. Good-night."

His eyes were moist as he pulled the front door open to leave.

"Colin."

He turned around.

"Yes?"

"Any reason to leave and come back in the morning? I've slept over at your house many times, and I'd like for us to be together tonight. There's a second bedroom here. I'll show you." When he hesitated, she asked, "Would it make you uncomfortable?"

"No, it's not that. Just thinking about Blue."

"Will he be anxious if you're not there overnight?"

"Haven't left him alone like this before. I guess he might be curious for a little while, then sleep through the night."

"Oh, I just thought of something. What about his medicine?"

"Morning will be fine."

"Well, there you go." She looped her arm into his, tugging gently. "And here we go."

With Paula's "I love you" slow dancing in his mind, and the memory of her in his arms a sensation he didn't want to let go, Colin struggled to quiet his mind as he lay in the second bedroom. He finally drifted off to sleep, awakened later with the realization … he wasn't alone.

Twenty-Two

Old acquaintances

"R emember me?" Paula whispered, as she pulled the covers back over them and pressed her naked body against his back, draping her arm over his chest.

Startled, his mind flew back in time to when he heard those very same two words from her as she stood in dim porch light their first night together in Colorado. It took him a moment to find his voice.

"I do."

"Colin, before what I want to happen, happens, and I hope you do, too, will you just hold me? It's been so long. I'm nervous, and I'm counting on you."

Colin didn't acknowledge his own nervousness as he turned to take her in his arms. Her hair fell feather soft against his cheek, and as she reached to brush it away, she kissed him. When he sensed she was receptive, they made love slowly with the familiarity of an eighth day at Three Oaks they never had.

As they lay in each other's arms, Paula said, "Now that's an affair to remember! You Cary Grant. Me. You know, what's her name."

"Deborah Kerr."

"I know. Just testing you."

"Really?"

"I've told you before. That's my word. And Danielle's. Yours seems to be truly. Or pick another."

When he didn't answer, she sat up in bed and looked toward the outline of his shape in the darkness.

"You're not feeling guilty about this are you? I mean, after all, I'm the one who climbed into your bed in the middle of the night, naked as the day I was born."

"No. Not at all."

"What, then?"

"Well, you limited me to one word. Just one word to describe how happy I am we found each other again. That we're together now."

"Tell me, Colin. Was it like this before when we were together? You know. The intimacy."

"It's as if time stood still and we were never apart."

Paula lay back down, reached to hold his hand, and listened to him breathing beside her as several minutes passed.

"Come up with a word yet?"

"I have," he answered. "Already said it."

"Care to say it again?"

"Love."

She ran her fingernails across his shoulder and down his arm.

"Me, too."

They made love again around sunrise before Colin returned home to see what surprise Blue may have in store for him. And to give him his medicine before coming back to prepare breakfast.

Paula occasionally accompanied Colin to a recording session or an audition he thought might interest her. They often dined out early in the evening before spending nights together at his house rather than Danielle's because of Blue. Even though at one time she was a highly regarded feature writer covering the city's food and entertainment scene, every place Colin took Paula was a new adventure for her. Weekends were planned so that Blue could make it a threesome. The reunited lovers had little interest being with anyone except each other, and time passed quickly.

"Mind if I ask a personal question?" she asked.

They were seated at one of Colin's favorite upscale restaurants. White table cloth. Exposed brick walls. Smooth hardwood floors at least a century old. High ceilings with slow-moving fans circulating the air without disturbing the diners. Their entrees had been ordered and they were enjoying their first glass of wine.

"Ask away."

"I've been wondering. Not too long ago, you spent half a day with me while I shopped for clothes. And you're always so complimentary of how I dress when we're together."

"Beautiful woman adorned in beautiful clothes. Why wouldn't I say something?"

"Either I'm blushing or it's gotten terribly warm in here all of a sudden. But thank you."

He raised his wine glass, hers met his, they each took a sip.

"As I was saying …"

"I thought you were wondering," he teased.

"Right. Wondering. I've been *wondering* about your wardrobe. I mean, you're an incredibly handsome man, with a, if I may say, a great body and ..."

"And like a good pair of jeans, I've gotten better over time while we've been apart?"

"Will you please stop interrupting? I've gotten myself into this, and you're making it more difficult. But since you mentioned jeans ..."

"Want me to make it easy?"

"Please."

"You want to know why I dress the way I do."

She nodded.

"Never seen me in slacks."

"Never."

"Always blue or black dress jeans."

"Always."

"Starched button-down long sleeve shirts, usually white, occasionally light blue."

"Keep going. And please don't mistake curiosity for criticism."

"I won't. On occasion, a navy or black blazer, never a suit. Leather slip-ons, no socks, never lace shoes. When I'm told the industry expects it, I'll dust off my one pair of cowboy boots I brought with me from Colorado." He paused. "Is that what you were wondering?"

Paula nodded again.

"Personal preference. Not trying to impress anyone or make a fashion statement. I dress for comfort. My comfort."

"Makes perfect sense. And whatever you're wearing when we're together, I think we pair up quite nicely."

"Indeed, we do. Even more when we're together and not wearing anything at all."

"Why, Mr. Collins, I ..."

The arrival of two waiters with their entrees interrupted her.

"Looks like we both made excellent choices," Colin said, when they were alone again.

"Are you speaking of food, clothes or no clothes?"

"Yes."

"Then I agree. Bon appetite."

An hour later, they were walking hand-in-hand along a brick sidewalk. Paula sensed Colin was both with her and not with her.

"Something troubling you?" she asked.

"I was just thinking about how sorry I am you have your problem. It's so unfair."

Paula stopped in front of a green metal bench anchored in concrete in a grassy area.

"Take a load off." When Colin was seated beside her, Paula said, "Like every other person, I want people to like me. And if it's not too much to ask, a few to love me. I have that in my daughter and Marla Jo. Not long ago, you and I found each other again and agreed to be friends. Hopefully, more."

"Much more."

"Okay, much more. But please, don't ever, ever, feel sorry for me."

"I'm just trying to understand. Truly I am."

"Then here's what I struggle with, as best I can explain. Doctors say I haven't given up IQ ground. Except for things I can't remember, I have the same ability to communicate. But people who've known me in the past, people I can't easily remember, or remember at all, now think I'm aloof. Or stupid. I think I told you that once. By moving to Nashville, I hope to leave that all behind. A new beginning."

Paula explained that with almost no sense of history, she had no choice but to live in the moment and had become comfortable doing so. She said it gave her a wonderfully positive outlook on living each day to its fullest, unburdened by the past and not worried about the future.

"And you're not bitter?"

"No. I was at first, but not anymore. After praying about it, I believe you can be just as happy or just as unhappy as you make up your mind to be. I've made up my mind to be at peace with what's happening. I don't think of it as any sort of tragedy. After all, I can't do anything about it. So why not look at it as a gift from God? It's one I don't understand, but I don't have to in order to be grateful."

"I confess I'm confused."

"Don't worry. So am I. I'm also confused why pizza is made round, then cut in triangles and put in square boxes. I read that somewhere. But I'm not going to get distressed about it. About me, that is. Not the pizza. Think about it this way, Colin. While I don't have pleasant memories to re-live, I also don't have painful ones. It's liberating to be free from regret, free from looking back so I can savor each day and look forward to the next. I don't worry about everything making sense now because of what it will mean in the future. Because for me, it won't."

Colin listened for a false note in what she was saying, and heard none. *That's what Danielle was talking about when she said her mother was free.*

The following Saturday afternoon, the weekend threesome was sitting at an outdoor table at a popular restaurant on a busy sidewalk in Midtown not far from internationally renowned Music Row. Colin had just settled their check and they were preparing to leave when two women approached their table.

"Paula, darling! I thought it was you! Never expected to see you here. It's been ages."

Paula recognized a woman she'd met at a Bowling Green Garden Club event Marla Jo had taken her to a few weeks ago while Danielle was rehearsing in Memphis.

"What a beautiful dog." Turning her attention back to Paula, the garden club member touched the arm of the women standing at her side. "And you, of course, remember my only sister. She's up visiting from Atlanta."

With no name given, Paula's lack of recognition was obvious in her expression and lack of response.

"I can't believe you don't remember me," the woman said, unmistakable indignation dripping in her overplayed Southern accent. "You were a guest in my home when you and Marla Jo came to Atlanta for that concert. And I know we've seen each other in Bowling Green."

Colin felt the pain of embarrassment Paula had to endure and watched in silence as the two women kept at it for a full minute before finally giving up and strutting away. He'd witnessed what Paula had told him she was living with, and what he knew would only grow worse over time. He reached to hold her hand and offered Blue's leash for her other as they headed off in the opposite direction as the two women on their broomsticks. A minute or so passed.

"I'm sorry they did that to you. It was so uncalled for."

"Their problem. Not mine. It's such a beautiful day, isn't it?"

The second time Paula accompanied Colin to a recording session, Paul Dean was there. Colin ushered her to a seat in the control room before pulling his colleague aside in a corner of the studio.

"Paula Chandler! I haven't seen her in I don't know when. How'd you find each other?" When Colin didn't answer, Paul added, "I never told you. She's the one who made it possible for you and me to meet."

"I know. But not from her. She doesn't know that I know. Truth is, she doesn't know anything about you and me. Doesn't remember anything. I don't have time to explain. Just trust me. Let me introduce you now. She won't recognize you. I'll explain everything later."

"You know that makes absolutely no sense. But whatever you say."

Paul followed Colin into the control room.

"I want to introduce someone very special. This is Paul Dean. He composes the music that goes with the words I write. His job is much more difficult than mine. On top of that, he's my best friend. Paul, this is Paula Chandler."

"Paula, it's a pleasure to meet you."

"My pleasure, as well. And you're so handsome. I can see why Colin hasn't introduced us before."

Paul was taller than Colin by a couple of inches and equally as fit-looking from regular visits to the health club where they both had memberships. Paul was a few years younger, but what really set them apart was his hair that was more copper than red – and shoulder length. He looked much more the part of the Nashville music industry scene than Colin, and they both relished the opposites-attract contrast people noticed on the rare occasions when they were seen in public together. It was almost always Paul who told Colin when it was time to dust off his cowboy boots for an industry gathering.

"Paul, I should've warned you. Paula is, by her own account, a notorious flirt. But harmless."

"Who said anything about harmless?" Chandelier smile.

"All right then," Colin said, taking his cue. "The landscape looks like this. Paul, you're my best friend. I saw Paula first. Now, may I tell you something you need to know about her?"

"You may, indeed. Anything and everything."

"Paul, I warned you," Colin said, feigning irritation.

"Keep it up," Paula said, clapping her hands, just as Colin had recently witnessed as her lookalike daughter playfully egged him on about certain silk blouse. "This is fun! Two handsome men fightin' over little ole me."

A light began flashing in the control room.

"We've gotta move this along. Paul, all you need to know, all I'm going to tell you, is that Paula is the mother of one of our most promising protégés."

"Who?"

"Danielle Chandler."

"Well, Paula, it pains me greatly to agree with Colin." Colin groaned in mock torment. "But this is one of the rare occasions when he's right. Your daughter *is* one of our most promising."

"That's wonderful!"

"She has talent in abundance, the drive to succeed, and a winning personality. And, if you don't mind me saying, it's certainly easy to see where her beauty comes from."

Paul's words about her daughter left Paula beaming, and she wasn't above having a final bit of fun at Colin's expense before the recording session began.

"Colin, don't you have someplace else to be? Say, for an hour or two? I'd like to hear what else Mr. Dean might like to say about me."

When the recording session ended, Paula informed Colin the bookstore at Green Hills was calling her name and asked to borrow his car. After she left, Paul entered the control room, dropped down beside Colin in the chair she vacated, and listened in stunned silence as he heard the story.

"As you can see, she's at once the same person … and a different one."

"And I can see something else," Paul said. "You're in love with her."

"That I am, my friend. That I am."

"Have you told her?"

"I have. And that's why it would be wrong for me to intercede to help her daughter."

"Let me guess. This is where I come into the picture to help you. Again."

"It is."

"Well, to put you forever in my debt, to have a marker I can call in when needed, I'd like to say what you're asking could be professionally risky and a tremendous imposition." He let his words hang in the air for a few moments. "But it's not."

"Because …"

"All the things I told Paula. Getting helpful, well-deserved breaks will pass anyone's sniff test. It would be an honor to help."

"I don't know how to thank you. I'll be forever in your debt."

"Ah, but you didn't let me finish. You're late to the party. The producers at Adelaide asked me to do the very same thing right after her audition. It's already happening while she's out on tour. But I'll let her tell you."

"I don't care who said what or when. Just know that I'll be eternally grateful. Buy you a beer?"

"Any day. And today's any day."

They pushed open the front door to Adelaide Studios, and as they walked toward a popular neighborhood pub to await Paula's return, Colin asked again that Paul not tell Danielle he'd asked for help on her behalf.

"Don't worry. Those expensive imported beers you're buying will seal my lips."

A week later, Colin's phone rang. Danielle calling.

"How are things with you and Mother? I try, but I can't get her to tell me anything. And lately, when we talk, it's sometimes difficult to hear her. Maybe it's just my phone."

Colin had also noticed the ever-increasing softness in Paula's voice, causing him, at times, to strain to hear her. But he gave no thought it might be a harbinger of a change in her health.

"And you thought I'd get between a mother and her daughter? Not in this lifetime."

"Well, I know she sold the brownstone and told Marla Jo her decision was Nashville, not Bowling Green. Since she knows I'm not going to be around much, one can only assume ..."

"You keep right on assuming, young lady. But enough about your mother and me. Not that there *is* a your mother and me. Tell me about you. And the tour."

"Exciting! All that I'd hoped for, and more."

"Tell me about the more part."

"Almost from the beginning, I've been getting to sing one solo every night. Imagine that! Out of the background, down front and center."

Colin now understood what Paul meant when he said, "I'll let her tell you."

"That's great!"

"You have anything to do with my good fortune? You know, bein' like the Wizard of Oz, pulling strings from behind the curtain."

"Each time you bring that up, you overestimate me. And my influence. Remember what I told you when we first met. I'm just a small town ..."

"Yeah, right. I guess that still makes me Patsy Cline. Although I guess I am gettin' started on my way to bein' like her in real life. Say, anything exciting ahead for you or Mother before I get back?"

Colin had no way of knowing a final trip for them back to Three Oaks was just days away.

"Not that I know of. Just more of the same. Writing every day. Meandering around town together from time to time, usually with Blue. Getting to know each other all over again. Nothing special."

"Well, I can smell the aroma of that bullshit all the way out here."

"Such language! What would your mother say?"

"If she'd tell me the truth, she'd tell me she'd fallen in love with you. Again. Now I'm going to ask you straight up. Forget meandering and any other words to keep from telling me the truth since I'm not there to look you in the eye. Have you fallen in love with my mother for a second time?"

His answer came without hesitation.

"Yes, I have. Deeply. As deep as the ocean."

"Have you told her?"

"I have."

"Fantastic! And she says?"

"That she loves me, too."

"Double fantastic! When're you gettin' married?"

"Don't know that we are?"

"Why not?"

"I haven't asked her."

"What! You haven't asked her yet? Why not? What are you waiting for?"

Colin was growing as accustomed to bantering with the daughter as with the mother.

"I dunno. Guess I'm waiting for the right time and place."

"Listen to me, Daniel Colin Collins. You've been waiting over twenty years. And so has she, although she doesn't understand it in the same way. I won't say anything to Mother. Hard as it will be, I'll continue to play dumb. But if you haven't asked her by the time I get back to Nashville, it ain't gonna be pretty between you and me. Do we understand each other?"

"Yes, ma'am, we do." Colin struggled not to laugh. "No confusion on my part."

"And please don't be confused about something else. If I was there, I'd throw my arms around you and give you the biggest hug you've ever had. I'm beyond happy for both of you. And I'm sure Blue is, too. Give him a hug for me, will ya?"

"Will do. First chance I get."

"Before I go, I want two promises from you."

"And they are?"

"Number one, of course, is a marriage proposal before I get back. And since I know Mother has to be in New York, you and Blue be there to meet the bus. Promise?"

"I promise."

Only one promise would be kept. Could be kept.

Twenty-three

Three Oaks, redux and after

The moment Paula stepped out of her car in Colin's driveway, she sensed something was wrong. Terribly wrong. When she reached the steps up to the porch where he was sitting, she could tell he'd been crying. She slowly eased into the chair beside him. In his lap, she saw a rectangular shape covered by a deep blue velvet bag with a gold draw string. Colin turned his hand over to hold hers, and told her in a halting voice that Blue had died overnight. No warning.

Everyone at the clinic where Blue was a favorite shared in Colin's agony, and arrangements for cremation had been expedited. An urn containing Blue's ashes was in a sealed box inside the bag.

"May I ask why you didn't call me?" He heard the hurt in her voice.

"I did. Voice mail."

Paula's free hand covered her mouth as she looked off to the side before turning again to the man beside her.

"Oh, Colin, I'm so sorry. I was writing and had it turned off. Forgot to check." She waited. "Do you wanna talk about it?"

"Sure."

"What're you going to do?"

"Don't know," he answered, shaking his head. "There's something about this that makes me more angry than sad. And that doesn't seem right, somehow."

"You told me about Baby Blue. Is this how you felt with her?"

"No. I knew she was sick. Had time to prepare. This was different."

"I'm so sorry. I know I'm repeating myself." She squeezed his hand. "What did you do when she died?"

"Same thing." He lifted the bag slightly.

"May I ask where you put it?"

"In a cabinet under the bookshelves. In my study."

Moments passed.

"I want to comfort you, Colin, but I don't know how. Don't know what to say."

"That's okay. Just being here is enough. More than enough."

"I do have an idea," she said, tenderly.

He nodded for her to continue.

"When Danielle and I went to Three Oaks, that delightful Annie woman told us about the two of you burying the first Blue beside the swing behind the house."

"We did. It was her idea."

"Then what would you think of taking Baby Blue and this Blue out there so they can all three be together?" She waited, but he didn't say anything. "You wouldn't have to go alone. I wouldn't let you. I'd go with you."

"It's not my house anymore."

"You can rent it, can't you? We did. I can call Annie and find out who to talk to. We can hop a plane to Denver, rent a car, and be back here in no time. Or stay longer if you want. All up to you."

"I don't think it'll be that simple. I doubt the owners would be all that interested in our notion of a graveyard for Blues."

"And that could be true. Another way to think about it is we just do it. Don't say anything. I was there. Sat in the swing. We can do it so no one will ever know but us. Colin, we can do this. If you want."

Paula took charge, making all the arrangements. The house was available to rent, and they arrived mid-day Denver time three days later. It was late afternoon when they reached Three Oaks. Walking up the steps, Colin was surprised he didn't feel more emotion given its connection to both Mallory and Paula, a house he built steeped in memories of the only two women he'd ever loved. After years of living in a much smaller exact replica in Nashville, he was struck by its size. For her part, Paula sensed Colin wanted to get right to the interments, but she insisted they wait until the next day.

"Why?"

"I have my reasons. I know they were your companions, but this was my idea. And by now you know you can trust me. Can't you? Really, it's only until tomorrow. Middle of the morning at the latest."

"Sure. But you're being very mysterious."

As day broke the next morning, Colin found Paula already up and dressed. She told him it was because of the time difference with Nashville, but as he showered, it occurred to him she'd been waking up early every morning the past several weeks. He'd learn later it was symptomatic of a change in her condition.

They journeyed the short distance to town for breakfast at The Diner with Paula commenting on the beauty of their surroundings. Colin was heartened to see his corner booth available, and before their breakfast arrived, they were joined by a fashionably-dressed woman Paula guessed to be in her 90s. Marlene was a widow again, still living in Denver, back for a visit to Three Oaks, one she told them she expected to be her last.

Colin told Paula it was Marlene who was responsible for them meeting for the first time.

"Quite a coincidence," Paula said. "You being here at the same time we are."

Before Marlene could answer, Colin said, "I guess God works in mysterious ways."

"Yes," Marlene said, her age-lined face broadening into a smile. "She does."

On the drive back to the house, Colin remembered hearing or reading somewhere that there's often a fine line separating coincidence from answered prayers. When the log cabin home came into view, he saw Annie standing on the porch waiting for them. A heartwarming reunion Colin hadn't anticipated, orchestrated by Paula.

"You being mysterious yesterday has turned into a wonderful thing. Thank you," Colin said, as their car pulled to a stop. As he opened the passenger-side door and took Paula's hand, he said, "Speaking of which, and now seeing Annie, did you by chance have anything to do with the Marlene coincidence?"

Waving, Paula replied, "Darling, if you knew everything I know, where would be the mystery?"

Where, indeed? He thought, as they walked hand-in-hand to greet Annie.

After they buried the two boxes with barely any disturbance to the ground next to the swing, Colin pulled Annie aside when Paula went into the house to make coffee.

"There's something I want you to have."

"I still have your wife's pillow. You know, the one that says *I believe in angels*. It was such a wonderful gift. I've treasured it ever since the day you and Baby Blue took off down the road."

Colin reached his hands behind his head, undid the clasp, and handed the Jerusalem cross to her.

"This was also Mallory's. And I know she'd want you to have it."

"Are you sure?"

He nodded.

"That's so kind of you. Help me?" she asked, spreading the necklace apart and turning her back to Colin.

Colin fastened the clasp as Paula returned with two steaming mugs of coffee.

"None for me, thanks," Annie said. "I need to be getting back to the clinic. Dogs a-waitin'."

"I'll walk you to your car," Colin said.

"No, let me," Paula said, reaching for Annie's hand as she looked Colin's way. "You say your good-bye here and stay put."

"Why?"

"Think of it as me being mysterious."

As they walked to the end of the stone pathway in front of the house, Paula asked for Annie's help with something she wanted to happen once she and Colin got back to Nashville. Annie assured her it could, and something she'd love to be a part of. A second time.

Paula returned to find Colin sitting in the swing and sat down beside him.

"Colin, last night, before I went to sleep, in my prayers I asked to be able to help you with your loss. At the time, I was thinking of Blue. But when I woke up this morning, something told me there's a much greater burden weighing on your heart. Is there?"

Colin's mind flew back in time to Mel's last birthday present, remembering each of the promises. He needed counseling then, but not now. He'd abandoned his friends then, but embraced the ones he now had. He'd long ago stopped fixing blame, and had returned to attending church regularly. He prayed daily. He'd sacrificed lawyering to transform from a poet to a lyricist. That left only one truly broken promise a quarter of a century later. Twilight. His glistening eyes answered Paula's question.

"If you love me, as you say you do, don't you think you should let me help you?" When he didn't answer, she asked, "Is it something you did? Or is it something you regret not doing?"

"Regret," he answered. She took his hand in hers.

"A few days before she died …"

Paula waited for him to compose himself.

"A few days before she died, Mallory gave me a poem and asked me to read it to her. Small print. Looked like it had been cut from a newspaper. No author. The title was *When Twilight Comes*. It's in her Bible at my house, between the same pages where she left it."

"What did it say?"

"Don't have it memorized, only the last two lines."

Paula's loving gaze wordlessly asked the question.

"God grant that life may leave us hand in hand, when twilight comes."

He wiped his eyes, cleared his throat.

"Am I right in guessing that twilight is the poet's word for death?"

"You are. Mel made me promise to find someone else to love and marry after she was gone. And she made me promise it would be someone she'd approve of. I remember asking her how I'd know, and she said, 'You'll know.'"

Colin stood, walked several steps away from the swing and looked off into the distance, to the poplar trees swaying in a stiff breeze that had come up suddenly. While Paula was trying to decide whether or not to join him, he turned around and walked back. He extended his hand and gently pulled her up, then put his arm around her waist. "Let's walk."

As they turned the corner at the side of the house and approached the stone walkway leading to the front porch where they'd be sheltered from the wind, Colin said, "Paula, my biggest regret in life, the burden that has weighed on my heart for all these years, is that I let you leave here without telling you how I felt. That I'd fallen in love with you. My second biggest regret is that I kept my word about not contacting you."

When they reached the steps leading up to the front porch, Paula looked at the two rocking chairs. "This is where it all began? This being you and me."

"It is."

"Shall we?" she asked, taking him by the arm, not waiting for an answer.

Comfortably seated, Paula said, "Thank you for sharing. It must have been difficult."

"Not really." He responded to her knowing smile by saying, "I know, I know. It's your word. But truly didn't seem to fit somehow."

"Just don't make a habit of it. Now, I have two questions for you."

"I hope I have the right answers."

"We'll know soon enough. Colin, do you think Mallory would approve of me?"

"Above every other woman on the planet."

"Then why don't you keep your promise to your first wife and ask me to be your second?"

"Here? Now?"

"Can you think of a better time? A better place?" She didn't wait for an answer. "You said you put the swing in the back yard where you proposed to Mallory. Right?"

"Right."

"Well, wife number two wants to be front porch not back yard. Let's get to it."

"Paula, will …"

"Oh, no you don't. Don't remember my first proposal, but I'm going to do all I can to remember this one. As long as possible. I'm a Southern gal. Down on one knee, Daniel Colin Collins."

Colin assumed the position, and as he held her hand, felt her hand tremble. Ever so slight, but a tremor nonetheless. At the time, he dismissed it as emotion.

Later that evening, walking arm-in-arm up the lane, Paula asked Colin about the paternity test.

"Do you want to know?"

"I do," he answered.

"Me, too. It may not be long before it won't matter in my life, but will in yours and Danielle's. One of us needs to talk with her, and it shouldn't be over the phone while she's away."

"Agree. You or me? Or better yet, together."

"Well, luck of the draw, you're gonna be the first one to see her."

"Why's that?"

"I remember because I wrote it down. The day she gets back to Nashville, I'll be in New York selling my house."

"Well, then, I guess that's settled."

"And while you're at it, in the time-honored tradition, …"

"What time-honored tradition?"

"One I'm making up just now. You also tell her about us getting married. Fits together nicely, don't you think? She'll being getting a father, one way or the other, and you'll be the one telling her."

"Paula, are you sure you want me to be the one to tell her about us?"

Colin decided not to share the two promises he'd made to Danielle the last time they'd spoken.

"No, I'm not. But sometimes things just happen the way things happen. And you're the better wordsmith between us."

"Don't know if I agree."

"You certainly are. Especially about matters of the heart. Don't think I haven't made it my business to listen to all your songs. By all the different artists. I have. Many times."

Colin was standing curbside among other family members and friends when the tour bus turned the corner and Danielle waved from her window seat when she saw him.

Hugging him, she said, "Where's Blue?"

Colin took her hand and guided her to a nearby park while the luggage and instruments were being unloaded.

"Blue's gone," he said, hesitantly. "He passed away during the night a not too long ago."

"Oh, Colin! I'm so sorry." Tears streamed down her cheeks as she wrapped her arms around him, trembling. They held each other tightly, and when she pulled back, he reached into his hip pocket for the ever-present handkerchief. Drying her eyes, she said, "I don't know what else to say. I know how much he meant to you. How much you meant to each other."

While waiting to retrieve her luggage, and continuing on the drive to her home, Colin shared details of the recent trip to Three Oaks, finishing while they were parked in front of the house.

"Mother's really something, isn't she?"

"That she is."

"Were you surprised when she asked you to marry her?"

"I was. But I was prepared, just like I'd promised you. Thought I had it all planned out. She just got there a few minutes ahead of me."

As they walked toward the front door, Danielle asked, "Different but related. Did you ever call Doc?"

Once inside, Colin told her about the brief phone conversation.

"Did it help you make peace with Mother as she is now?"

"It did. Truth is, I've fallen in love with her all over again. Not the Paula of Three Oaks. We know she's gone forever. The Paula of today. And whatever tomorrow brings."

Settled comfortably in her living room, Danielle spent several minutes answering Colin's "Tell me all about the tour."

When she finished, he said, "I couldn't be more thrilled for the way things are breaking for you." He sipped freshly-brewed iced tea. "Your mother, too, as I'm sure she's told you."

Danielle set her glass on the table between their chairs.

"When you said 'whatever tomorrow brings,' it gave me an idea for a first step in that journey. Stay where you are. Don't move. I'll be right back."

Danielle returned, holding her mother's leather-bound journal.

"You've persuaded me you're now mature enough to read this."

Finally holding it in his hands for a second time, something only he knew, Colin knew it was an anchor to the past, not a pathway to the future.

"No, I don't think I'll read it."

"Are you sure?"

"As sure as I am about my love for your mother. And you."

"That's sweet. And so like you."

"I don't know that it serves any purpose. For anyone. Would you consider getting rid of it?"

"Absolutely. Thought about that often. Any ideas?"

"The fire pit in my back yard."

"Let's go."

They stood a few feet away from the fire, watching the journal curl up and shrink, first turning black, then gray as the flames died down before burning out.

"That's done," Danielle said. "From the looks of you, I'll bet your mind is churning lyrics, imagining what's in those ashes you never read."

"Mind-reader."

"If you only knew," she laughed. "And now I have to ask. How did mother coax a marriage proposal out of you? I wanna file it away for future reference."

"Odd, in a way," he answered, leading them toward his back door. "How it happened, that is. She asked me to tell her about my first wife. I told her about a poem Mallory asked me to read to her a few days before she passed away. And a promise she made me make that I would find another woman to love, to marry, to share my life with. Seems like that's all your mother needed."

"It's worth repeating. She's really something."

"Speaking of something," Colin answered, opening the door, "I want to show you something. And give you something."

Danielle counted with her fingers as she stepped in front of him to go inside.

"You just said *something* three times. Does that mean you're going to give me three things?"

"No such luck. But hopefully, you'll be happy with the one I have in mind. Meet you in the study."

Colin returned with Mallory's Bible, holding it in both hands as he sat across from Danielle.

Danielle nodded, assuming it was the Bible he was giving her. He opened it to the place still marked by the silk ribbon and pulled out the *Twilight* clipping. He set the closed book on the table beside his chair.

"I don't mean to be melodramatic. I don't." Colin handed her the clipping. "Mallory knew your mother was out there, and that our paths would cross. I know that she and your mother would both want you to have this."

When Danielle finished reading, she carefully refolded it, averting her eyes, though Colin still saw her tears.

"I wish I could have known Mallory."

"Me, too."

A half-minute passed before she asked, "Can we talk about one more thing?"

"Of course."

She moved to kneel at the side of his chair and reached to touch his cheek with the palm of her hand. "I want us to take the test. We know Mother wants us all to know, and there'll come a time ..."

"I agree. Let's do it."

A few days later, sitting at the table they now considered "theirs" at the urban coffee shop, Danielle asked Colin if he was disappointed.

"I am. Very. I was hoping for a different outcome."

"Hope can be a tricky thing."

"You're not disappointed?"

"Nah," she answered, without hesitation and with a smile. He wouldn't have anticipated either her answer or her smile.

"You're not?"

"I can't resist. Think of your favorite word."

"Okay, I get that. But why not. Why aren't you disappointed? I thought it was something we both wanted. Your mother, as well."

"Well, maybe you and Mother are thinking too much like the writers you are."

"May need a little help making sense of that."

"Think about it. You turning out to be my father would've been an unbeatable script for a Hallmark movie. Not that all the rest wouldn't, mind you. It would. It's just that life seldom turns out that way. Not really Mother's life, is it? Or yours."

"What about yours?"

"Mine? Not to worry. I've already got a handsome fairy godfather who's got a thing for my mother helpin' me along with my life and my career. Even though you say it isn't you behind the curtain, I think it is. And anyway, after you and Mother marry, you *will* be my father. One step removed."

"Clever," he replied.

"Thank you. I thought so, too."

"Or..." he said, dampening the moment.

"Or ... what?"

"After your mother and I marry, I could adopt you."

The ever-present traffic noise gave Danielle time to take in what she'd just heard. Her eyes narrowed when she asked, "Now why would you want to go and do a thing like that?"

"Selfish. On my part. In my old age, maybe even earlier, I'd have legal bragging rights after you become rich and famous."

"Clever."

"Thank you," he answered, straight-faced. "I thought so, too."

"I guess you know we're beginning to repeat each other."

"I know," he said. "Just like in a song." He paused, grinning. "I thought you knew that's what I did."

Well, he just stepped into it knee-deep.

"Speaking of which." Return volley. "How's that for a segue?"

"Won't know 'till I hear it."

"Okay, here it comes. Until you and Mother make you and me legal, how 'bout steppin' up as my fairy godfather and granting me a wish? Just a small one."

Her thumb and forefinger spread apart slightly to emphasize "small," and every ounce of her body language and facial expression conveyed the answer she wanted.

"I have a feeling it isn't small, but the answer is yes. What is …"

"Really!"

"It was yes until I heard that. Now I …"

"Oh, *no*, you don't! It's you and me writing songs together. I know you don't need any help, and certainly not from me. But it's a dream of mine to be a songwriter as well as a singer." Colin's stoic face flooded hers with disappointment. "Please at least think about it, will you? I don't have much time."

"There's nothing to think about," he said, his countenance softening. "I've never tried writing with anyone before, but there's no way I'm going to say no. But please understand. What you're setting about to do is extremely difficult. Do you know how long it took Paul and me to have our first number one hit?"

"I do. Ten years. But I'm not asking for that."

"What then? And what did you mean you don't have much time?"

"All I want are a few songs Mother can know you and I wrote together. You can't imagine how happy that would make her. And me. The rest can wait."

"Danielle, from reading the journal and what I know you've learned from Marla Jo, you have to know I owe your mother everything. We'll make this happen. Together."

After an early evening dinner at a Hillsboro restaurant, the young singer and not-so-young songwriter enjoyed a leisurely stroll back to Danielle's home.

"Colin," she said, gripping his hand firmly, "I'm so happy Mother and I found you. Or rather that God put us in each other's path."

When he took three steps without answering, Danielle thought he was ignoring her. Then she saw his chin quivering and heard him say,

"If it was your intent to make a grown man cry in public, you succeeded." Eyes dried, they continued walking. "The day after your mother left me in Colorado, I knew how I wanted the movie to end. And still do."

"How?"

"Happily ever-after. For all three of us."

"Well, we'll just have to work doubly hard to see that it does. Say, now that that you're gonna be family, can I tell you a secret? Something even Marla Jo doesn't know?"

He thought back to Marla Jo telling him about the name change known to the two of them, and Paul Dean, but not to Danielle. Now he was about to be told something that had been kept from Marla Jo. Hoping his own memory would serve him well in the future, he asked, "That's always a risk, isn't it?"

"Meaning?"

"A true secret is something only one other person knows."

"I'll risk it. You know about Mother's writing. And her public speaking."

"I do."

"Well, here's something else. She is, or was, quite an artist. Studied for years in New York. Even had a few exhibitions of her sketches in small galleries there, but wouldn't let them publicize her name. Always anonymous."

"That *is* a secret. At least one kept from me. I'd love to see them."

"That's the thing. Mother forgot all about that part of her life, and since she never told Marla Jo, all the sketches were sold a few weeks ago along with furniture and other things. When I found out, it was too late. We don't have a single one of them."

"Any chance she might pick it up again?"

"Who the heck knows? The way our lives have been going since you and I first met, I guess anything's possible."

They reached Colin's car parked in front of Danielle's house. He reached into his jeans pocket with his right hand, then using his left to spread a small number of coins across his palm, he found the object of his search. He returned all of the coins to his pocket except for a quarter.

"Mind if I ask what you're doing?" she asked.

His face had no expression. "Thought we'd flip for who gets to tell your mother about the test results."

Standing close enough to land a good roundhouse punch, Danielle put her hands squarely on her hips and tried to affect her sternest possible look. "I thought I'd broken you of that bad habit."

"Which one?"

"Thinking for yourself, of course."

It was a contest of wills to see who could hold out and laugh last. Danielle lost.

"You're impossible! Come here and give me a proper father's hug."

When he'd closed the car door, she leaned toward the open window a few feet away. "Wanted you to know I had a chat with Mother. About names."

"And?"

She stepped back, stood erect, smiled and said, "Good-night. FATHER!"

Twenty-four

New beginning; old ending

"When I learned the two of you took that test, I prayed Danielle would finally have a father." Paula turned to Colin. "And if we could've gone shopping for one, there would have been none better."

Paula was sitting on the couch in Danielle's living room, her daughter on one side, Colin on the other. She tried to persuade them her tears of sadness and disappointment were more for her daughter than herself.

"But Mother, Marla Jo has always said what a fine man Reverend Chandler was. We couldn't help it he was taken from us when I was too young to remember him."

Colin took Paula's hand in his. "And even though I never met the man, I know that to be true."

Paula's eyes met his. "How could you possibly know that?"

"Because I know you. You married him, planning to spend the rest of your life together. And the choice you made resulted in his beautiful child."

"And Mother, there's more than one kind of father."

Paula turned to her daughter. "Meaning?"

"The stepfather kind. And Mother, you took your own advice."

"What was that, dear?"

"The night you met Colin again for the first time, at the restaurant, you told me not to let him get away. And *we* haven't. You and I. So right back at ya."

A few hours later, the new mix-and-match family, as Paula had earlier referred to them, was finishing a celebratory dinner at a restaurant that had become Paula's favorite from among all the venues Colin had taken her.

After toasting her about-to-become parents with raised glasses of champagne, Danielle asked her mother about wedding plans.

"Simple. Small. Here." Paula answered.

"A bit more, if you please," her smiling daughter urged.

"Okay. No fuss. No bother. No more guests than can be counted on two hands. With fingers left over. And I was going to ask your help finding a small church in my new hometown."

"We can do all of that," Danielle said, thinking to herself that all ten fingers would be needed. Hopefully.

Paula and Colin were married on October 23rd in a small chapel at Belmont College, a stone's throw from the larger Vanderbilt University campus in Nashville. Marla Jo and her husband, Ben, were there, along with Doc McGinley and his wife Grace Ann. The Judge rounded out the Bowling Green delegation. Paul Dean stood as Best Man to Danielle's Maid of Honor. As they were gathered together in the minutes before the appointed hour, Danielle appeared visibly distracted.

"Dear, it's my wedding. I'm the one who's supposed to be nervous. What's got you so anxious?"

Danielle was about to answer her mother when the door at the back of the chapel opened and two women, six decades apart in age, walked through. A stunned Colin knew whose hand had held the baton to orchestrate a reunion that brought everything full-circle when he saw Danielle rush to greet Annie Hayworth and Marlene McKenzie. Colin asked everyone to gather for introductions, then briefly shared the importance of a little redheaded girl from Colorado at a pivotal time in his life.

"And to you, Marlene," he said, bowing, "tonight would not have been possible without you."

Marla Jo and Danielle had read Paula's journal, so they understood Colin's meaning immediately as they watched him gently lift Marlene's hand and kiss it as he would royalty.

Seeing the puzzled looks on the faces of the others, Colin said, "Yes, there's a story there, and I promise to tell it over dinner. But for now, I've waited far too long and I don't want to wait a minute longer. Let's get on with the wedding before Paula changes her mind."

"In a word, ocean. The rest is up to you."

Weeks before the wedding, Paula had answered Colin's question about a honeymoon destination, so he followed up by suggesting Pawleys Island, South Carolina, a day's drive from Nashville. Paula agreed, saying she'd heard about it but never been.

"Anything special about it other than sand and waves?"

"It'll be my first time, too," Colin answered, "But from others I'm told the locals refer to life there as being arrogantly shabby. Tourist shops even print t-shirts and other stuff with the slogan."

"How could we possibly not enjoy a place like that? I can hardly wait."

The setting lived up to its reputation, and the weather for the end of October was ideal the entire week. But Paula became easily fatigued, cutting short their walks on the beach at sunrise and sunset. Beginning with their trip to Three Oaks, Colin had been adding things up in his mind and became increasing worried. Ever-softening of her speech. Early rising most mornings. The slight tremor in her hand. He kept his thoughts and fears to himself, and the morning of their last day at Pawleys, Paula confessed to not feeling well, a first for her. He suggested they see a specialist when they got back home to Nashville, and she didn't resist, but said. "I'd like Doc there with us. It's time the two of you got better acquainted, anyway."

The following week, with Danielle on tour again, Paula and Colin, accompanied by Doc, got the Parkinsons confirmation they'd once feared. Paula heard the two words she'd forgotten from the silent stroke diagnosis. No cure. Life repeating itself in a dreadful way. One difference. Her Parkinsons was anticipated to progress rapidly, with amnesia and dementia overtaking the memory loss she was already fighting a losing battle. After Doc left Nashville to return home to Bowling Green, Paula told Colin if she'd known, she never would have married him. Never would have wanted to be a burden to him in that way. They were slowly walking near Colin's house they now shared.

"Paula, there's no way on God's earth you will ever be a burden to me."

"Colin, I love you with all my heart, but we both know that isn't true. But it's fixable."

He squeezed her hand gently to stop them, and turned to face her. The inevitability of what lay ahead was breaking his heart, and for the first time since she came back into his life, she appeared weak and vulnerable.

"Fixable. What do you mean?" he asked.

"I don't know. It's the word that came to mind. Spoke without thinking. Sorry."

But Paula *had* been thinking, and the week after Thanksgiving, sitting in their living room, she told Colin she'd found "a fix." With Marla Jo's help, she'd done a lot of research, and while she was still strong enough, physically and mentally, with the help of another friend, The Judge, Paula had purchased with her own money the last available suite (living room, kitchen, bedroom, bathroom) in a converted mansion in the city of Franklin, Tennessee, near Nashville.

The historic Lanneau Estate was a sprawling, nearly two-hundred-acre compound that had been turned into an upscale retirement community with gated entrances and private security guards that would provide everything Paula could possibly need. Three meals a day in a dining room or her suite. Housekeepers and laundry. A limo service if she needed to go anywhere and Colin was unavailable. Health care professionals always on-site with physicians on-call. As her health deteriorated, caregivers would come to her suite as-needed twenty-four/seven.

"Only eighteen of them," Paula said. "I bought the last one. Only about a dozen are occupied. The rest are waiting for me and the others to arrive when our time comes. When I pass away, the company buys it back at a price we've already negotiated. I ..."

"To say that I'm surprised doesn't begin to ..."

She interrupted his interruption.

"Colin, I pray constantly that God takes me before I'll ever need to go there. But know this. As certain as God is in Heaven, I'll know when that time has come, and I'll be the one to decide."

"And there's nothing I can say? Nothing I can do?"

"There is. You can make a decision."

"What decision?" His heart was in his throat.

"I love you with all my heart, and I thank God every day He brought us back together. But that promise you gave Mallory. The one that got you down on your knee on the porch in Colorado. It wasn't this. And there are no words you can say to persuade me to hold you to it."

"But Paula ..."

"I'm giving you two choices."

He slumped in his chair.

"You can fight me, and I'll have our marriage annulled."

Her words overwhelmed him, but he decided to hear her out rather than the two of them continuing to interrupt the other.

"The Judge tells me it can happen quickly, and he's got lawyers working on it. But they'll also have documents naming you as my guardian, along with Danielle. If that's something you'd want. I hope and pray you would, but neither of you could stop me from going to Lanneau when I say the time is right. And staying there until I die. I refuse to be a burden to either of you, and that's the way it's going to be."

It was becoming clear to Colin that Paula had taken control over the remaining days of her life, however many they might be, while she still had the power.

"What's my other choice?"

"We stay married. You sign a piece of paper saying you agree I get to decide when to go to Lanneau, and that you can't change the arrangements I've made. I know you love me, but I'm not going to let you wreck your life, and probably Danielle's, trying to take care of the mess we both know I'll be. Not gonna happen. You don't have to decide this minute, but soon. Door number one. Door number two."

"Anything else?" His voice barely a whisper.

"There is. Whatever you decide, I want you to promise to join me in praying that God takes me before I have to leave you and go to that place. And I have something I think may help. I'll be right back."

Paula returned and handed Colin a gift-wrapped box. In it, he found a small, highly polished copper watering can. On one side, in white enamel paint, the words: Matthew 21:22 "If you believe, you will receive whatever you ask for in prayer." On the other side, in the same paint and in the same unsteady cursive handwriting he recognized as hers: Matthew 7:7 "Ask and it will be given to you; seek and you will find; knock, and the door will be opened to you."

Colin's heart pounded as his mind brought back the image of Paula with the watering can at Danielle's house, and then their less-than-a-minute conversation that evening when he shared with her Mallory's prayer-and-garden metaphor. Paula had not only remembered; she'd understood how much it had meant in his life and created a gift that would transform it into a tangible remembrance. His eyes filled. He gently returned the gift to the box, set the box on the floor beside his chair, and moved to kneel in front her.

"I'll give you my answer now. Door number two."

"That's the answer I was praying for."

"One thing I ask. Please never tell Danielle I was given a choice."

"I won't. I promise."

He leaned forward, kissed her, and said "Thank you." He returned to his chair. "Paula, I know we have to take your illness one day at a time. Nothing we can do about that. But I must ask. Do you have any more surprises planned for me?"

Her face brightened instantly with a knowing smile and twinkling eyes, so when she shrugged slightly and answered "maybe," he knew the answer was "yes."

As with her declining health, Paula had no control over her surprise, so when it failed to materialize as she'd been led to anticipate, she became distraught. She said nothing to Colin, and he never asked. Then one morning, she focused on the two passages of scripture on his watering can. She decided to turn the surprise's uncertainty into something to live for every day. She drew mental, emotional and physical strength from her prayers during the day, and at night, when she rested her head on her pillow, she had something to look forward to because tomorrow might be the day for the surprise.

Twenty-five

Older dog, newer beginning

"And who might this be?"

Colin had waited to ask until Paula and her companion exited her car and reached where he was sitting.

It was an early March afternoon, and her symptoms were progressing more slowly than her doctors had anticipated. In fact, they'd noticed she'd been growing stronger rather than weaker, an anomaly for which there was no medical explanation. None of the doctor's factored in the power of prayer.

"Why Blue Four, of course. Annie found her for me at a shelter right here in Nashville. Perfectly healthy. Oh, except she's full grown and can't have puppies."

"Her?" Colin asked.

Paula dropped the leash and the dog quickly climbed the porch steps, tail wagging.

"Annie and I didn't plan it. Just turned out this way. Boy, girl. Boy, girl."

"Honestly, with all that we've got going on, I'd given no thought to another dog. Why did you?"

Blue climbed into Colin's lap as Paula eased into the chair beside them, wrapping herself in the blanket they kept folded across it. She pulled both feet underneath her and settled back.

"Because you've told me, and so have Marla Jo and Danielle, you weren't alone when we met in Colorado. Or when I left you. We know I'll leave you again, in a different way. Before I do, I wanted to make things the way they were for you the other times." She paused. "So you won't be alone."

Colin's eyes began to tear as he rested his hand on the dog's head. "Is she the surprise you mentioned way back before Christmas?"

"She is. Took much longer than Annie and I wanted." She reached for his hand. "But so did I."

How is it even conceivable this woman will be taken from me?

Paula insisted Danielle keep to her commitments to touring and studio work, especially during the holidays, but they played havoc with the desire she and Colin shared to work together as songwriters. It wasn't until February they were able to begin writing together in earnest, with Danielle becoming the quick study Colin anticipated. They collaborated long hours with Paula ever-present in both of their minds, bringing in Paul Dean when appropriate. Blue joined them from time to time after her arrival on the scene, spending the rest of her time keeping Paula company.

Among their first ideas for titles were: *First Impressions / Second Chances; City Girl / Country Heart; I Believe in Angels; Lost then Found; New Beginnings; The First Door on the Right; Sweet Surrender; Chandelier Smile; Dreams Never Come True (for those who never dream).*

Their urgency began with a desire for Danielle to record at least a few of their creations while Paula was still able to enjoy them. Then Adelaide Studios brought to Dean and Collins an even more pressing deadline to create three original songs for the soundtrack of a production already underway in California in time for a lavish, media-rich gala to launch the movie in June.

Danielle, Colin and Paul wanted the upcoming Hollywood event to be a wonderful surprise for Paula. Things didn't work out that way. During one of her visits to the recording study to watch and listen to her daughter, a slip of the tongue from an Adelaide employee spoiled everything. Paula broke the news to The Three Amigos over lunch at a casual Mexican restaurant. Their disappointment was painfully obvious.

"Mother, can I share something really cool about going to California in a few weeks?"

"Certainly, dear."

"The movie studio is sending a private jet for the four of us. And a few people from Adelaide Studios. Isn't that exciting?"

"Exciting? Yes. Accurate? No."

"What do you mean?" Colin asked.

"Only that the math is wrong. It'll be four minus one. I won't be going."

"Why?" Paul beat the other two in asking.

"Two reasons. Don't want to be that far away from my doctors. And I don't want to be a burden in any way. You people paying attention to me as I know you will and not to the reason for your trip."

Danielle and Colin took turns trying everything they could think of to change Paula's mind, but to no avail. When it appeared she was unmovable, Paul finally spoke up.

"My turn." All three turned to look at him. "I've been keeping something from all of you. A few days ago, I learned, and was sworn to secrecy, that Danielle would be performing live at the event. In front of all that Hollywood and music industry royalty. And the press."

"What!" Colin exclaimed. Loud enough to draw the surprised attention of other diners at tables surrounding them.

"You heard me. Adelaide and the movie people wanted to surprise Danielle after she got there. I've now spoiled that, but hopefully with good cause."

"Mother, what about it? Will you go with us now?"

Paula reached over to hug her daughter, promising to think about it.

When a few weeks later the sleek Gulfstream jet lifted off from an executive airfield near downtown Nashville, the passenger manifest agreed with Paula's Mexican restaurant math. But she was there to see them off, with Marla Jo at her side, and both were there to welcome them home three days later.

The movie studio had arranged for Danielle, Colin and Paul to have three adjoining rooms at an iconic Beverly Hills hotel. The men insisted Danielle take the corner room with the best view, and Colin ended up in the middle. Their second night, after the gala, he heard Danielle come in at two in the morning. When he and Paul meet at the hotel restaurant for breakfast, Paul requested a table for three.

Seated in a circular corner both ideal for morning celebrity sightings, Colin said, "May only be the two of us. Danielle got in very late."

"And you know this how?" Paul asked, as the coffee arrived.

"You'd think a place that gets these kinds of prices would have thicker walls."

"You sound worried."

"Do I?"

"You do. Paternally so. You, my friend, are officially a father. And she officially became an adult a few years ago."

"Shouldn't both of us be concerned, Paul? Wondering where she was? Who she was with? What she was doing?"

"No, no, no and no. We may be curious. You certainly are. But she's a grown woman, and it's none of our business. She's as levelheaded as they come, and strong in the Christian values column. And let's not forget, she was raised by a working single mom, not in rural Iowa but in New York City. She came through that experience with flying colors." When Colin didn't join in, Paul added, "Please tell me you're not going to say anything."

Colin stirred his black coffee.

"Colin?"

"All right. I won't say anything."

The two men enjoyed a hearty breakfast vastly overpriced by comparison to virtually any place else in the country. An opinion Colin offered when he signed the check to their suite.

"You know, buddy. Travelling with you is like dragging a concrete block of sensibility. This is Los Angeles. The City of Angels. And we brought one of our own with us. Maybe the meal price, which by the way Adelaide is paying, includes seeing all the movie stars sitting around us. Who knows? Anyway, I'm going for the papers to see what they said about last night."

"A bit premature, don't you think? It was just a few hours ago," Colin said, as Paul slid out of the booth.

Dropping his expensive cloth napkin with the hotel's logo on the table next to his plate, Paul said, "And this, my friend, isn't Kansas. Isn't even Iowa. Ye of little faith. You'll see."

Paul returned a few minutes later with one thick newspaper.

"The entertainment tabloids will arrive a bit later. They'll bring them to us."

Colin and Paul were devouring the *Los Angeles Times* when they looked up to see Danielle approach. The excitement of the prior evening's festivities, and the crowd reaction to her performance, masked any hint she'd only gotten a few hours of sleep. She was glowing.

"I'm famished. I was too nervous yesterday to eat anything after breakfast."

Minutes after their waiter took Danielle's order, the hostess arrived with the morning edition of the two main entertainment tabloids.

"Here you are, Mr. Dean," the smartly-dressed, very attractive women in her forties said as she handed them to Paul. With a smile meant only for him.

Watching the slender woman walk away, Colin looked at Paul and asked, "What was *that* all about?"

"The Dean charm," Paul answered. Danielle whispered 'bullshit' under her breath, but loud enough for them both to hear. "And a twenty-dollar tip."

"Twenty bucks? Are you crazy?"

"No, Colin, I'm not. We got the papers we wanted, right?" He didn't wait for an answer. "And she's thinking about being my date this evening." Paul pointed to a phone number hand-written at the top of one of the tabloids.

"Atta boy!" Danielle chimed in. "Maybe we can double-date. Leave the grouch to enjoy his grumblings over a room service dinner."

"Two against one," Colin said. "Fair fight."

Colin returned to the *Times* while Paul handed the tabloid without the phone number to Danielle.

Less than a minute of page-turning later, Paul said, "Well, we made the big time. Correction. One of us made the big time." He spread the paper on the table in front of him. "Says right here the newest country music star has burst onto the scene, and LA is claiming bragging rights because it happened here last night instead of in Nashville."

Colin set his paper down, hoping to spark some mid-morning playful fun with their tardy breakfast companion and extract a bit of grouch revenge.

"Well, it has to be one of the three of us, doesn't it? Does it say which one?"

Danielle spun her head toward Colin, but a mouthful of avocado-cheese omelet silenced her. She had to content herself with wrinkling her nose and squinting at him, looking for all the world like her mother would in the same situation.

"May I read aloud?" Paul asked.

Danielle responded with a circular motion of her hand and Colin nodded.

All roads leading to Hollywood are paved with over a century of broken dreams, but last night a new star appeared and captivated even the most jaded among us. Now that her record company has pulled back the curtain, Nashville will want to claim her, but we saw her first. Her name is Danielle Chandler. Beauty beyond belief, a traffic-stopping figure, legs that go from here to tomorrow, and a voice to make the angels weep.

"What!"

"What what?" Paul asked, unable to suppress a smile.

"You think this, this is funny?"

"Easy, Danielle. Remember where we are. This is Hollywood. They invented shameless here."

"But it's *me* they're talking about. Me! And that thing about my legs. *They* made me wear that short skirt. You know that. They said it was in our contract to do what their wardrobe people said. I never would have done it on my own. Mother's gonna kill me! If I don't die of embarrassment first."

"Danielle, Paul's right. What they wrote is shameless. Tasteless. And I'm sorry it happened. But one thing's for certain. Last night, the entertainment world stood up and took notice. Your world has changed, Patsy. In a huge and positive way."

"I should just forget about what they wrote?"

"Only the stupid stuff," Paul answered. "You're on your way, and you can always depend on two things, wherever you go and no matter what happens."

"What are they?"

"Your father. And me."

They were about to leave when Coin's cell phone vibrated with a call from an Adelaide executive asking for a lunch meeting. Looking at his breakfast companions, Colin asked, "All three of us?"

Over an elaborate lunch in the Adelaide hotel suite, The Nashville Three heard the executive say he'd read the trade publications.

"They got many things right," said the man with features chiseled by skilled cosmetic surgeon that made it impossible to guess his age. "Nashville, and more specifically we at Adelaide, are claiming Danielle Chandler. And the two of you, Mr. Collins and Mr. Dean, we're counting on you to help us protect Danielle from the West Coast sharks that'll come swimming her way."

Danielle listened to the assurances from the two men so important in her life, now and in the years ahead.

"Anyone interested in what's on my mind?" Danielle asked.

The man from Adelaide fell all over himself to assure her they were.

"How soon can we leave for home?"

After learning the private jet would be "wheels up" at nine the next morning, all three went sightseeing together. In the middle of the afternoon, Colin asked what would interest the others for their last meal in Tinsel Town. Danielle acted slightly embarrassed when she told her companions she had plans. Both men waited for the elaboration that wasn't forthcoming.

"I guess it'll be just you and me, partner," Colin said, looking Paul's direction.

Paul wasn't the slightest bit embarrassed when he revealed he also had plans. A dinner-then-dancing date with a local.

"Miss Morning Newspapers?" Danielle asked, a mischievous smile spreading across her face.

"Since the two of you haven't had me out of your sight since we arrived, that wasn't a lucky guess," Paul said. "It was the only guess."

"Well, I'm happy for the both of you," Colin said, with unmistakable insincerity. He was ambivalent about his best friend's evening plans, but far from uncaring about his daughter's. Choosing not to probe any further with Danielle, he added, "For my part, I'm going to follow my daughter's suggestion to order the most expensive meal on the room service menu since we're not paying for it. Then, before retiring earlier than either of you, I'll end my day with a long phone call, talking with the love of my life."

At eight the next morning, Colin called Danielle's extension to ask if she was ready to accompany them to breakfast. Thinking she might be in the shower, he waited another ten minutes before calling again. Still no answer. Concerned, he knocked on the door separating their rooms. Still no answer, so he slowly opened the door, calling her name. Silence. Looking around, his eyes found a bed that hadn't been slept in. He turned to re-enter his room as the phone was ringing.

"On my way," Colin said to Paul, who was calling from the courtesy phone in the restaurant. He left hurriedly, forgetting to close the door between his room and Danielle's. She joined them an hour or so later. Both men rose and she kissed each of them on the cheek.

"If you'll excuse me for a moment. Want to say good-bye to Miss Morning Newspapers."

As soon as Paul had departed, Danielle sensed uneasiness on Colin's part and, because of the opened door and undisturbed bed, knew what was on his mind.

"Colin. Dad. I'll say this, and only this."

When she didn't continue, Colin asked, "Yes?"

"Ask me no questions; I'll tell you no lies." She didn't want there to be conversation around what she'd said. "Now, what do you recommend? What did the two of you have?"

On the plane that morning, somewhere over the vast expanse of western states, Danielle could tell that Colin, sitting in the plush leather chair at the window across from hers, had something on his mind. Ever her mother's daughter, she chose not to suffer in silence.

"Hey, Dad," she whispered. When he looked her way and their eyes met, she added, "Yes, you. Everything okay? And by okay, I mean you and me. Like you asked me that day at the coffee shop."

"Yes, we are." He reached for her hand.

"Then what has you so deep in thought?"

"You mentioned the coffee shop. I was reminiscing back to the day we met. When we were crossing that busy street on our way to Adelaide. You said you wouldn't tell me your last name because you might change it on your way to becoming rich and famous."

"I remember."

"After your performance a few nights ago, that option is gone."

"Does that trouble you? Doesn't me."

"Not in the least. You're Reverend Chandler's daughter. You know it. For now, your mother knows it. I know it. And now, the world will know you as Danielle Chandler."

The time difference with the West Coast brought the travelers back mid-afternoon, squarely between normal dining hours. Instead, they all agreed to gather at Colin's home to celebrate.

"I want to hear all about the trip," Paula said, when they were comfortably seated, each with a glass of what had become her favorite chardonnay. Meiomi from California. "But first, I want to hear about Danielle's performance."

"If I may," Paul answered. "In a word. Stunning. Your daughter was a stunning success!"

"I don't know about that," Danielle said to her beaming mother, thinking back to her orchestra-accompanied performance to an overflow west coast audience. "But I don't think I embarrassed any of us. And …"

"And what?" Paula asked.

"I was just going to say I did like the attention. Even if it only lasted for a few minutes."

"Were they Patsy Cline moments?" Colin asked, straight-faced.

"They were! All I dreamed of, and more."

"Patsy Cline?" Paul asked, recalling Colin had called her Patsy at breakfast the morning after her performance in Los Angeles.

"It is something special between Danielle and me that began almost the moment we met."

After Colin briefly explained, Paula asked, "Danielle, sweetie, which of the three songs did they pick for you to sing?"

"My favorite, Mother. And the most appropriate."

Dreams Never Come True

When I was just a little girl / my Mama said to me
I can be anything / my dreams will let me be
She said dreams never come true / for those who never dream

Mama said it won't be easy / life don't work out that way
But she made me promise her / to keep dreamin' every day
'Cause dreams never come true / for those who never dream

Mama said don't take things as they are / keep dreamin' things that
can be
'Cause I can be anything / my dreams will let me be
Dreams never come true / for those who never dream

Others may suffer heartache and pain / that's not the world I see
I'll be just as happy / as my mind will let me be
'Cause dreams never come true / for those who never dream

I never knew my father / he didn't want my mother and me
Mama said it didn't bother much / and it left me to be free
To become anything / my dreams would let me be

When I became a woman / Mama said I done her proud
I kept followin' my dreams / and got all that God allowed
'Cause dreams never come true / for those who never dream

I knew it would happen / didn't know it would be today
The angels came from heaven / and took my Mama away
I remember when I was just a little girl / Mama said to me
I can be anything / my dreams will let me be

My dreams have always been my wings / to carry me in flight
And when each day is done / and I say my prayers at night
I want to become half the woman / who always said to me
I can be anything / my dreams will let me be

Danielle, Colin and Paul had taken turns recounting some, not all, of what had happened during their brief time away. For their part, Paula and Marla Jo were a rapt audience, taking it all in.

"Danielle, Colin mentioned seeing celebrities in the hotel restaurant," Marla Jo said. "There must have been plenty of them at the big event. Right?"

"There were. I recognized a lot of them, but one thing surprised me."

"What's that?" Paula asked.

Danielle said she was surprised many of the male movie stars and Hollywood royalty weren't very tall.

"Neither was Colin's doppelganger," Marla Jo dryly observed, recalling Paula's journal mention and her frequent re-telling over the years of her week in Colorado.

"His what?" Danielle asked. "Sounds dirty."

"Trust me," Colin said, "it's not. It means someone who's very much like another person. Their appearance. Their mannerisms. Right down to the way they walk, the way they talk. Marla Jo's being clever, or at least trying to be. At my expense."

"I still don't understand. Who's the dopple whatever that's supposed to be just like you."

"Steve McQueen," Marla Jo answered. "And Colin knows he should be flattered."

"Dead is what he is," Collin stated flatly. "For about forty years."

"Colin acts all sensitive about the comparison," Paul offered, "but like all of his dogs, McQueen had blue eyes." Paul delighted in continuing, for Danielle's benefit, with the details of the Collins/ McQueen sameness.

"Enough already. Or I'll start writing songs, naming names. And they won't be flattering."

"Don't worry, Colin." Danielle said. "And for the rest of you, now that I know what the dopple thing means, you might be interested to know there's another McQueen guy. Sorta. Met him on our trip."

"And?" Marla Jo asked

"And what?"

"Well, details, of course. Inquiring minds want to know."

Danielle cast her eyes from one person to the next to the next, ending with her mother

"Not a chance," Danielle answered, firmly. Seeing her mother's wink, she added, "Not now, anyway."

A week after the California experience, Paula asked Danielle to pose Colin and Blue on the porch and take their picture while she stood watching from the front yard. Sitting in the rocking chair as instructed while Danielle positioned Blue beside him, Colin's eyes found Paula. The physical attraction was undeniable and ever-present, but he also adored the complete essence of the woman who was slipping away from him in slow-motion with each passing day.

Her daughter's arm wrapped tightly around her, Paula said, "When I get down on my knees and say my prayers tonight, I'm going to ask God to let me remember this for as long as I can."

Paula ended her professional writing career with the Parkinson's diagnosis that had remarkably only caused a slight trembling in her hands. In addition to reading, she spent a few hours every day sketching, never saying a word, just one day picking it up as if she'd been doing it all along. The study in Colin's home had been converted into a studio for her because it had sunlight in the mornings as was the case with the larger, identical home in Three Oaks. The small watering can Paula had made for Colin occupied a place of prominence on the window sill where she could see it all day long.

Sensing her need was greater than Colin's, Blue chose to be her constant companion. With the arrival of the "surprise," Paula's fatigue quickly returned and she needed to rest more frequently during the day. And it was evident to everyone she'd become less and less sure of herself standing or walking. Paula readily embraced having a licensed caregiver in their home because it would lessen or eliminate burdens falling Colin's way. Rochelle Williams, a devout Christian woman of unwavering kindness to everyone she encountered, told both Colin and Danielle that caring for Paula wasn't work. It was a privilege; something to look forward to every day.

On one particularly bright and sunny September morning, Paula asked Rochelle to fetch her embossed and scented stationary. She wrote two short letters, sealed the envelopes and gave them to Rochelle when she returned with her lunch on a tray.

"Rochelle, if the Lord takes me away before I go to that Lanneau place, promise me you'll give these to my husband and daughter as soon as you see them, and not a minute before. If they do pack me off to Lanneau, please make certain these letters go with me."

"I certainly will, Miss Chandler."

"And Rochelle, I think of you as my friend, and I hope you think of me as your friend. It would warm my heart if you would call me Paula. Not Miss Chandler. Or Ma'am. Just Paula."

"Yes, ma'am, ... I mean Paula. I will. I surely will."

Later that same day, bundled up against the afternoon chill in the hour before sunset, Paula sat with Colin on their front porch with Blue nestled between them.

"Penny for your thoughts," Colin said, as they held hands, looking at each other.

"Worth much more than a penny, a coin I doubt you have in your possession at this very moment. Am I right? About both?"

"You are. As always."

"I'll answer anyway. I was wondering if in the life I've lived, I did something so terribly wrong that God punished me by keeping us apart."

"I don't believe God works that way," he answered, reassuringly. "In fact, I'm certain He doesn't."

"Good. I don't either. But if I did do something wrong so long ago, something about you and me, do you think He's forgiven me?"

"You didn't do anything wrong. But even if you did, He's forgiven you."

"How can you be so certain?"

"Easy. He wouldn't have given you back to me to love again, now would He?"

"And for me to love you. You're right."

Paula squeezed Colin's hand as she closed her eyes.

"Colin, do you want to know what else I'm thinking?"

Though fearing where the conversation might lead, he had no choice.

"Yes."

She opened her eyes.

"That Lanneau place is getting closer and closer. Truth is, I pray every day not to have to go there. And you're supposed to be doing the same. Are you?"

"I am." He lied. He feared anything that would keep him away from her, and wasn't going to pray for it.

"When I'm not reading, or sketching, or praying, or thinking about you and Danielle, I'm thinking about when I'll know the time has come."

"And how will you? For certain, I mean."

"Two ways, I think. I read the other day the Scottish have a word. Gloaming. And when this gloaming comes, I think it's gonna be kinda like reading at night and the light flickers 'cause the plug isn't all the way in. Make sense?"

"It does." *What else can I say?*

"I'll know it's time to go when my light begins to flicker."

There was never a time in his life when Colin felt so helpless, so powerless, swept along as if in a canoe without oars on a river's current in a thunderstorm.

"You said two ways."

"The other is the very moment I think I'm being too much of a burden to you."

"Paula, you know I love you so much I'll fight you when you tell me that time has come."

"And you know I love you so much I'll fight you right back. And I'll win.

He knew she was right. Even before she stuck her tongue out at him.

"That's eloquent," he said, grinning, "and a first in our relationship."

"Been savin' it. Afraid if I didn't do it now, I'd forget to do it later." Her blue-green eyes brightened. "I have told you I've got this memory thing goin' on, haven't I?"

Colin would remember until his dying day how for a few precious moments the sudden return of Paula's chandelier smile in all its radiant glory banished the darkness her maladies had inflicted upon her, and he was certain her prayer would be answered.

Twenty-six

Comes the gloaming

O n a clear, crisp, October afternoon one year, three months and thirteen days after the paths of Daniel Colin Collins and Elizabeth Danielle Chandler crossed at a sidewalk café in Nashville, Rochelle brought Paula Chandler Collins' lunch into her studio.

"I'm not hungry. But please sit with me, won't you?"

"May I see what you've drawn this morning,?" Rochelle asked, as she pulled a chair alongside. "Why that looks just like both of them. I think it's the best picture you've ever done, if you don't mind me sayin'."

"Thank you, Rochelle. Needs some more work. It's a first anniversary present for Colin."

"When will that be?"

"It's marked on the calendar over there. A few weeks, I think."

"He'll be delighted. I know he will." Rochelle waited a few moments. "Are you sure you don't wanna eat just a little somethin' before your nap? To keep up your strength."

"No, but thank you." Paula's loving caregiver started to leave. "Before you go, may I ask you to pray with me. That's the strength I need." Rochelle sat back down. "I have to talk with Colin when he gets home. It's about something we both knew was coming. Not going to be easy. For either of us."

"Mr. Collins, this is Rochelle."

She didn't have to say her name. Colin recognized her honeyed Southern accent.

"Say, Mr. Collins..." She had never before called him, and her pause conveyed her message before her words. "Paula has gone ta be with tha Lord. I was with her, holdin' her hand. Only a few minutes ago. It was tha most peaceful passin' I ever seen. The angels jus came down and lifted her away. Miss Danielle was upstairs and she's with her mama now."

Colin kept his composure, thanked for her call, for all she'd done for Paula, and said good-bye. He sat on the floor, leaned against the wall of the soundproof room at Adelaide where he and Paul were working, and wept. Paul had stepped away a few minutes before the switchboard put Rochelle's call through, and when he returned, he knew without asking.

Rochelle, eyes moist, opened the door when Colin and Paul arrived and led them down the hallway to the studio where Danielle tearfully hugged first Colin, then Paul. She took them by the hand to kneel with her in front of the chair where Paula sat serenely, eyes closed, hands resting in her lap. Minutes passed. Danielle was the first to speak.

"I must call Marla Jo."

While she was gone, Paul offered to call the funeral home.

When Danielle returned, Paul left and Rochelle said, "Now might be tha best time ta give you these."

She handed a letter to Danielle. *To my daughter. Do not open until I die.*

Then Colin. *To my husband. Do not open until I die.*

Despite the Parkinson's, they were addressed in Paula's easily recognizable hand.

"You first," Danielle said, as they sat side-by-side on the oversized sofa Paula had selected.

"May I read it out loud?"

Danielle nodded.

Colin carefully opened the envelope.

Colin, my love~

I'm gone. I hope my prayers were answered and I'm not at that Lanneau place. Either way, please do these few things I ask.

No marker in a cemetery somewhere to come visit, or feel guilty when you don't. I'm not there anyway. I once saw a tea towel that said: "Cremation: My last chance for a smokin' hot body." That's want I want.

I found an old stone church. Pescatarian, of course. Sits on a hillside outside Nashville. I've drawn you a map. I went there often to pray. Every time, a breeze was blowing. I thought of it as God's breath of life. That's where I want my ashes spread. Into the wind. If they're able, I'd like a few dear friends to be with you and Danielle when you do. Marla Jo and Ben. The Judge. Doc and Grace Ann. Paul Dean. And Blue, of course.

I know the life I can't remember must have been filled with joy and happiness because God blessed me with my wonderful daughter.

And with loving you. Twice. How many women can say that? Promise me you will honor our love by living the rest of your life without regrets. Especially about me.

All my love,

Paula

Colin swallowed hard, re-folded the letter, slipped it into the envelope.

"I'm supposed to be the word guy."

"Mother was really something, wasn't she? I find myself saying that a lot, I know."

"Yes, she really, really was."

Danielle smiled at his intentional word choice, opened the envelope she'd been holding in both hands and read aloud.

To my darling daughter Elizabeth Danielle~

I know you've always been the most precious thing in my life even though my memories were taken from me. That was such a cruel thing I'll never understand.

I've left you all my money. They tell me you'll never have to worry about a thing. Follow your dreams and sing your heart out with God's rare gift. May it bring you happiness and others pleasure.

Colin will need someone to look after him. He'll say he won't, but he will. Don't listen to him. I often didn't, and he didn't seem to mind.

Even though I didn't live to see it, I hope you fall in love and have a family. But if you don't, it wasn't God's plan for you. But get yourself dogs. Your life won't be complete without them. Colin has shown us that it's true. True Blue.

When you think of me, please remember I loved you more than life itself.

Mother

At that moment, Danielle and Colin turned to look behind them to the sound of someone crying softly. They'd completely forgotten

Rochelle, who apologized, drying her eyes with a handkerchief Paula had given her with her embroidered PC initials.

"There's something I ...."

When she didn't continue, Colin asked, "What Rochelle?"

"May I go with them when they take her away? I don't think Paula would want that ta be a burden on you, and I don't think she'd mind. Jus don't want her to be all alone. You know. With strangers."

The silent hugs from both Danielle and Colin gave Rochelle her answer.

The dirty limestone church had seen far better days and likely hadn't been home to a congregation, Presbyterian or otherwise, in decades. Broken windows, a twisted, storm-damaged green metal roof, it was enshrouded by overgrown trees and bushes and perched somewhat precariously on a steep hillside. Reaching it from the road below wasn't for the faint of heart. Paula's letter to Colin explained she was repeatedly drawn to it as a place to pray, but how and when she found it remained a mystery.

Mysterious to the end, Colin thought to himself.

All those Paula had asked for, hoped for, were present. Plus one. A man a few years older than Danielle, looking for all the world as if he were the son of either Steve McQueen or Colin Collins, stood by her side, holding her hand. They'd met at the gala, and spent a night together at his home, but not in the way Colin had feared. They were still just talking, becoming friends, when the sun came up that morning and she left to return to her hotel. After that, they talked often by phone, planning a way their separate professional lives might allow them to once again be together. Danielle had no idea he would be there until the moment she saw him walking toward her among the broken gravestones in the small cemetery adjacent to the church. She would later learn Paul Dean had called him.

Standing six feet tall with snow-white hair teased by the gentle breeze Paula had recalled in her letter to Colin, Judge Benjamin Taylor, like his life-long friend Doc McGinley, looked much younger than his seventy-plus years. He carried himself with the grace and dignity befitting the Southern Gentleman all who knew him acknowledged he was, putting many to mind of the late movie star Gregory Peck's portrayal of the small-town lawyer Atticus Finch in *To Kill a Mockingbird.*

"All of you knew Paula better than I," The Judge said. "Longer than I. But for some reason, and Paula always had her reasons, she asked me to say a brief word on this occasion. Emphasis on brief. With that in mind, I remembered reading something a long time ago that I hope you will agree is apropos."

He extended his arms to lift the urn with both hands. "At this place of her choosing, as we release Paula's ashes into the wind, what she described as God's breath of life, it's as if we're waving good-bye, saying 'There she goes, gone from us forever.'" He paused. "But what we cannot see, those of us who are Believers, and Paula certainly was, are others on a distant shore, waving their arms in welcome, saying, 'Here she comes.'"

The Judge handed the urn to Danielle. She also used both hands to slowly wave it back and forth as Colin, holding Blue's leash, lifted his eyes to follow the ashes upward as they disappeared into the cloudless blue sky above.

Paula's new beginning.

Although dinner was planned for that evening at Paula's favorite restaurant, none wanted their time together to end. Colin invited everyone back to his home.

When they arrived, they found Rochelle busy tidying up things that didn't need to be. An excuse for her to be there, to show them something. When everyone was assembled, she led them to Paula's studio and motioned toward the easel left untouched. Moving closer, they could see a partially completed drawing and a photograph paperclipped to the lower left-hand corner. Looking back at them was an easily recognizable sketch of Colin in the rocking chair on his porch, Blue at his side.

"Danielle," Rochelle said, "your mother used the picture you took ta help her. Mr. Collins, she said it was gonna be your anniversary present. It's the last thing she saw before she closed her eyes and went away."

Danielle stepped closer and leaned in before dropping down on one knee. She touched the lower right-hand corner with her finger. "Look here. Look what Mother wrote."

Everyone gathered around the easel. Colin knelt beside his daughter, put his arm around her shoulder.

Blue by you.

FINI

Author's Notes

If you enjoyed *Blue by You*, please consider taking a few minutes to leave a review on my author page at Amazon https://www.amazon.com/author/larrygildersleeve. In today's online world, reviews will make a huge difference to the success of an author by helping others find me.

And please share my www.larrygildersleeve.com web site because it contains the first three chapters of my other three novels that anyone can read before considering a purchase via a direct link to my page on Amazon.com.

I discovered the poem *When Twilight Comes* just as I described in the book – a tiny newspaper clipping yellowed with age I found in my late father's Bible. No author's name or date, and I searched to no avail for someone to give attribution. My best guess is the clipping itself is over a hundred years old.

The inspiration for The Judge's remarks when releasing Paula's ashes was this quotation believed to be attributed to Henry Scott Holland (1847 – 1918), Canon of Christ Church, Oxford, England:

"I am standing on the seashore. A ship spreads her sails to the morning breeze and starts for the ocean. I stand watching her until she fades on the horizon, and someone at my side says, 'She is gone.' Gone where? The loss of sight is in me, not in her. Just at the moment when someone says 'She is gone,' there are others watching her coming. Other voices take up the glad shout, 'Here she comes!' And that is dying."

I had a professional colleague in London by the name of Colin Collins who found his Twilight with his beloved Maggie before his passing in 2019 while living on Tenerife in the Spanish Canary Islands.

Annie Hayworth is a nod to the late actress Suzanne Pleshette, one of my favorites, and her character in the iconic Alfred Hitchcock movie *The Birds*.

When the late Hollywood icon Carl Reiner (actor, director, screenwriter, author) was asked by Dan Rather in 2020 to name his favorite movie of all time, without hesitation, he said, "Random Harvest." The day after I saw the interview, I watched the movie for the first time and wove the title and the leading lady's name it into my manuscript.

Thank you so very much for joining me on my journey.

With best wishes and kindest regards.

Larry

The Author Guy

Acknowledgements

As has been true with all four of my novels, *Blue by You* would not have become a reality without my outstanding editor Lynda McDaniel who patiently stays with me from the first draft to the finish line. She lives in California, the sun rises for me in Kentucky, and we've never met. I hope someday that changes.

A wonderful new resource I found is Dr. Cherri Randall, a professional editor on the staff of Writer's Digest in New York City. Her review of my manuscript contained brilliant insights and suggestions that enabled me to take the story to places I hadn't envisioned, yet when my imaginary friends and I went there, Cherri's ideas made all the sense in the world. It was Cherri who persuaded me I could, like my protagonist Colin, become a country music lyricist – if only I'd try. It took me less than two hours to write *Dreams Never Come True*.

The Reverend Charles Flener has been a source of inspiration, ideas and encouragement since I began writing novels in 2015. Decades ago, he was my favorite high school teacher and later he followed a calling to the ministry, eventually becoming a police chaplain in Louisville, Kentucky. I helped "The Rev" realize his dream of publishing a memoir, *The Adventures of Charlie Chaplain*, before his death in late 2021. I miss him greatly.

As an author, I have a following of folks interested in my writing and curious about what the future holds. At the risk of offending others, and I certainly don't mean to, one person has to be at the top of the list, and that person is my friend of over four decades – Carlos Barbera.

Cover design and interior formatting by www.arashjahani.com

CPSIA information can be obtained
at www.ICGtesting.com
Printed in the USA
JSHW062023160822
29345JS00001B/5